Bow of the Moon

The World In-between Series
Book 2

IE Castellano

Laurel
Highlands
Publishing

Bow of the Moon
Copyright © 2012 IE Castellano
All rights reserved.

Cover by JosDCreations

Laurel Highlands Publishing
Mount Pleasant, PA
USA

http://LaurelHighlandsPublishing.com

ISBN-13: 978-1-941087-03-9
ISBN-10: 1941087035

This book is a work of fiction. Names, characters, places, and
incidents either are products of the author's imagination or are
used fictitiously. Any resemblance to actual persons, living or dead,
events, or locales is entirely coincidental.

To believing in magic

Chapter One

Home Again

B erty stood, waiting in the large, circular room with its wood grained walls and brass chandeliers dressed in his gold trimmed green shirt and matching pants. A young man roughly two and a half feet tall hurried into the room, then bowed.

"Theodore," said Berty, "is everything ready?"

"Yes, Emperor," Theodore answered.

Pleased, Berty walked up the few steps to the dais landing. He glanced at the huge Sages' Seal carved into the back wall of the dais. The massive tree relief had seven differently decorated circles superimposed from top to bottom. It framed the lone elegantly carved wooden throne upon which he finally sat.

While he waited, Berty recalled the events of the past two weeks. After returning home from the Dragonlands, he and his Advisory Council discussed the best ways to repair the Hidden Treaty, which ceased the war between the ever-feuding Goblins and Trolls. Trying to diffuse a budding new war, they penned a tentative Second Hidden Treaty. The Heads of the Empire had to approve the new treaty before the Goblins and Trolls would sign it. However, both the Goblins and Trolls banned Berty from any further proceedings. He felt quasi-good about at least bringing them together on something.

The arrival of his Advisors brought Berty back to the present. Theodore stood at the entrance to the Reception Room from the Receiving Room below, ready to announce the Heads.

Finally, Theodore announced whilst bowing, "Goscislaw, Prince of the Dwarves." A regal man, no taller than Theodore, walked to the dais wearing a dark brown traveling cloak. After greeting Berty with a bow of his head, he stepped to the side.

"Avery, High Elf," announced Theodore. Approaching the dais was a tall, thin, young man with light hair and a forest green cloak. Although Avery looked a bit unsure of himself, Berty saw his Advisor, Alfred, watching his grandson proudly. Avery, too, bowed his head at Berty, then stepped next to Goscislaw.

"Elrick, King of the Fairies," Theodore told the room, "and Telor, Crown Prince of the Fairies." Elrick smiled warmly at Berty as he walked into the room a step ahead of his son. When both Fairies reached the dais, Telor followed his father's lead bowing his head in respect.

"Thank you for coming," said Berty. "The task ahead of you will not be easy. My Advisor, Hatcher, will remain as Gatekeeper, but has recused himself from the proceedings for obvious reasons." The Troll bowed his triangular head, then left the room. "Lord Darnell and Chief Miercia will arrive tomorrow. Per their request, I will not be present nor will my Advisor, the Watcher, Declan. Empire Scholar, Alfred, and Empire Historian, Delyth, will greet the Goblin Lord and Troll Chief when they come. I advise that you start as soon as possible."

"You are leaving us now?" asked Goscislaw in his low growl.

"Yes," Berty answered. "The Goblins and Trolls do not feel that I have a stake when it comes to the treaty."

"Are they mad? You are the Emperor," said Goscislaw, raising his voice.

Berty smiled, then said, "I am simply a steward of the Empire."

"And why is Declan leaving?" asked Elrick.

"They do not feel that Watchers have the Empire's best interests at heart," Berty replied.

"That whole thing is nonsense, if you ask me," said Goscislaw.

Standing, Berty said, "I will see you again once the treaty has been signed." He stepped off the dais. "Avery, Telor, it has been an honor meeting you both." Sweeping his claret cloak off his shoulders, he nodded to Declan who followed him up the stairs.

On the landing at the entrance to the Roundtable Room, Berty asked Declan, "Do you need anything?"

"My bag is in the room," answered Declan, "and Delyth has my locket in case they need to communicate with us. Unfortunately, we cannot watch the negotiations."

"I am not sure if I want to," Berty said.

Declan agreed as they entered the Roundtable Room. Passing the large Roundtable in the center of the room, Declan grabbed his bag off of his chair and secured his bow to his back. At the opposite end of the room was the magically barricaded entrance to Berty's private staircase that connected his chambers to almost every level of the Empire Tree. Grabbing Declan by the elbow, Berty pulled him through to the small landing on the other side.

Berty and Declan ascended the stairs carved into the trunk of the tree until the staircase came to an end. Seeing a dark hallway in front of him, Berty turned, leading Declan across a narrow rope and plank bridge covered in snow. The bridge took them to a wooden platform in front of a snow laden bundle of branches inside which were Berty's chambers. Turning again, Berty brought Declan across a short bridge to another platform in front of another bundle.

When they walked through the arched entryway, Declan took a quick look around. The round room had a carved wooden desk with bookshelves on the curved wall behind it. On the other side of the room were a couple of yellow couches separated by an oblong coffee table. Berty picked up his shoulder bag off a couch, then proceeded to the back of the room where a smaller version of the Sages' Seal was carved into the back wall.

Behind the Sages' Seal hid a staircase up which Berty led Declan. At the top of the stairs was a well-appointed bedroom with a slight feminine touch. Declan looked a bit confused as they passed the large bed.

Noticing Declan's expression, Berty explained, "Elder

Hunter's chambers when she was Empress."

Berty stopped in front of the wall where a tapestry hung depicting a stag in a woodland scene.

"Wow," exclaimed Declan. "I have never seen a portal look like this."

As a Watcher, Declan could see magic constantly in use. Curious, Berty asked, "What do you mean?"

"The portals that lie off of Portal Road," began Declan, "are elongated shimmering blue discs. Here, the whole tapestry is alive. The trees blow and the stag runs in-between them. Had I not known that we were heading through a portal, I would never have known that this was a portal."

Berty thought it interesting because the scene stayed still when he looked at it—like a tapestry should. "Ready?" Berty asked.

When Declan nodded his head, they stepped through the tapestry.

"Wow," Declan said again as he gazed around the Victorian bedroom.

Walking past the pair of wing chairs, Berty placed his bag down on the carved wool rug, leaning it against the four poster bed's footboard. Turning around, he saw Declan still standing near the fireplace through which they came. "Declan," said Berty as he hung his cloak on a wooden valet, "pick out a bedroom for your stay."

Finally, Declan stepped further into Berty's bedroom following Berty into the bright hallway. "There are three other bedrooms," Berty said pointing at the paneled doors. "Choose one and take off your cloak." Pulling a white metal pocket watch from his pocket, he opened it glancing at the one side that told him that it was Friday afternoon. "We are heading out, so I need to change."

Berty left Declan wandering into a bedroom while he changed out of his gold threaded garb into corduroys and a cable knit sweater. Grabbing his notebook from his bag, he walked down the hall to find Declan exploring his new bedroom.

Knocking on the open door, Berty said, "Bring your gloves. We have to go."

With his gloves in one hand, Declan went to grab his bow. "You will not need that," said Berty. Leaving his bow, he followed Berty down the steps into the wood paneled foyer.

Opening a panel near the stained glass front door, he grabbed two knit scarves and hats. Handing one of each to Declan, Berty also found a puffy winter coat for Declan to wear.

Getting ready to face a cold day, Berty had to show Declan how to use a zipper. He ignored the rooms off the hallway as he led Declan towards the back of the house. Before opening the door where the hall ended, Berty opened a small panel. Out of the small cubby he grabbed his cell phone and car keys.

Pushing open the last door, they entered the old-fashioned kitchen. "I have never seen a house like this before," Declan remarked. "But since I have never been on this side of the portal," Declan stopped speaking when Berty opened the back door. Stepping into the cold, Declan asked, "What is that?"

Berty walked off the stoop and over to the driver's side door of his silver sedan. "My car. Get in," he answered. He showed Declan how to open the car door and how to fasten his seatbelt.

To Berty's relief, his car started. They turned onto the street with Declan clutching the door handle. At a stoplight, Declan let go and relaxed. Plugging his cell phone into the charger, Berty turned on his phone. Declan sat silently looking out the windows at the modern world he had never seen.

Realizing he had a message, Berty put his phone on speaker. "Hey, Berty; it's Jon." Declan turned his attention to the small phone. "This weekend is Matt's last before he leaves for Japan. He got a job in Tokyo. Anyway, Teresa wants a small farewell get-together on Sunday. We're combining it with a Super Bowl party. Let us know if you can come. Please, please come. Bye."

Declan was still staring at the phone, so Berty explained. "The phone works a lot like the Watcher's Lockets, except it transmits voice."

Looking out the windshield, Declan asked, "What is that?"

Tall buildings stood in the distance before them as they drove on the highway. "That's the city skyline," Berty answered. As they drove into the city, Declan tried to look up with his head plastered onto the door window.

Finding a spot, Berty parallel parked. "Come on. You get to meet my boss," said Berty as he opened the car door.

Berty deposited change into the meter while Declan asked, "The Emperor has a boss?"

Not answering, Berty walked to the front of the building. Declan followed him through the glass doors. Inside the lobby, he pushed the up arrow button as Declan watched the numbers change above the elevator door. Berty heard the familiar ding when the doors opened. After pushing the circle marked fourteen, the elevator began to move.

Declan grabbed the bar in the back. Stabilizing himself, he asked, "My Lord, is this magic?"

"Electricity runs the elevator," Berty explained, "and mostly everything else."

"What is electricity?"

Berty had never thought about electricity before. He had always accepted its existence. Living without it in the Land of Sages never phased him. The doors opened to the fourteenth floor. He said, "I'll explain later. Let's go."

A woman behind the receptionist desk smiled at them as Berty asked, "Is Mister Hunter in?"

"I haven't seen you around in a while, Mister Chase," she said, picking up a phone receiver. "Mister Hunter," she spoke into the phone, "Mister Chase is here to see you." She smiled at him again. Putting down the phone, she said, "He says to go right in. And you really shouldn't be such a stranger." She jotted something on a piece of paper, then handed it to Berty.

"Thanks," said Berty.

As they walked down the carpeted hall, Declan asked, "What did she give you?"

Opening the paper, Berty answered, "Her number." He threw it in the nearest garbage can, then continued walking.

A door at the end of the hall opened. Stepping out of his office, a silver haired man said, "Berty, my boy, come in."

"So good of you to see me on such short notice, Martin," said Berty. "I would like you to meet Declan."

After they entered Martin's office, Martin closed the office door. "The Watcher." Smiling, Martin shook Declan's hand. "Great to meet you. Sit down, both of you." While Berty and Declan sat on chairs, Martin walked behind his desk. "I see you have more chapters of *The Adventures of Leigh and Marcus* for me," he said, eyeing Berty's notebook.

Grabbing a section of newspaper, he walked over to Berty, then said, "Look at this. It is the first installment." Martin dropped the paper in Berty's lap. "Let me get your notebook photocopied." Berty opened his notebook to the proper page before handing it to Martin.

Looking at the paper, he read, "The Adventures of Leigh and Marcus by Berty Chase, Part One." When Martin left the office to find an intern, Berty told Declan, "I wrote a somewhat fictitious account of my time in the Land of Sages."

Martin returned, handing Berty his notebook. "I am printing an installment every week," he told them. "Just like they did in the old days. What do you think?"

"It's great," said Berty. "Thanks, Martin. Unfortunately, we need to get going."

"Of course," he replied as they stood. Shaking hands, Martin opened the door saying, "Nice meeting you, Declan. See you soon, Berty."

In the elevator, Declan remarked, "I do not know why you called him your boss. He seems to work for you."

Again, Berty did not respond, but thought Declan's observations were astute. When they returned to the car, Berty had the heater running as he said to Declan, "I need to make a call."

With the phone on speaker, they listened to the ringing. "Hello?" said a woman's voice.

"Teresa," Berty said.

"Berty," said Teresa, "I hope you are calling me to tell me that you are coming this Sunday."

"I am," Berty replied. "A friend of mine from work is staying with me for a few days. I hope you don't mind if I bring him along."

"Of course not," said a cheerful Teresa. "Jon's college friend is coming with his family. The game starts somewhere around four so you and your friend should be here before two."

"Okay. Should I bring the chips, dip, soda or beer?"

"Nothing. You have brought quite enough lately," Teresa answered. "Hope wears that cloak you brought for Christmas all around the house." She laughed. "Her bus should be coming soon. I need to pick her up at the stop. See you Sunday."

"Yup. Bye."

Closing his phone, Berty began to drive out of the city. "I better fill you in on some things, Declan. Teresa is married to my brother, Jon. They have a young daughter named Hope."

"She's the one you bought the doll for in the market place."

"Yes. And before I forget, Matt is Teresa's brother. I'm sure our parents will be there, too."

Nodding his head slowly, Declan looked as if he were absorbing it all. "Your boss, Martin Hunter," he began, "knows about the Land of Sages. What is his connection to Elder Hunter?"

"They are brother and sister," answered Berty. "He explained the age difference as simply, time was strange."

"But your family still has no knowledge?"

Berty sighed. "Only Hope has an inkling. On Sunday, it would be wise to call me Berty instead of referring to me as Emperor."

Arriving home, Berty opened his inherited cookbook in the kitchen to a hearty soup recipe. Declan watched as Berty read the recipe out loud. Magically, a pot waited on the stove while vegetables and meat chopped in mid-air before settling into the pot.

"What is the Super Bowl?" asked Declan as Berty sat at the plank kitchen table.

"The biggest football game of the year," Berty replied. "Most people get together and watch it regardless of whom is playing. My mom likes to see the commercials more than the game." He laughed.

They filled bowls with steaming soup. Sitting at the table, Berty spent the evening explaining football to Declan.

On Saturday morning, Berty introduced Declan to coffee. While Berty searched his Victorian family room for a book to read, Declan paused at the window asking, "What is in the building out there?"

Berty looked out the window at the old two-story garage with blue siding. "I don't know," he answered. "I've never been in there. Let's find out."

Donning coats, they trudged through the snow. When Berty opened the side door, gas lights ignited, illuminating two extremely old carriages. Entering the garage further, Berty got a good look at numerous saddles, harnesses and tools that Berty had no idea what they did.

In the back of the garage was a narrow staircase, which both of them climbed. On the second floor, Berty shockingly found all manners of weaponry from swords, axes and spears to longbows, shortbows and crossbows. Accompanying the weapons were practice dummies, armor and targets. With the weaponry spanning the ages, Berty figured that only a museum would garner a more complete collection.

"My Lord," asked Declan, "may I take this target outside and practice?"

Not seeing the harm, Berty agreed. While Declan set up to practice his archery, Berty returned to the house to read. When it got too dark to see the target, Declan returned to the house to have dinner.

After dinner, Berty spent the evening explaining television and electricity to Declan.

"A television also works like a Watcher's locket," reiterated Declan, "but is more of a box that runs off of electricity. I am not really sure that I understand electricity, my Lord."

Berty sighed. "It would be easier if I were able to show you the wires, plugs and switches, but my house does not have any." He looked at the natural gas lighted sconces on the walls. "Silvia feels that electricity interferes with magic." Seeing the confused expression on Declan's face, Berty corrected, "Elder Hunter."

In his bed, Berty stared out the dark window watching the snow fall in the street light. He thought about Silvia—her wild dark red hair, her warm brown eyes, her inviting smile. Her last order as Empress was to make sure a second Hidden Treaty was going to be drafted. As he lay awake, Silvia was on the other side of the portal, somewhere, with Estelle. While in the Empire Tree, treaty negotiations ensued. Knowing that he was not letting her down, Berty fell asleep easily.

An easy night morphed into an uneasy morning when Berty realized that he had nothing to bring to his brother's house for the game. Clutching his mug of coffee, Berty stood in the kitchen hoping to get some inspiration. While he stared at his large old multi-oven range, Declan poured some coffee from the French press. Taking his coffee, Declan left Berty standing in the kitchen to shoot some arrows in the snow.

The quick burst of cold air from Declan opening the door jarred Berty's mind. "Cookies," Berty said to the kitchen. As the magical cookbook flew towards him, he said, "Oatmeal cookies." The cookbook landed on the plank table opened to an oatmeal cookie recipe. Reading the recipe out loud, the cookie batter mixed itself in a bowl. After three dozen cookies baked and speed cooled, Berty boxed them to go.

At noon, Berty and Declan got ready to leave. In the car, Declan kept gazing at the modern world while Berty reminded him that his brother's house was different.

When they turned into Jon and Teresa's development, Berty joined Declan's peering at all the similar looking homes. Finding his brother's house, Berty parked in the driveway behind a dark blue BMW X3.

Box of cookies in hand, Berty led Declan to the front door where Berty rang the doorbell.

A thin man with dark hair and glasses opened the door, then said, "Hey, Berty, come on in."

"Jon," said Berty, giving his brother a one armed hug, "this is my friend, Declan."

Extending his hand towards Declan, Jon said, "Nice to meet you."

"And you," replied Declan as he shook Jon's hand.

While Jon hung their coats in the hall closet, Berty asked, "Whose SUV?"

"Matt's," answered Jon with a smirk. "He'll tell you all about it."

"Can't wait," said Berty.

Jon rolled his eyes as he led Berty and Declan down the hall. As they stepped into the gleaming modern kitchen, a tall, thin woman with chin length brown hair said, "I told you not to bring anything."

"Nice to see you too," replied Berty placing the box of cookies on the counter. "Your new haircut looks nice."

She smiled saying, "Thank you."

"Teresa," Berty said, "this is Declan."

All Declan could muster was a small hi.

"And that is Matt," Berty told Declan referencing the tall man with messy brown hair standing next to Teresa and desperately in need of a shave.

"Berty was admiring your new car," Jon said to Matt.

Matt's eyes lit up as he said, "It's just a little happy divorce present I bought myself."

"The divorce went through already?" asked Berty.

"Apparently she already had another husband in queue," Matt elaborated through his teeth. "Rachel's father pulled some strings to get it through the courts faster. Ended up not having to give her a thing. She even paid all the court costs. So, I sold the house and traded in the cars for the beauty you saw outside."

Declan looked a bit confused, so Berty explained. "Rachel is Matt's now ex-wife. She was, uh, unbearable to put it mildly. I don't know what you saw in her, Matt."

11

"She wasn't *that* bad," said Teresa reprovingly.

"You're right," Berty said. "She was worse when she drank, which was all the time."

Teresa shook her head while Jon and Declan chuckled.

"Uncle Berty," screamed a little girl running into the kitchen. Her bouncing brown curls could not hide the wide smile on her face.

"Hope," said Berty crouching down to give her a hug. "I want you to meet a friend of mine. This is Declan."

She scrutinized Declan before saying, "Hi."

Declan smiled, saying, "Hi."

"What's in the box?" Hope asked.

"Oatmeal cookies," Berty answered.

"Raisins?" Hope scrunched her face in disgust.

"Nope."

Her face relaxed. "Can I have one?"

"No," Teresa said firmly. "We are going to eat once your grandparents get here."

"Okay," Hope said. "I'll wait by the window." She ran out of the room.

With Hope's footsteps echoing through the house, Berty turned to Matt asking, "When are you leaving for Tokyo?"

"Tuesday," Matt answered. "All my stuff is being stashed at my parents' house except the new car. Teresa says she'll keep it safe here for me."

Berty wondered why Matt bought the car at all, but decided against asking.

"I already have an apartment near my work," Matt continued. "Fully furnished and westernized. The change of scenery should be nice. I can't wait."

"That's great," said Berty. "Good luck with everything."

Matt's thanks was interrupted when Hope ran back into the kitchen yelling, "They're here. They're here."

When she ran out of the room again, Jon followed her.

While Teresa checked the food, Matt continued to talk about his new job to Berty and Declan. The only thing that made him slow down was the arrival of his parents.

A tall, thin, blonde haired woman hugged Teresa saying, "We aren't actually going to watch that lurid game, are we dear?"

"Not unless you really want to, Mom."

"Sorry we're late, Teresa," said a tall silver haired man as he gave his daughter a kiss on the cheek. "I couldn't find where I stashed this." He held up a bottle filled with a dark golden liquid.

"No problem, Dad," she looked at her brother, then smiled. "Matt's been able to keep everyone entertained."

Carrying Hope, Jon entered the kitchen with his and Berty's parents. After giving Teresa a hug, Berty's father made a beeline for the group of men.

"You must be Berty's friend from work," his father said to Declan.

"Dad," said Berty, noticing the snowflakes melting in his father salt and pepper hair, "Declan."

"It is nice to meet you, Declan. Please, call me George." He shook Declan's hand.

"It is nice to meet you as well, George," said Declan.

A woman with chin length brown hair and a streak of silver cascading near her face hugged Berty, saying, "How are you, Berty?"

"Fine, Mom," answered Berty.

"This is Kate," George said to Declan. "Have you met Robert and Lillian yet?" He indicated Teresa and Matt's parents.

"Not exactly," said Declan.

"Come. I'll introduce you."

Declan let George steer him away from Berty and Matt. Finally, Teresa called everyone into the dining room for dinner.

Once everyone was seated, Robert lifted his glass saying, "To Matt: May this new chapter of your life bring you happiness, prosperity and perhaps a little love."

Berty and Declan joined everyone in toasting Matt with their glasses. Food and conversation worked their way around the table.

"So, Declan," said George, "are you a writer as well?"

"No. I'm an Advisor," Declan answered.

"In what way?"

Berty almost choked on his food.

"Are you connected to Berty's story in the paper?" Kate asked Declan.

Trying to save Declan from his parent's questions, Berty jumped into the conversation. "Yes. I have been spending an almost excessive amount of time in the woods lately. Declan is very knowledgeable and has been an invaluable guide."

"Well, I can't wait to read further installments," said Kate.

"Thanks," Berty said with a smile.

Kate picked up her glass, asking, "So, how is Silvia?"

Berty's insides sank, but he replied nonchalantly, "She is doing well. Right now she is taking her student, Estelle, on a field trip. Silvia is trying to improve Estelle's interactions with other people."

"This girl is socially backwards?" asked Lillian.

"Estelle was abused as a child," Berty explained. "Her social skills suffered as a result."

"Poor thing," said Lillian.

"Do you think we will be meeting Silvia over Easter?" Kate asked.

"Mom," said Jon, "Easter is not for months yet."

"I can make suggestions," Kate said with a wave of her hand.

Breathing easier, Berty finished his dinner.

Looking around the table at all the empty plates, Robert suggested, "If we all grab a plate, then we can get the table cleared and watch the pre-game."

After the table was cleared, the men retired to the family room while the women kibitzed in the kitchen.

As they took seats on the sectional, Jon turned on his big screen television. "I miss a large screen TV," said Matt.

"What happened to yours? It was nice," Jon asked.

Matt sighed. "One of the only things I lost in the divorce. She said she needed it. I didn't quibble. I just wanted her out of my life."

Smirking, Jon left the room.

"It had tons of apps, too," Matt reminisced. "After selling the house, I moved into my parents' guest room. Let's just say that they don't watch TV. Of course in a Rachel free world, I don't really need it."

Berty laughed with Matt while Jon returned with bottles of beer for everyone.

After taking a sip, Declan grimaced, asking, "What is this?"

"Beer," replied Jon, looking confused.

Declan glared at the bottle's label commenting, "*This* is not beer."

The doorbell drowned Berty's laughter. When Jon left to answer the door, Robert handed Declan a glass of brown liquid.

Jon returned to the family room with a light brown haired man hiding behind him. Nudging the man into the room, Jon said, "This is my college buddy, Peter." As Jon named everyone in the room, Peter just stood sheepishly in his thick-soled boots. Being the shortest man in the room, Peter needed a couple of beers to feel comfortable with them.

During the first commercial after kickoff, Teresa and a short, plump, blonde woman brought an assortment of snacks.

After placing the trays on the coffee table, Teresa said to the woman, "Jane, you are so helpful. Thank you."

"Oh, it's nothing," Jane said cheerfully. "I can't let my Peter go without my famous seven layer dip during a game."

Berty saw Teresa smile her I-am-so-annoyed smile as she followed Jane out of the family room.

His attention was brought back to the screen when George yelled, "Who are you throwing to?"

"This is exciting," Declan said to Berty before all of them rose out of their seats yelling, "Go! Go! Go!"

During the commercial, Hope walked into the room with a plate of the oatmeal cookies that Berty made. Grabbing a cookie, she set the plate on the table. Hope sat far back on the couch between Jon and Berty. After taking a bite of her cookie, a blond haired boy squeezed his way in front of Hope.

"What are you doing?" he asked, flapping his arms. "We are playing alien invasion."

"I'm eating my cookie," Hope replied matter-of-factly.

"Hurry up," the boy demanded.

She took a small bite of her cookie.

"You have to be the alien monster from the fifth dimension," whined the boy.

"I want to eat my cookie," said Hope, looking only at the cookie in her hand. Her mouth opened to take another bite of her cookie, but the boy snatched it out of her hand. "Hey! Give me back my cookie, Charlie!"

"Only if you promise to get off the couch and play," Charlie taunted.

Jon glanced at Peter who was completely oblivious to his son's antics. "Charlie," Jon said calmly, but sternly, "give Hope back her cookie. She has the right to choose whatever she wants to play and when she wants to play it."

Charlie's blue eyes narrowed and his pink face scrunched making his nose look like a pig's snout. Looking from Jon to Hope maliciously, he stuffed the whole cookie in his mouth. With his cheeks puffed and pink, he ran out of the room.

Hope slid off the couch like nothing happened. Taking another cookie from the plate, she said, "I didn't want it after he touched it anyway." She ate her cookie while she sat on the couch watching the game with her head cocked to one side.

When halftime began, Hope grabbed another cookie, then skipped out of the room. Feeling his pocket vibrate, Berty excused himself. Walking into the foyer, he extracted his large, gold Watcher's locket from his pocket. He glanced at the carving of the eye in the center of a six-pointed star before opening it.

Inside, he read, "My Lord, the treaty was signed tonight. All the Heads are staying the night and wish to greet you in the morning. You must approve the signed treaty for it to be validated into law. —Delyth"

Taking the rod part of the clasp, Berty wrote, "Declan and I will return in the morning. —E"

As he closed the locket, Declan approached quietly asking, "What is the news?"

"It's done," answered Berty. "We can go back as soon as we are finished here."

"I knew it," Hope said with delight. "You are going to the Land of Sages. I'm coming with you. I'll get my cloak." She ran out from under the hall table up the stairs.

"You're not coming," Berty said to her over the railing. Berty heard her footsteps come to a sudden halt.

"What are you doing?" Hope yelled from upstairs. "Get out of my room!"

Berty realized why he had not seen Charlie in awhile.

"No!" Hope screamed shrilly. "Don't touch her!"

Scrambling up the stairs, Berty found Charlie in the middle of Hope's room. Everywhere Berty looked, Hope's belongings were torn or broken and discarded on the floor. A wicked smile plastered across Charlie's face as he held her wooden doll, Ashley, over his head.

"I'm going to rip her arms off first," taunted Charlie.

"Don't," cried Hope as tears began to gush from her big, brown eyes.

"Put the doll down, Charlie," said Berty. "Don't you think you have done enough damage already?"

"I want her to pay for not playing with me," Charlie said through his scrunched up mouth. His eyes delighted at the sight of Hope crying.

Berty heard adult footsteps thundering down the hallway behind him. Teresa ran to Hope's side while Jon made a beeline for Charlie. As Jon grabbed for the doll, Charlie squirmed through Jon's legs.

Charlie ran wildly for the door that Berty guarded. With a squeal, Charlie slipped past Berty's open arms running down the hall with the doll high over his head. Before he reached the stairs, Berty made him trip with magic. As the boy fell on his face, Berty made sure the doll gently touched the floor.

Berty snatched the doll off the floor while Jon towered over Charlie saying, "We are going to have a talk with your parents."

Charlie sniveled as Jon marched him down the stairs where everyone gathered in the foyer. Teresa held Hope's hand as they descended halfway down the steps. Looking at Hope's tear streaked face, Berty sat on the top step with Ashley securely in his arms.

Nudging Charlie towards Peter and Jane, Jon said, "Your son destroyed my daughter's room."

Jane laughed. "Oh, he wouldn't have done such a thing," she said in her singsong voice.

"You are welcome to see her room," said Jon.

"Your daughter didn't want to play with our Charlie," Peter replied with his hand on his son's shoulder.

"Excuse me?" said Jon raising his eyebrows. "Hope's things are strewn all over her room in pieces."

"Perhaps you need to teach your daughter to treat her things with more respect," Jane suggested.

"We cannot be held responsible for *her* actions," added Peter.

"How dare you," said Teresa, her voice cold. She stepped deliberately down each step as if the wrought iron railing was restraining her from tearing both Peter and Jane to bits. "You do *not* accuse my child of anything when you stand there turning a blind eye to your own child's destructive and selfish behavior."

"Aren't we high and mighty," Jane said as her head rocked from side to side with each syllable.

"Get out," Jon gritted through his teeth. The closet door swung open, hitting the wall with a thud. Grabbing their coats, he threw them. He opened the front door. Still grasping the doorknob, he said, "Out of my house."

A fearful Peter ushered his wife and son over the threshold, clutching their coats. As Jon slammed the door behind them, Jane could be heard saying, "I never."

Removing her red knuckled grip from the railing, Teresa took a few deep breaths. She looked at Jon and a wisp of a smile returned to her face. Turning to face Hope, she said sweetly,

"Come on, I'll help you clean up your room."

Kate and Lillian looked at each other. Following Teresa upstairs, Kate paused to put a hand on Jon, telling him that he did the right thing.

Berty stood to let them through. Hope waited beside Berty for her mother and grandmothers to pass. Crouching next to her, Berty handed over her doll.

"Thanks, Uncle Berty," said Hope in a small voice. "I guess I'm not going to be able to go with you tonight."

Looking at her disappointed face, he said, "The right time will come. Besides, you can't miss school tomorrow."

She shook her head, hugging her doll. "Ashley says thanks, too."

"You are both welcome," he said with a smile.

"Also, she wants me to tell you that a leaf has a special connection with a root." Smiling weakly, she ran down the hall.

When Berty returned to the foyer, he ignored Declan's raised eyebrows. Entering the family room, Berty grabbed a bottle of beer before flopping on the couch. The game was on pause as Jon vented about his so-called good buddy, Peter.

Chapter Two
Staves of Life

By the time they finished watching the game, Jon was in better spirits. Hope's room regained a semblance of order. Berty had not had a chance to think about Ashley's words. On the way home, Berty pushed them from the forefront of his mind.

Driving on the snow covered roads past the city kept Berty's mind occupied. Declan gazed at the passing city lights. The skyscraper's lights reflected on the calm river the highway followed. Breaking the silence, Declan said, "You have a great family."

Surprised, Berty answered, "Thank you."

"They'd accept it if they knew," Declan added before he turned his head to look at the passing snowy scenes. Berty waited to see if Declan was going to say more. When he did not, Berty left it alone.

When they returned to Berty's house, Berty put everything back while Declan collected his things. Standing in front of the fireplace, Berty plunged the house into darkness before they stepped through the portal.

The night was still as they walked onto the frozen platform. Berty led Declan across the rope and plank bridge into the trunk of the Empire Tree. Turning right, the Watcher followed him through the dark, narrow hallway. The hallway ended at a door. Grabbing Declan's elbow, Berty guided him through the door.

They stepped into a wide, well-lighted hallway. "Hallway for the Watching Rooms," said Declan. He turned to Berty saying, "Thank you for bringing me."

"You are welcome," Berty said. Turning, he faced the wall out of which they had just come. "See you in the morning," he said before stepping through the wall. Alone, he had nothing but his thoughts to accompany him as he walked to his chambers. Ashley's words swam into his thoughts, but he had no idea what they meant.

In the warmth of his study, the words, *leaves* and *roots*, played over and over in his mind as he emptied his bag. Finishing, he sat on a club chair. His eyes roved while his mind acted like a broken record. They rested on a box in which he kept his coins.

"Coins," he muttered. "Roots." He leaned forward. "Coins are kept in the vaults. The roots of the tree surround the vaults. She didn't say leaves." His eyes found the Sages' Seal carved into the front of his desk. "A leaf has a special connection with a root. Not leaf, but Leif. Of course, Leif's old vault."

Berty went to bed knowing that Leif, the previous Scholar, had no time to clear the Scholar's Vault before Silvia dismissed him.

The morning found Berty sitting in the Reception Room at a large table with the Advisory Council and the Heads of the Empire. No one dared disturb the still air as Berty looked over the treaty that Goblin Lord Darnell and Troll Chief Miercia signed the day before.

Pleased that the treaty will keep the peace between the Goblins and Trolls, Berty said, "I accept the Second Hidden Treaty." After stamping it with his wax seal, he handed the treaty to Delyth.

"Thank you, my Lord," Miercia said, bowing her inverted triangular head so that her long white curls touched the table. "The Empire Tree has saved us from a costly war, which neither Darnell nor I wanted. To show our gratitude, we advise you to seek the counsel of the one who sees on God Mountain."

"It is a good time to journey to Veleda," squeaked Darnell as he looked at Berty with his dark beady eyes. "A word of caution, my Lord, beware of a former Advisor."

With bows, both the Troll and the Goblin rose from the table. Summoning their traveling parties, they descended to the room below.

"Our work here is done," said Goscislaw in his low growl. "I must return home. It has been an honor, Emperor." The Dwarf climbed off his chair to bow to Berty. After fastening his cloak, he disappeared below the floor.

"Telor," Elrick said to his son, "send word to your mother that we are coming home."

"Yes, Father," said Telor.

After Telor ran up the stairs, Berty and the others arose from the table to say their good-byes.

"Why did Lida not come?" Berty asked.

Sadness momentarily spread onto Elrick's face. "After finding the onslaught of traitors, we felt it best to not let anyone think that we have let down our guard. Besides it gives Telor," he watched his son enter the room, "some well deserved experience."

After hugging Delyth, the Fairies shook Berty's hand, then joined their guards who were waiting outside.

"I am afraid that I, too, must return home," said Avery. "Once I return to Irmingard, the vote for Low Elf can be counted. We had four excellent candidates vying for the seat this term. I wish that I could stay longer as it is my first visit to the Empire Tree, but like duty called me here, duty calls me home."

"I understand duty all too well," Berty said. "You are welcome to return at anytime, Avery."

"Thank you, Emperor," said Avery as he bowed to Berty. "It has been an honor to have met you. Grandfather," he said facing Alfred, "I will let you know who the new Low Elf is as soon as I can."

Smiling, Alfred hugged Avery while saying quietly, "I am so proud of you."

After Avery said goodbye to the rest of the Advisory Council, he followed the same path as the Fairies before him out of the Empire Tree.

"Declan," said Delyth, "I need to return your locket. Come while I file the treaty." She picked the paper scroll off the table before leading Declan up the stairs.

When the Advisory Council began to go their separate ways, Berty turned to Alfred saying, "Walk upstairs with me."

The aged Elf followed Berty up the stairs into the Roundtable Room. Sitting in his ornately carved chair, Berty watched the light of sconces dance on the reflective tabletop of the Roundtable.

Once Alfred took his seat, he asked, "What is it, my Lord?"

"Darnell confirmed what I have been thinking," began Berty. "Have you been to your vault?"

"Yes, whilst researching the Hidden Treaty," Alfred replied confused.

"But have not looked at everything?" Berty asked.

"No," said Alfred. "I am afraid I am not following."

"If you couple Darnell's warning with what my niece said last night, it all points to one place."

"The Wood Listener?"

"I feel that Leif may have left something behind in the Scholar's Vault," Berty said.

Alfred gave Berty a calculated look while Berty stood to walk around the table.

"Perhaps, I am reaching," Berty said as he walked. "It is just that he has been conspiring against the Empire. I want to be able to do more than merely take stabs in the dark."

Alfred's eyes followed Berty around the room. "Being Scholar for three Empresses, he would have accumulated a lot of stuff down there. I will need help."

Through the open doorway, Berty saw Declan and Delyth arrive on the landing from the bridge. "Help has arrived," said Berty.

Declan and Delyth accompanied Alfred down into the Vault Room while Berty waited. When they returned, they dumped piles of leather bound books, covering the shiny tabletop. "All of these are Leif's personal notes," Alfred told Berty.

"There are more books that we could not carry," said Declan.

Berty grabbed a book from one of the many piles, saying, "There has to be a hundred books here."

Taking a book off another pile, Delyth sat, asking, "For what exactly are we looking?"

"I am not sure," answered Berty. Cracking the spine, he began to read.

Dozens of books later, Declan put down his newly opened book, asking, "Is anyone reading something that does not have to do with the scepter? Every book I have read is about the scepter."

"So are all these," said Delyth.

Peering over his half moon reading glasses, Alfred said, "All his assumptions about the scepter are wrong."

Berty, too, only read about the scepter. "Elder Hunter did mention Leif's fascination with the scepter ever since he became Scholar."

Declan flipped through the pages of the book in his hands. "Fascination? This is a sick obsession. He sits in the Scepter Room, staring at it while forgetting to eat. I think he was having hallucinations from starving himself. In one of these books, every page is a drawing of the crystal." Placing the book on the table, he ran his fingers through his sandy hair while shaking his head in disbelief.

Two days later, they had moved onto the second load of books from the vault. Halfway through the mounds of books, Declan declared, "Here's a book about Astrology," then his tone turned bitter, "and how it relates to the scepter. Nevermind."

On their third trip back from the Vault Room, Alfred said, "These are all his books."

Berty looked at the towering piles of books not feeling any better. So sure they would find something, he felt his reading enthusiasm wane as he picked another book at random off the table.

Hours later, Delyth stood on her chair to see over the piles, saying, "My Lord, listen to this: 'The scepter is not the only crystal bearing staff. The legendary Staff of Lightning has been favored by generations of Warrior Mages. If only I could find this staff, then perhaps I could tap some of the scepter's power. According to Florian, this staff has been lost to history. When he retires, I will then be able to gain access to his vault. Perhaps I will be able to pick up the trail.'"

"Who is Florian?" Declan asked.

"The Historian before Millicent," answered Alfred.

"Did Leif find out what happened to it?" Berty asked.

Delyth turned pages as her eyes quickly skimmed the words. "No. According to Leif, the last Warrior Mage disappeared without a trace."

Closing his book, Berty called for Theodore. When the Dwarf arrived, Berty said, "We need to see Sean, now."

As Theodore left, Declan grimaced. Privately, Berty agreed with Declan as Sean was still the enemy to him. In the silence, Berty's mind wandered to that fateful day—the day that changed everything. Sean and his followers attacked the Empire Tree. He scoured the tree, searching for Silvia. Intent on claiming the scepter for himself, Sean finally found Silvia. Berty remembered watching helplessly as Sean's dagger flew across the scepter room, killing her. Closing his eyes, he shook the image from his mind.

Sean arrived in the Roundtable Room with Theodore closely by his side. "You wanted to see me, my Lord," said the mousy voice that Berty despised.

Looking at the source of the voice, Berty cringed inside when he saw straight black hair framing a flat nose and gray eyes bearing a glimmer of hope. "Thank you, Theodore," he said.

Bowing, the Dwarf left.

"Sean," Berty said with an acrid taste in his mouth, "do you remember when you told me that you had been searching far and wide for your great-grandfather's staff?"

"Yes, my Lord."

25

"He was a Warrior Mage. Was he not?"

"Yes, he was."

Berty took a deep breath to help suppress his loathing for the man standing between the door and the table. "It pains me to say that you were led astray when you came here seeking knowledge because of another's covet."

Sean's face scrunched with confusion. "I do not understand."

"Delyth, if you would be so kind to show Sean what you have found," Berty said while each word made his stomach turn. The old adage of forgive and forget became a trudge through quicksand on a beach as high tide crashed onto the shore. Dealing with Sean was more palatable when Silvia wanted him to do it.

Still standing on her chair, Delyth held the open book in Sean's direction. With hesitation, Sean stepped towards the Fairy. His unsure hands barely touched the book while his gray eyes read Leif's handwriting. When he finished, he looked up at Delyth who recoiled slightly. As he turned his head, Berty saw his chest begin to swell.

"He lied," Sean said with strength that Berty never had seen. "For his greed, he lied."

"So did you," reminded Berty. His eyes glanced at Sean's gray crystal resting against his brown tender's uniform.

"But *I* was not a scholar," Sean justified.

"That doesn't matter," muttered Declan loudly.

Trying to diffuse a potential volatile situation, Berty asked, "This Staff of Lightning is the one you seek?"

Closing his eyes, Sean breathed deeply. When he opened them, his eyes lost the hardness and edge Berty always saw. "Yes," Sean answered. His right hand caressed his crystal while tears streamed down his face.

Berty wanted to avert his eyes, but they would not obey his thoughts. He was forced to watch another man cry no matter how indecent he thought voyeurism was.

Sean's soft mousy voice broke the stunned silence. "What have I done? I have made such a mess. All over lies. That

Scholar fed me lies and I devoured them like a starving man. And look how my life has turned out."

Hearing a gentle thud, Berty's eyes moved towards the sound. Off of her chair, Delyth approached Sean carefully. Tenderly, her arm reached out for his. In her soothing soft voice, she said, "There are always repercussions from our decisions. Come with me."

Delyth gently pulled the depressed Sean out of the room. He barely could place one foot in front of the other.

Declan sprang off his chair.

"Leave it," Berty said.

Declan's arms shook as he managed, "He... her."

"Breathe," Berty ordered Declan.

Breathing, he sounded like a bull ready to charge.

"Slower." Berty watched Declan's body fill with air while he inhaled. "She is fine," Berty told him.

Slowly nodding, Declan painfully sat in his chair. His eyes never left the door.

Quickly returning to the room, Delyth said, "He acts like a child—an overgrown child." She looked disgusted as she returned to her seat.

Sitting comfortably, Declan smiled.

"He needed to know," said Alfred.

With a murmur of agreement, they continued to pour through the piles of books still on the table.

When the final book was read, Declan leaned back on his chair, saying, "Well, that was boring."

"Though insightful," added Alfred.

"We will help you return these books, Alfred," Delyth said.

Alfred gave Delyth a fatherly smile. Books in their arms, the three of them left Berty sitting at the Roundtable.

The brass sconces flickered to life on the smooth walls of the Roundtable Room. Flames dancing in the reflective tabletop mesmerized Berty. He wondered if Leif would have challenged Silvia for power if he had found the Staff of Lightning. Hearing the wind howl through the Empire Tree, Berty's thoughts changed direction.

Closing his eyes, he saw a long table filled with people eating and drinking. Light from the candles on the tables and from the fireplace flickered so furiously that the light almost seemed steady. At the table sat a laughing woman whose wavy dark red hair began to sweep past the bottom of her earlobe. Her warm, brown eyes looked at another woman with light blonde hair resting on her navy blue shoulders. Sitting around them were burly men drinking tankards of alcohol.

When the women stood, one of the men asked, "Where are you going?"

"Retiring for the evening," answered the blonde.

"It's too early for that," another man said as the group laughed.

Yet another said, "There's not going to be much to do with that storm brewing." He winked.

"Stay," said a man sitting next to the redhead as he grabbed her golden sleeve. He drunkenly attempted to pull her back in her seat.

"Let go of my arm," she said sweetly.

"Stay," he insisted, tugging with force.

"Will you please let go?" she asked.

"You're gonna need someone to keep you warm tonight," he slurred while his grip did not slack.

"I did say please," she said calmly. Lifting her arm, the man rose off his seat. She shook her arm as if she were shooing a fly. The man flew across the room, crashing into a nearby wall, then sliding to the floor.

Silence blanketed the room. She smiled as she adjusted her golden sleeve. "It is much easier if you had just listened the first time." Turning to the blonde, she said, "Ready, Estelle?"

"Of course, Ellri," Estelle answered with a smile.

With every pair of eyes following them, Silvia led Estelle to the stairway behind the stacked stone fireplace. Before she ascended the stairs, Silvia turned to glance at the silent room once more, smiling. As she stepped up the stairs, Berty noticed a royal blue crystal peeking from behind the gold collar of her gown.

Opening his eyes, he looked down to find that his hand had extracted his own dark red crystal from inside his shirt.

"Good, you are still here, Emperor," said Alfred as he walked into the room. When Berty's eyes found him, he continued, "I have been thinking."

Glancing at Alfred's forest green crystal hanging around his neck, Berty allowed him to elaborate.

"Do you think that Leif is out there searching for the Staff of Lightning?" the Elf asked.

"It is possible," Berty replied. He found the dancing light in the tabletop again. "What I wonder is how much Millicent knows."

Sitting in his chair, Alfred said to Berty, "You are going to have to find it first."

Seeing the grave seriousness in Alfred's blue eyes, Berty asked, "How?"

"By following the advice of Miercia and Darnell," answered Alfred.

Berty nodded before rising from his chair.

The tree creaked in protest as the wind howled while Berty climbed his private staircase. Reaching his rope and plank bridge, he watched as it swayed in the bitterly cold wind. As he crossed the bridge, the snow began to blow in front of his face. Berty could only feel the wood under his feet and the rope in his gloved hand. When he reached his platform, he turned his head seeing only white instead of the massive dark brown trunk of the Empire Tree. Entering his warm chambers, he knew that Alfred was right. He also knew that he could not leave until the blizzard was over.

For three days, snow blew furiously. Heavy snow covered all the platforms and bridges so fast that the Tenders had a difficult time keeping the walkways clear. In the afternoon of the fourth day, the snow finally began to wane. Sitting in the Reception Room, the inhabitants of the Empire Tree felt relieved that the blizzard was ending.

Spearing a potato, Hatcher said, "The gates of the Sages' Grove are snowed shut. We can start clearing the snow this afternoon."

"People are snowed into their homes," Alvar mentioned. "Some of the snow is higher than their windows and it falls in their houses when they attempt to open the door."

"Captain," said a young Elf, looking up from his food. When Alvar looked at him, he continued, "The Empire Guard is getting restless."

"What do you propose, Edwin?" Alvar asked his Lieutenant.

"That we employ the guards to help clear the snow," replied Edwin. "It will help with their cabin fever plus, it gets the Sages' Grove moving more quickly."

The normally stoic Elf smiled at Edwin, saying, "You have a lot of good insight, Lieutenant. After the snow has been cleared, I give you my blessing to go collect your bride."

Edwin's face lit. "I must go to Irmingard first," he said.

"I would expect no less," Alvar said. "Emperor, may Lieutenant Edwin collect his bride?"

"Of course he may," answered Berty. "Lark will be ecstatic."

"Thank you, Emperor, Captain," Edwin said with a wide smile.

After lunch, Alvar approached Berty on the steps to the Roundtable Room. "To commemorate Edwin's honor," said Alvar, "I must draw up Blessing Papers for him to give to her parents. We both have to sign."

"When they are ready, I will sign," said Berty.

Alvar nodded. "My Lord, I have a related issue which I would like to discuss with you."

Walking into the Roundtable Room, Berty sat in his ornate chair waiting for Alvar to begin.

Sitting, Alvar said, "In the current climate, I do not wish Edwin to travel alone. As capable as he is, love sometimes clouds the mind."

Berty could see the concern in Alvar's eyes. "Perhaps Declan should accompany him as my representative," he suggested.

"Declan would be an excellent choice," Alvar said with fleeting delight. "Do you think that he would agree?"

"Let's ask him." Berty called for Theodore.

The Dwarf told him that Declan was in the Vault Room, out of his reach.

After dismissing his Head Tender, Berty extracted his large, gold Watcher's locket. Using the rod part of the clasp, he messaged for Declan to join them.

While waiting for Declan, Alvar constantly rubbed his fingers. Berty wondered why he was so nervous.

"Sorry I could not come sooner," panted Declan as he approached the Roundtable. "I was helping Delyth with her research materials."

Not wanting to know what that entailed, Berty gestured for him to sit while asking, "How would you like to be my representative on a journey to Irmingard?"

A large smile crept onto Declan's face as he descended into his chair. "Really? I mean, it would be an honor, my Lord."

"You will be accompanying Edwin as he begins the marriage tradition," explained Berty.

"As a high ranking Lieutenant in the Empire Guard," Alvar added, "Edwin needs to show his family that he has the full support of the Emperor."

"You will need to wear your locket so that they know that you are my eyes and ears," said Berty. "And remember, I met Lark and her family. They are good people. I wholeheartedly approve."

"Of course," Declan said looking from Berty to Alvar. "Do you think Edwin will face opposition?"

"It is possible," Alvar conceded. "Especially with his family being who they are. And Lark is not from Irmingard."

Declan nodded. "The journey to Irmingard could be dangerous, I better ready my arrows."

When Declan left the room, Alvar stated, "At least one of them will have his head on straight. Thank you, my Lord."

Ascending two flights of stairs, Berty opened an arched

wooden door. He walked into a narrow room that followed the curvature of the trunk of the Empire Tree. Standing next to the only table in the room, he looked at the miniature model of the Sages Grove before blowing into the trunk of the miniature Empire Tree. Instantly, a blanket of white buried all the thatched roofs of the cob buildings. Around the village, Edwin orchestrated Empire Guards as they removed the snow from the paths and away from doors and windows.

Once the doors were clear, villagers emerged from their homes helping the guards and their neighbors. Watching the likeness of Edwin, Berty felt happy for him. Edwin had spent roughly three months away from Lark. Although they wrote letters to one another constantly, Edwin missed her terribly. Berty knew exactly how he felt.

He had been separated from Silvia for almost as long, but Berty had no idea when he would see her again. His misery without her rooted deeper than his lieutenant's. Even if he and Silvia were reunited, she could not return with him because the crystals that hung around their necks made it so.

Berty did not quite understand the crystals. Seven crystals of different colors hung around seven necks. He often pondered how the crystals connected them to the scepter and to each other.

Refocusing on the miniature before him, he realized that most of the snow had been cleared and that evening was fast approaching. Breathing stillness into the model, Berty returned to the Reception Room for dinner before retiring for the evening.

Sunlight poured into his bedroom as he lay in his large bed. Descending his spiral staircase into his sun-filled study, Berty knew that he had to give Declan proof of representation. In his desk, he found paper with the Sages' Seal watermark.

Pen in hand, Berty wrote, "I hereby declare Advisor Declan my official representative. Accept this as proof of his honor and loyalty to me." After signing it, "The Emperor," he stamped it with a wax seal like he did the treaty.

While waiting for the wax to dry, Berty heard his wind

chimes. "Come in," he said.

Theodore entered, then stood in front of Berty's desk. "Alvar has Edwin's Blessing Papers ready. He wants to know if you could sign them before breakfast, my Lord," the Dwarf said, extracting papers from his cloak.

Perusing the papers, Berty did not read all of Edwin's honors and achievements since he joined the Empire Guard. He simply signed the last page next to Alvar's signature. With both documents secured inside his cloak, he brought them to breakfast in the Reception Room.

Berty handed Alvar Edwin's Blessing Papers before he sat at the table. When Edwin entered the room, Alvar said to him, "Excellent job, Lieutenant. I have your papers. Is he ready to go, my Lord?"

Edwin looked at Berty with hopeful anticipation.

"Almost," said Berty. He extracted the wax stamped paper from his pocket. Handing it to Declan, he said, "Declan will be joining you." Looking at the two men, he said, "Have a good journey men. And be careful."

Jumping off his chair, Edwin managed to say, "Thank you," before heading to his chambers. After Declan left to return to his chambers to gather his things, their breakfast companions scattered leaving Berty with Alvar and Alfred.

Alfred looked around the room. Satisfied, he turned to Berty asking, "When will you leave for God Mountain?"

"Once I know that Edwin and Declan have arrived in Irmingard safely," Berty replied.

Chapter Three
Ramparts White Glare

Berty stayed in the Reception Room until Edwin and Declan disappeared below the floor. Retreating to the relative seclusion of the Roundtable Room, Berty held the large gold locket in his hand. With the clasp's rod, he depressed the pupil of the eye surrounded by a six-pointed star. Opening the locket, the one side acted as a mini television screen while the other emitted sound. He watched through Declan's eyes as they walked through the gates of the Sages' Grove, beginning their westward journey.

"Have you ever been to Irmingard?" Edwin asked Declan.

"No," answered Declan. "How long has it been since you have been back?"

"Roughly two years," Edwin replied. "Right before I became a lieutenant."

Declan said nothing. Berty wished he could see Declan's expression.

"It will be nice to see everyone," continued Edwin. "My brother was just elected Low Elf. My parents are Ørgranden on the Ráðþing." Edwin paused, looking at Declan. "Ørgranden are lead council and the Ráðþing is Irmingard's legislative body. I really hope they give their blessing. Wait till you meet Lark. She is... wow... the most wonderful woman."

Berty tuned out Edwin's rambles about Lark, realizing that he would be leaving soon without Edwin and Declan. Open locket in hand, Berty climbed the stairs until he found himself in a wide hallway looking at curved doors. Finding the door he wanted, he walked into a room full of practice weapons and dummies hanging from the ceiling. He placed the open locket on the side table, then passed his hand over it. The picture and sound left the confines of the locket, resting as a hologram in the room with Berty.

Changing into leather sparring gear, Berty cranked a dummy into the center of the room. He unsheathed his sword, took his stance, and then began to attack the dummy the way Edwin had taught him.

Trying to keep one eye on the hologram caused Berty to be careless. In one fluid movement, Berty cut the rope that attached the dummy to the pulley system on the ceiling. The dummy dropped to the floor with a thud.

Chuckling, Berty's eyes scanned the room for more rope. Seeing a trunk with rope spilling out of it, he walked across the room. A scraping noise made Berty stop. Thinking he sensed movement, he turned around in time to see an axe being swung at him. Ducking quickly, he somersaulted out of the way.

Scrambling to his feet, he saw the dummy turning around, ready to attack. "This is new," Berty murmured.

He turned the hilt in his hand before blocking the attack. The dummy attacked Berty relentlessly. As Berty got tired and worn out, the dummy kept chasing him around the room.

Adrenaline overtook exhaustion. Finally, Berty disarmed the dummy. Falling to its knees, the dummy surrendered. "That is enough," said Berty. The dummy fell lifeless to the floor. Berty left the training room thoroughly exhausted, but willing to do it again.

As Edwin and Declan traveled towards Irmingard, Berty practiced with his untethered dummy. A few days after they left, Berty finished a sparring session to watch Declan gaze upon huge gleaming white ramparts. From the outside, Irmingard appeared to have many castles nestled inside a fortress with its many towers and spires.

Edwin smiled as he faced his childhood home. Collecting the locket, Berty returned to his chambers as the two men approached a bridge spanning a deep moat. Declan looked down into the murky water, saying, "A moat full of magic. Interesting."

On the other side of the bridge, they passed under a series of raised gates made of wood, metal and stone. Before entering the expansive grounds inside the ramparts, two white armored Irmingard Warriors stopped their progress. "No weapons of any kind allowed inside," said the youngest of the two men.

"Excuse me?" Edwin said.

The other guard scrutinized Edwin's cloak clasp before saying, "I am sorry, Lieutenant. He's new and did not recognize your Empire Guard rank. You may keep your weapons on your person, but your friend must surrender his."

"He's an Advisor to the Emperor," said Edwin. "Surely he does not have to, if a lowly lieutenant does not."

"Ummm...." The guard clearly was uncomfortable. Turning to the young guard, he said, "Get the Commander."

Edwin and Declan waited in the tunnel-like archway while Berty began his lunch. A large man with a highly decorated white metal breastplate walked out of a side doorway.

"Lieutenant," said the man, "Edwin?"

"Commander," Edwin began, "this is Declan, Advisor to the Emperor."

The Commander looked directly at Declan saying, "I do apologize for the confusion. Not many advisors visit and my men were naturally confused. Of course, Advisor, you are not required to leave your weapons at the door."

"Thank you for the clarification," said Declan.

The man sharply nodded his blond head. "Would you at least let us know what weapons you both are carrying?" he asked. "For our records."

"Of course," answered Declan.

"I am carrying a sword and a bow with a full quiver," Edwin said to the guard who was taking notes.

"Just a bow and quiver," said Declan.

The guard looked up from his notes. "Thank you."

Berty saw an unsettling look in the Commander's eyes as Edwin and Declan stepped forward.

"Lieutenant," the Commander called, "what is the reason for your visit?"

Turning, Edwin smiled saying, "To see my parents."

"They are in the Garden as we speak," said the Commander, catching up to them. "Allow me to escort you. It has been a while since you have lived here."

From the tunnel, the men walked into a vast stretch of snow covered ground before entering a locked door, which the Commander unlocked. Inside the white inner wall, a few torches on the stone walls dimly lighted the narrow corridor. The Commander opened another wood door through which they entered a large stone room.

"This does not lead to the Garden," Edwin said, not walking any further.

"It is a shortcut," said the Commander.

"I may have permanently left Irmingard over a decade ago, but I know where I am," Edwin stated firmly.

"Watch your tongue, Lieutenant," threatened the Commander as he turned sharply to face Edwin. "Do not let being an Empire Guard go to your head."

"Jealous?"

"I am Commander. You are Lieutenant. Know your place!"

Berty thought steam would escape the Elf's nostrils at any moment. He did not understand what Edwin was doing.

Edwin looked steely as he stared at the Commander. "Know yours," he said, his voice hard. "Empire law states that as a lieutenant directly serving the Emperor, I outrank you."

"Be that as it may," the Commander uttered through his clenched teeth, "you are bringing into my city a man possessing sacred weapons."

Glancing at Declan, Edwin asked, "Are you out of your mind? I was right, you brought us into the Warrior Realm."

"The Dominatrix will sort this out," the Commander yelled.

Berty almost choked on his drink.

From somewhere in the shadows, a woman's voice cut through the tension. "Enough, Marshall."

"Mistress," said the Commander as he turned saluting the shadows.

An elderly woman wearing dark leather armor walked towards them with the help of a cane. Her many long silver braids shone in the relative darkness of the room. Although she walked with a cane, her small frame emanated power.

Approaching Declan, she said, "I am the Dominatrix— Irmingard's weapon expert. Apparently, our Commander believes that an Advisor to the Emperor would carry something forbidden." She sighed. "Unfortunately, the only way to quell rumors is to indulge them. Would you forgive me if I asked you to hold out your bow?"

From under his brown cloak, Declan held in front of him the elegantly curved bow that Berty had seen him use on numerous occasions.

"It is beautiful," the Dominatrix said. "From where did you get it?"

"My grandfather gave it to me," Declan answered.

She smiled giving her hard lined face softness and warmth. "Do you craft your own arrows?"

"I do."

"But?"

"I haven't had to in a while," answered Declan. He glanced at Edwin, "since Eirawen."

A tear streaked down her face. She laughed, filling the room with laughter. "Use your grandfather's gift well, Advisor." Turning away, she said, "Marshall, I believe the Lieutenant would like to see his parents."

Berty finished his meal as Commander Marshall led Edwin and Declan through a series of poorly lighted corridors. Thinking about his next excursion away from the Empire Tree, Berty realized that instead of returning to the Training Room, he needed to speak with Alvar.

Commander Marshall opened a door, saying to Edwin with disgust, "You know the way."

Edwin stared at the Elf as he stepped out of the corridor ahead of Declan. The door slammed behind them. Declan casually gazed at the white stone wall in front of him as Edwin got his bearings. Looking up, the high ceiling arched like a gothic church. To the right was a distant door.

"The Garden is this way," said Edwin, leading Declan left. They proceeded down the wide, empty hall while Edwin explained, "This is the House of Reason where the Ráðþing meet. The Ørgranden like to spend time in the Garden. My parents say that it helps with the thought process."

Light shone into the hallway before them through a one-sided colonnade making the white stone sparkle. As they passed the columns, Declan peered through the openings at lush greenery. Trickling water could be heard in the distance.

Halfway down the colonnade, Edwin stepped down a few marble steps. Declan followed him into a vast garden. Declan's eyes caught a blue butterfly fluttering from flowering bush to flowering bush. Glancing upwards, he saw a beautiful metal and translucent glass dome. Nearby voices caused his head to look in front of him.

Turning a corner, a handful of Elves gathered around a pond full of koi, sitting on stone, metal and wood seats.

"Looks like we have visitors," a man said.

"Edwin," said a woman whose braided brown hair was pinned in a bun. Standing, she approached Edwin with open arms.

"Mother," Edwin said with a smile. When they hugged, Berty could see the streaks of silver in her hair. "Hello, Father," said Edwin warmly as his mother stood back drinking in her son's appearance.

"It has been too long since we have last seen you," his mother said. Her smile was wide. "To what do we owe this surprise visit?"

"Who is your friend?" asked a mostly white haired man with

vestiges of dark behind his ears. His blue eyes pierced Declan with suspicion.

"This is Declan," Edwin answered. He turned to Declan, "My mother and father."

"He is not a fellow lieutenant of yours," his father said without letting Declan speak, "but he can carry weapons through our city."

"Father," said Edwin undeterred, "Mother, I have news which I would like to share with you."

"Whatever you wish to share can be shared with the other Ørgranden," his father stated.

Edwin paused for a beat. Berty knew that Edwin wished that he were talking only to his parents. "Declan is an Advisor to the Emperor," Edwin began. "He is here as the Emperor's official representative." While a few eyebrows raised, his father's expression instantly changed from suspicious to curious. "The Emperor and Captain Alvar have signed my Blessing Papers." The Elves looked happy as if they knew what Edwin was going to say next. "I have met my bride and I wanted to get your blessing as well."

"Edwin, that is wonderful," his mother said while hugging her son again. "Declan, welcome to Irmingard. I am Femke. My husband is Ryker. Please, wait for us at our home. We will have a great meal and discuss this young lady."

"Thank you," said Declan. "It is a pleasure to meet you both."

Passing his hand over the locket, Berty returned the picture and sound to the confines of the ovals before fastening his cloak. As he descended his private staircase, he took a peek at Edwin and Declan strolling through narrow streets of a white stone city. In the Roundtable Room, he called for Theodore. He told the Dwarf that he wanted to see his Advisory Council.

When the Advisory Council took their seats around the table, Berty glanced at the empty chair beside him, saying, "As you know, Declan has accompanied Edwin to Irmingard. They arrived today unscathed. Which means, I can leave for God Mountain. However, because of Darnell's warning, I need to bring more than just Sean with me."

"My Lord," said Delyth, "I wish to go. My use of Fairy Dust is second to none. In addition, I have expanded my training with my sword."

Berty considered her for a moment. Leif did not work alone. The previous Historian, Millicent, aided him. Knowing that they had no other weapon against a Fairy, Berty agreed to let the Fairy Princess accompany him.

"I, too, will join you, my Lord," said Alvar. "My men are busy with the patrols. That is the one thing they can do without me."

"Very good," Berty said. "Alvar, Delyth be ready to leave in the morning. Everyone else, practice vigilance." Rising from the table, he disappeared into his private staircase.

Back in his study, Berty passed his hand over his locket. A cloth-covered table around which Declan, Edwin and his parents sat filled his study.

"I had a chance to read your Blessing Papers," Ryker said. "Reporting directly to the Emperor, you bring us such honor."

Edwin looked pleased that he made his father proud.

"Now," said Femke, "what is the young lady's name?"

"Lark," Edwin answered without being able to suppress a smile.

"Have you met her Declan?" Femke asked.

"No, I have not had the pleasure," replied Declan. "But by the way Edwin speaks about her, I feel as if I already have."

Femke laughed, turning her attention to her son. "What of her family?"

"Her parents, Thaddeus and Charlotte, are the proprietors of Violet's Inn in Calledin," Edwin said.

Femke and Ryker exchanged a look of concern.

"The Emperor has," Declan began.

"Excuse me for a moment, Declan," said Ryker. He faced his son. "Calledin? Those are not Elves worthy of anything."

Looking hurt, Edwin exclaimed, "Father."

"Your father is right," said Femke. "The Elves of Calledin have renounced our ways."

"They had to," Edwin explained, "or else they would have lost everything."

"Some things are more important," stated Ryker. "I forbid this union."

Standing, Edwin said firmly, "No."

Taken aback, Ryker said, "Excuse me?"

"I am not here to get your permission," said Edwin. "I wanted to share this with you." Throwing down his napkin, he walked away.

Once Edwin left the room, both Ryker and Femke looked at Declan as if he held answers regarding their disobedient son.

"Edwin met Lark and her family when he escorted the Emperor to Calledin," Declan elaborated. "Traveling incognito, neither the Emperor nor Edwin revealed their true identities. Without that knowledge, Lark and her family willingly helped them escape Calledin, defying Governor Manfred's laws."

Femke looked at her husband. Ryker nodded. "Excuse us," she said to Declan. They rose from their chairs, following their son out of the room.

When the three Elves returned, Berty had begun his dinner.

"Your mother and I have come to a new decision," Ryker said as they sat.

Chapter Four

Fairy Ring around the Dragon

"**W**ith Irmingard Warriors, we will be joining you on the road to Calledin," announced Femke with a smile.

"We will leave tomorrow," Ryker said. "First thing."

Berty felt relieved that Edwin and Declan would have the extra protection of Irmingard Warriors. He finished his meal trying not to think about his own morning embarkment.

A sense of purpose followed Berty as he went about his morning routine. In his study, he secured his sword to his belt and fastened his cloak. Stepping onto his platform, the smell of spring found his nostrils.

Entering the Reception Room, Berty found breakfast and supplies for his journey waiting for him. As he sat at the table with his breakfast, Alvar and Delyth joined him. Not long after, Sean appeared in the room, sheepishly joining the table.

"My Lord," said Delyth, "do you still have the map I drew?"

"Yes," Berty answered. "It is with my things."

"There is a road through the Dragonlands that leads to God Mountain," explained Delyth.

"Then that is the road we take," stated Berty.

After gathering their supplies, the four of them walked out of the Empire Tree into the cold morning air. Alvar led the group beyond the wooden gates of the tree-walled Sages' Grove. They strode into the forest towards the perimeter road.

Morning wore into afternoon before they finally stopped for a well-deserved break. Consulting the map, they traveled further towards the unknown. As the sun began to fall rapidly towards the horizon, Alvar said, "We should make camp."

Berty nodded. "Where?"

"I know of a place," said a familiar voice from behind them.

Spinning around, Berty saw two women approaching them. Smiling, Berty asked, "Coincidence?"

Laughing, a dark redheaded vision cloaked in light blue answered, "Goblins. They know that God Mountain cannot be traversed without a little heavenly guidance." She glanced at a midnight blue cloaked blonde, then strode past Berty, saying, "This way."

Silvia led them to a small clearing that no one saw. Lifting her right arm above her head, a large walking stick sprung from her palm. After encircling her head, she brought the stick down in front of her, tapping the ground once. A campsite sprung up around them with two tents and a fire. Walking over to one of the tents, she said pointing to the one in front of her, "Girl's tent." Pointing to the other, she said, "Boy's tent," then ducked inside the first tent.

Emerging without her walking stick, Silvia sat on a log next to Berty. "Elder Hunter," said Alvar, "what did you mean by heavenly guidance?"

"If you were to look at a map of the portaled Empire," Silvia explained, "you would not find any roads or anything depicted for God Mountain."

"No," affirmed Delyth. "That is why I did not draw it on the map except how to get there."

"But," Silvia continued, "once you arrive, paths abound though signs are scarce. Good thing we have Estelle."

Alvar looked confused.

Silvia smiled explaining, "Estelle is a true Stjarœðan. To find what we seek, we must navigate its labyrinth using the stars."

"I'll take first watch," announced Alvar.

"No need for that, Alvar," Silvia said. "The Empire Tree's

magic creates an impenetrable magical barrier around our camp. Reserve your energy for our trek into the Dragonlands tomorrow."

In the morning, Alvar led them further towards the border.

"There is one thing that I don't know," Silvia said to Berty as they walked through the thawing forest. "Why?"

Leaning over towards Silvia, Berty inhaled the berry pie smell he missed before whispering, "What is lost needs to be found." He glanced over his shoulder at Sean. The look in her eyes told Berty that she understood.

Cautiously, they approached the perimeter road. Seeing no one, they avoided the mud caused by the melting snow as they crossed the derelict exterior road.

After letting the forest engulf them, Alvar said, "I thought it would be wise to have a meal in the border town of Dorian to save our supplies."

Before Berty could answer, Delyth shouted, "Stop!"

"What is it?" asked Berty.

"A Fairy Ring," Delyth replied. She pointed to brown mushrooms growing in a circle through the thin layer of melting snow.

"Knownots," muttered Sean. Looking around wildly, he clutched his sword and cloak tightly around his body.

"No," said Delyth. "This is not some benign Knownot party. Those mushrooms have brown spots. No one can go any closer."

"Are you sure?" asked Alvar, squinting.

"I am a Fairy," Delyth answered. "You would not be able to see them until it was too late."

"I don't understand," said Berty.

"Brown spots on Fairy Ring mushrooms indicate Fairy Dust," Delyth explained. "Cover your faces. I am going to stir up the dust."

As Delyth cautiously walked forward, the others all brought their cloaks in front of their faces.

After a few minutes, Delyth said, "You can look now. The dust has settled."

Lowering his cloak from his face, Berty saw Delyth standing in front of them.

"I would suggest that we walk around the Fairy Ring as a precaution," suggested Delyth. As the group continued towards the border town, they gave the circle of mushrooms a wide swath.

"My Lord," said Delyth, "did not Colvin say that one of the coins associated with the poisoning comes from a border town?"

Berty recalled Colvin telling him about the coins Millicent paid Kayla for poisoning Delyth. "Yes." Searching into Delyth's violet eyes, he knew that she was thinking. "Do you mind sharing?"

Looking at Berty, Delyth bit her lower lip before saying, "I think it was a trap. They banked on Kayla being caught. They knew that the coins would have been traced. I believe they thought that you would send someone to check this town—someone who was not a Fairy."

Delyth raised her hood over her long dark brown curls as rain sprinkled upon them. Raising his own hood, Berty glanced at Silvia, who raised her eyebrows. Berty figured that Silvia apparently thought Delyth held something back as well.

Mulling over what Delyth had said, Berty realized that she was right. "Delyth," Berty said quietly, knowing that rain amplifies sound, "Stay in front and keep an eye out for anything."

Nodding, she kept stride next to Alvar.

A little after noon, their path took them to a cluster of wooden buildings. The border town of Dorian had no walls for protection. No guards of any kind patrolled the area. The muddy paths through the small town were empty as the rain fell harder.

Ducking inside a pub like establishment, older men indulging in a liquid lunch occupied many of the small tables. In the back of the dark pub, Alvar and Sean pushed two tables together. The six of them sat with Alvar and Berty facing the rain lashed windows.

46

An older woman walked out from behind a swinging door. Approaching them, she asked, "What'll ya have?"

Looking around, Alvar asked, "Do you serve food here?"

"We do indeed," answered the woman. "Not like any of *them* would know." She jerked her head to the patrons behind her. "Six?"

"Yes, please," said Alvar.

A light conversation about nothing flowed around the table as they waited for their food. The people in the pub lived their lives mostly on the insides of a tankard. Berty and the others were able to eat in peace.

The rain had not subsided by the time they had finished their meal. Raising their hoods, they walked into the heavy rain. With all the puddles on the path, Berty expected Sean to complain. He looked over at the uncharacteristically quiet Sean. Sean kept stealing glances at Estelle. Rolling his eyes, Berty savored the silent Sean.

The muddy road from Dorian led directly to the Dragonlands. A few weathered signs cautioned them about the dangers of encountering Dragons. Not reading the signs, they crossed the border. They stayed on the road, traveling in silence through the steady rain. The soft rhythmic beating of the rain on the ground kept pace with their footsteps as they ventured deeper into the Dragonlands.

Through the wetness, the smell of smoldering vegetation reached Berty's nose. His eyes scoured the trees, but they found no sign of burning. Walking cautiously, he knew that the Clan Wars had rekindled.

"Where should we make camp?" asked Alvar.

The burning smell increased as Silvia answered, "Not here."

Berty could feel the tenseness in the group while they continued on the road.

"Fire!" said Sean, pointing in the distance.

"We should be able to avoid it," Silvia said. "Let's keep walking."

The dark afternoon increasingly darkened. Opening her

hand, Silvia's walking stick sprung from her palm. With a tap, light emitted from the top, illuminating the road and the raindrops. As they walked, Berty reminisced about how he loved to sit and watch the rain fall in the light of a street lamp. His reminisces were disturbed when he heard a ferocious roar.

They stopped walking. Berty could feel the fear of his companions as everyone studied the sky and forest.

A bluish Dragon flew into the beam of light from Silvia's staff. Berty saw horns on its head that followed its spine to the tip of its tail. A yellow-orange flame erupted from its mouth that shot across the sky causing the group to take a step backwards.

"Your time is finished, Angana," bellowed the blue Dragon.

A silver Dragon, glowing brightly in the staff light, flew into view. Berty remembered the First Dragon of the Clan of Cian older looking. Since Eirawen's death, Angana's magic had been restored to her, thus, Berty rationalized, restoring her vitality.

"Only the rest of Mitrah will know the gravity of your mistake, Nagend," Angana bellowed in return.

Both Dragons inhaled deeply, ready to unleash their fire. Pushing past Alvar and Delyth, Silvia screamed, "No!" Grabbing her staff with both hands, she lifted it high in the air, then slammed it on the ground. The Dragons' exhaled fire hit an invisible barrier causing them to search for its source.

Nagend spit fire at Silvia. Taking her left hand off her staff, Silvia merely held her open palm in the Dragon's direction to capture Nagend's fire. With a pulse of her hand, Silvia sent the stream of flames into the dark sky.

"Stop! Both of you! You should be ashamed of yourselves," scolded Silvia.

"Elder, Emperor," Angana said. She landed on her side of the barrier.

"Don't kiss up to the Emperor, Angana," said a disgusted Nagend. He, too, landed on his side of the barrier. "You have wronged us. The Clan of Cian does not deserve to be custodians of this land."

"And the Clan of Mitrah does?" asked Angana. She laughed.

"Enough," Silvia said. "Look around you. The Dragonlands are in disarray. Keep burning everything in your path and the Dragonlands will die. If the Dragonlands cease to exist, then you would be forced back into the lands that abandoned you. Your numbers have dwindled because they decimated you with their Dragon slaying and their wars."

"I want my revenge!" shouted Nagend.

"If you wish to be annihilated," Silvia said, "I can grant your wish now." Smoke rushed out of Nagend's nostrils. "Is your revenge worth the extinction of all Dragons?"

Nagend glared at Angana through the barrier, then shook his head. "As First Dragon of Mitrah, I bear a responsibility to my clan," he said. "Just because Angana neglected hers, does not mean I should shirk mine. I will call off this war, Angana, but the First Council will meet and decide your fate." He looked at Silvia, saying, "Thank you, Elder." Looking at Berty, the Dragon bowed his head, saying, "My Lord." Without another glance at Angana, Nagend spread his blue wings, then flew into the darkness.

Angana watched Nagend fly away. Turning her shining head, she said, "Thank you. With wisdom comes responsibility. Somewhere along the way, I misplaced both."

They watched her fly in another direction until the darkness devoured her silvery skin. Silvia tapped her staff twice to remove the barrier, which plunged them into darkness. Berty thought he saw Silvia stumble a little, holding onto her staff for stability. Before he could ponder, a set of glowing gold globe-like eyes appeared suspended over the road in front of them.

A thin gold mustache appeared, then Berty heard, "Emperor, we meet again."

"Tong," said Berty, "how have you been keeping?"

"Hidden," Tong replied. "It is not easy being without a clan at the moment. For what are you searching?"

"How do you know that I am searching?" asked Berty.

"Six in a search party."

Remembering Dragons' fascination with numbers, Berty answered, "God Mountain."

"It takes lone men four days to walk from border to border," said Tong. "And you need a safe place to spend the night." Tong's sleek black body and boxy head became visible as he turned. "Follow me."

As they stepped off the rain soaked road, Estelle walked up to Silvia saying quietly, "*Stjatollen, Ellri.*" Silvia allowed Estelle to walk ahead of her while she used her staff to steady herself in the mud.

Knowing that the exchange was not meant for his ears, Berty wondered what Estelle had said in the ancient tongue. Silvia clearly understood, but to Berty it only sounded like gibberish.

Tong brought them to a small outcropping of rocks in which nestled a cave entrance. Immediately inside, the Dragon started a small fire, illuminating the large cavern. Sitting near the fire, Berty was glad to have shelter from the cold, steady rain. Sipping a core-warming beverage, Berty thought that he should check on Edwin and Declan.

Extracting the large, gold Watcher's locket from his pocket, Berty depressed the center of the eye. He opened it to see Declan sitting around a fire next to Edwin. Edwin's parents rose, retiring to a tent while Irmingard Warriors patrolled the campsite. Silvia curiously peered at the locket, so Berty passed his hand over it for everyone in the cave to see and hear.

"I can't believe we will be in Calledin tomorrow," Edwin said. He looked happily at Declan. "I can't wait for you to meet her, you'll...." Stopping mid sentence, Edwin began to look concerned.

"What's wrong?" asked Declan.

"You. They don't approve of magic."

"Lark's family?"

"Calledin. They execute magic users," Edwin explained. "You will need to hide your wand well. The Emperor transformed his wand into a blade when we visited Calledin. The guards never knew." His eyes widened. "The Emperor! You are the Emperor's representative. Show them the paper first. I bet they will not inspect any of us." He smiled.

50

If Declan responded, Berty never heard it because Sean began to scream from across the cave.

"You knew!" Sean walked towards Berty, wearing the accusatory expression Berty loathed. "You knew my plans," Sean shouted. "You knew we were coming. All because Declan was a spy!"

With the utmost contempt, Berty asked, "Are you angry over what you did or over how it turned out?"

Sean seemed to realize that everyone was staring at him. He refrained from answering.

Berty continued, "You must realize that if you fight against magic, then it will never be on your side."

Seething silently, Sean slunk into the rain.

"He wanted to hate Declan for switching sides," said Silvia.

"Now he can hate Declan for infiltrating his 'army,'" Delyth said, rolling her eyes.

"He's lost and angry," Estelle interjected from another part of the cave. When all eyes found her, she continued, "He's angry because he's lost and he's lost because he's angry." Her fingers caressed her star amulet. "I know how that feels."

Berty closed the locket before Sean returned to the cave, temper cooled by the rain. They rested their heads on their bedrolls, falling asleep beside the dying fire.

By morning, the rain had ended. Tong led them through the forest. "This way is faster than the road," Tong stated.

The sun began to peek through small breaks in the clouds when they stopped for a rest. Berty scanned the group. Sean sat on a rock drinking from his leather canteen while Alvar kept checking every noise as he leaned against a tree. Silvia and Estelle were having a conversation. Sitting away from everyone, Delyth stared at the Dragon.

Opening his locket, Berty watched Declan and the Elves reach the gates of Calledin. He saw the familiar gray stone wall and lanced guards flanking the arched wooden gates. As they stepped under the raised locks, the grayness of the city with its gray stone buildings and gray cobblestone streets was magnified by the gray sky.

A guard wearing gray metal armor said to them, "Raise your arms." He was ready to perform a weapons search.

Declan held out the paper that Berty had given him saying, "That will not be necessary."

The guard took the paper and read it. After giving it back to Declan, he whispered to a nearby guard. "Wait here," said the guard to the group.

"I could get a complex," muttered Declan.

A third guard approached them. "Is this in regards to the Nelson girl?" he asked. Berty knew that he was referring to Estelle's escape a few months prior.

Declan glanced at Edwin who barely shook his head. "No," stated Declan. "I am here representing the Emperor so that his Lieutenant may collect a bride."

"You will be leaving with an Elf girl?" asked the guard. When Declan nodded, the man said to the other guards, "Let them all through." Turning to Declan, he said, "Whatever we can do for the Emperor, sir, let us know. It will be worth having one less Elf to look after."

Edwin looked murderous. Declan replied, "All I ask is for us to be left alone for the nuptials. We will be on our way in no time."

They proceeded down the gray cobblestone streets with the Elves full of disgust. Declan whispered to Edwin, "Sorry about that. I figured it was best not to provoke them. Let's focus on your happiness. I can't wait to meet her."

Edwin walked a few steps before cracking a smile. "You are right. Their inn is down the next street."

Closing the locket, Berty approached Delyth. "He's fine. They never checked him."

Delyth smiled, saying, "Thank you for letting me know, my Lord. I was worried about him."

They continued walking through the dark, dank forest until they found a relatively dry clearing for camp. The cold, early spring night made everyone huddle around the fire. Across the fire from Berty, Estelle and Silvia were having a reluctant conversation, at least on Silvia's end. Berty wondered about their topic of discussion when Delyth sat next to him with a look on her face that Berty could not read.

"My Lord," said Delyth, "could I have a word in private?"

Delyth's question stopped the discourse between Estelle and Silvia as Silvia watched the exchange between Berty and the young Fairy.

"Yes, of course," Berty answered. He followed Delyth into her tent whilst Berty felt Silvia's eyes follow his path.

When he entered the tent, he saw the map folded on a cot. "Sorry, I borrowed it," said Delyth. "I need to show you something." She opened the map on the cot. Once Berty was looking at the hand drawn map, Delyth pointed, saying, "This is the road to God Mountain." Moving her finger much further north, she said, "This is where I believe we are. I have no idea where the Dragon is taking us, but it is not God Mountain."

"Knock, knock," said Silvia's voice from the tent entrance before Berty had a chance to respond.

"Come in," Berty replied.

Silvia walked into the tent looking from Delyth to Berty. "I sense a problem."

"Tong might be taking us elsewhere," said Berty. When he said it out loud, he could not believe that the Dragon would deceive him, his equal.

"I'm sure he has his reasons," Silvia said. "I would not worry about it so much, Delyth."

"You trust him?" asked Delyth.

"Do not mistrust everyone," Silvia advised.

"I don't," said Delyth with defiance in her voice. "I am just being careful."

"There is a point where one can become too careful," Silvia stated. "Learn from mistakes. Do not let them take over your everything."

Delyth's fair skin rushed with pink. "I will take that into consideration," she replied. Grabbing the map, she jumped off

53

the cot. She hastened out of the tent while trying to fold the paper neatly.

"She will be okay," Silvia said after watching her leave.

"What about you?" asked Berty.

Taken aback, she asked, "What do you mean?"

Berty took a step closer. "You and Estelle."

"Oh, that." Silvia shook her head. "That's nothing." When she smiled, Berty took another step closer. "Woman talk, you know."

Berty knew that to mean, *not for your ears*, so he dropped it. Gazing into her warm, brown eyes, he found solace. Deeply, he inhaled the intoxicating berry pie smell. He lost all desire to think as his hand reached for her dark red hair. His other hand found her golden covered waist as he pulled himself closer to her. He wished for nothing more than to get lost in her soft, brown eyes and dark red hair. As Berty's head lowered to gently collide with hers, delicate fingers pressed softly against his lips.

"Berty," said Silvia softly.

He kissed her fingers before she slipped out of his grasp.

"We can't," she said.

"No one will bother us for a little bit," replied Berty inching closer to her.

"It's not that," Silvia said. "I'm an Elder, Berty."

Berty did not want to think at that moment, so he threw her a blank look, hoping she would elaborate.

"Do you know what being an Elder means?" she asked him.

His hopes were dashed as he answered, "You cannot return to the Empire Tree."

"And?"

"And you wander about imparting your wisdom, like you were with the Dragons on the road."

"That's only part of it," said Silvia as she made a tour around the tent. Turning towards Berty, she continued, "Because of your sacrifice, we are connected." She stepped in front of him. "My life is wrapped in yours. If you were to get sick, then so would I. If you die, then I die with you. No matter how far apart we may be." Glancing away from him, she said, "It is called the Elder's Curse." She looked squarely into his brown eyes saying, "This is very ancient magic. You should not mess with it."

"Okay," he said though he could not suppress his longing for her. He watched her wander around the tent again. "But I do not understand."

"You will," she stopped to look at him, "or at least that is what Estelle says." Approaching Berty, Silvia placed her hand on his arm, then said, "Please, I beg you, let this run its course."

Staring in her warm, brown eyes, they pled with him. He nodded his head.

"Thank you," she said.

Leaving Silvia in her tent, Berty glanced at the others huddled around the fire before he proceeded into his tent. Sitting on his cot, he placed his face in his hands. After a moment, he slid his hand into his dark brown hair while resting his elbows on his knees. He wished he understood more. Silvia had always known more than he, but he never minded. He found her knowledge and insight to be one of the most attractive things about her. However, Berty felt as though he was being purposely left in the dark. Lifting his head out of his hands, he muttered, "She always lets me figure things out for myself." Feeling a little better, he readied himself for sleep.

The morning felt colder to Berty than it should have been during early spring as they packed their belongings for another day's journey.

"My Lord," whispered Alvar as they began to trod through the frosty forest, "something is amiss." The Elf looked poignantly at the Dragon who led the way.

"So I have been told," Berty said. He glanced quickly at Delyth who walked in front of them. When Alvar raised his eyebrows, Berty knew that Alvar and Delyth had not discussed anything.

"Give it some time," answered Berty. Lowering his voice, he said, "Law of equals always trumps."

After a couple of hours of walking in the dark, silent forest,

Berty began to feel the increasing uneasiness of the group. "Tong," said Berty, "where are you taking us?"

He closed his globe-like eyes as he faced Berty. Upon opening them, he said, "Forgive me, Emperor. I am taking you to God Mountain via a small detour."

"Explain this detour, Tong," said Berty, stopping in his tracks.

Sighing, Tong explained, "Another clanless Dragon is the reason for my detour. She was doing her duty for Cian when things went wrong. No one knows what happened. If she does, she is not telling. All she says is, 'Stardust from the Earth.'"

Delyth gasped. "That's impossible."

"What's impossible?" asked Berty.

"Fairy Dust does not work on Dragons," she answered.

"How do you know that it's Fairy Dust?" asked Alvar.

"That phrase is a classic symptom of Fairy Dust abuse," Delyth replied.

Tong turned his attention to the Fairy. "You will help?"

"I will see what I can do," she said.

Smiling, Tong said, "She is just around here." He led them past some trees to a large rocky outcropping.

A loud sneeze brought everyone's attention to the top of the rocks. A large serpentine yellow Dragon curled herself around the rocks the way a small child would cling to a stuffed animal or security blanket for safety.

"Go no further," warned Delyth. "She seems to have had an allergic reaction to Fairy Dust." Cautiously, she walked towards the rocks. Opening her wings that glistened in the diffused morning light, the Fairy took to the sky.

Berty watched Delyth place a hand on the yellow Dragon's boxy snout. After a moment, she backed away. Thinking he blinked, all Berty saw was a glowing lavender sphere encompassing the Dragon.

"What's going on?" asked Berty.

"She's flying very fast," answered Silvia.

"Fairies can do that?" Sean asked skeptically.

"She's not just any Fairy," said Silvia. "She's the Princess.

Royalty usually have special abilities."

When the lavender sphere disappeared, Delyth flew to Tong. "She needs plenty of water and a lot of rest. Any lingering Fairy Dust should be flushed through her system in a couple of weeks."

"Thank you, Princess," said Tong. "I have kept you from your objective long enough. Allow me to take you to the border in an unorthodox way." The black Dragon landed, saying, "Climb on."

Chapter Five
Veleda

Berty looked at the waiting Dragon with trepidation. Somewhere in his memory, he remembered riding a pony. Barely four years old, he and Jon rode ponies at some fair wherever their parents brought them. The ponies were attached to a metal contraption that sat in the center of a barricaded circle. Their ponies rode slowly around and around. Berty could not enjoy himself because Jon cried the entire time on the pony opposite him.

A pony is not a Dragon. Trying to pretend that they were one in the same, he approached Tong. He could no longer play pretend when he realized that there was no saddle.

Berty found climbing on the Dragon's back surprisingly easy. Tong's black hide looked scaly until he straddled the Dragon's back. The scales were actually tiny black feathers that lay close to the skin. As he felt for a place to hold on, he marveled at how smooth the feathers felt under his hand.

"Everyone ready?" Tong asked.

A general murmur of agreement from behind Berty made him panic about how they would stay on Tong's back once they were flying through the air.

As the Dragon sped off the ground, Berty's panic was exchanged for exhilaration. He flew through the sky faster than Berty had ever gone. His stomach fell as if he were on a roller coaster. Berty highly doubted that anyone besides Delyth had

58

ever gone as fast before.

Trying to look around, Berty saw nothing but brown blurs interspersed among the gray. Feeling nauseous, he closed his eyes until he felt himself in a free fall. When he opened his eyes, nothingness surrounded him. All he saw was dull white. Berty felt the might of the Dragon reform underneath his body. His eyes registered a return of black, brown and gray. The brown blurs began to slow and tree shapes formed. Berty knew they were descending.

Tong landed softly on the muddy ground. "The border of the Dragonlands and God Mountain, Emperor," announced the Dragon. "I can go no further."

Berty slid off of Tong's back alongside everyone else.

"Good luck with your search," he said. Tong sprang into the sky, disappearing as a black streak against the gray.

"*That* was insane," remarked Sean. He stumbled a little until he got his bearings, then smiled wide.

Looking as if he had always ridden on the backs of Dragons, Alvar stated, "Without him, it would have taken us another day, at least, to reach the border."

"Instead," said Estelle, looking at the sky, "it took us less than half an hour." She started to walk forward. Stopping, she turned. "Are you all coming?"

Berty turned his attention to the path that crossed the border into God Mountain. The sun peeked through the clouds, illuminating bare tree-covered long rolling mountains. The further he looked, the bluer some of the mountains appeared. "God Mountain is a mountain range?"

"All the more reason why we need Estelle," answered Silvia.

Estelle took over point leading them into the forest-covered mountains. After many hours of nonstop up-hill walking, Alvar approached Estelle.

"We are going to have to find a place to camp soon," said Alvar.

"Yes, I know," said Estelle, keeping her head forward. "We are almost there."

She finally led them to a small clearing a third of the way down from the ridge of the mountain where they made camp. While eating dinner, Berty opened his locket.

Declan sat at a round table with a glass of heady stout in front of him while watching Edwin and Lark dance in the common room of Violet's Inn.

Carrying a pint of beer, an Elf sat next to him, asking, "Tired of dancing already, Declan?"

"Pacing myself," Declan answered. "What about you, Cesare?"

Cesare laughed. "There are two more days of celebration to go. Need to keep my strength." He lifted his glass to his mouth, taking a long drink. Placing his glass on the table, Cesare gazed at Lark and Edwin. The couple laughed while doing steps to an Elf folk dance. Finally, he said to Declan, "You know, Violet and I have only been married for three years. But, we practically grew up together. I've known Lark just about her entire life. She is more of a little sister than a sister-in-law." His smile faded a little. "The Sages' Grove will fully accept her and any children they may have?"

Berty thought that Declan smiled before he answered, "They will have a great life in the Sages' Grove. You and your family will not have to worry about her."

The smile returned to Cesare's face. After finishing his beer, he said, "We couldn't have asked for a better husband for her. Lieutenant, how awesome is that?" He began to laugh.

When Declan joined Cesare in laughing, Berty closed the locket.

"Are they doing well in Calledin?" Silvia asked Berty.

Surprised to see her sitting next to him, Berty answered, "Very." He took the moment to linger in her warm, brown eyes. His heart welled with a desire to hold her close to him.

"I am sorry that it is difficult," said Silvia as if she were reading his mind. "It should not have to be. Certain things should be easy. Is life not hard enough?" She searched into his brown eyes. "Please know that I am trying to protect you."

"From what?"

Without answering, she stood. Berty watched her walk into her tent.

The morning wind chilled Berty thoroughly as they trudged up the gentle mountain. When they reached the mountain ridge, the road split in five different directions. Estelle stopped, so Berty surveyed the view.

The sky threatened rain. The expansive valley had a small winding river cutting through it. Flanking the river, the trees began to speckle with buds. In the distance, the light blue and purple rolling mountaintops went on forever.

Estelle glanced at the mountains as her hand clasped her amulet. Tugging gently on her silver chain, it began to extend so that Estelle could place the gray stone over her eye. She looked as if she were wearing a starburst monocle. "There," she said while pointing to a mountain across the valley. "That lavender looking mountain is where we will find Veleda." As she tucked her amulet into her navy dress, the chain shrank to its original length.

"This way," instructed Estelle. She led them on the path that kept them walking parallel with the mountain ridge, roughly a third of the way from the top.

"Don't we have to cross the valley?" asked Sean.

"Yes," Estelle answered.

"Then shouldn't we be down there?"

"Only if you want to deal with magical creatures that have not been seen for centuries or longer," Estelle replied.

Sean glanced warily at the benign scene below, then stuck close to the group. Estelle kept everyone walking until it was close to sunset. She found a place to spend the night with a view of the path. Sitting around the campfire, Berty watched the fog settle in the valley.

When they embarked on the path in the morning, Berty saw that the fog had grown overnight, devouring most of the valley. Estelle kept to the path, checking the sky every so often.

The valley fog lifted slowly. Around noon, they were able to get a clear view of the winding river below between the trees of the thick forest.

A rustling in the woods below the path made them stop. Berty thought he heard large creatures moving very fast.

"Protect Estelle," whispered Silvia.

Alvar grabbed Estelle placing her behind him as he drew his sword. Berty, Sean and Delyth unsheathed their swords and waited.

Five men in bronze breastplates and red capes emerged onto the path from between the trees. Their swords were drawn, but Berty thought that they were running from something not running to attack them. When the men saw them, they looked surprised. One of the men said something to the others in a language that Berty did not know.

Silvia stepped forward with her staff speaking to them in the same language. The men sheathed their swords.

After one of the men spoke, Silvia translated, "They mean us no harm."

"We were escaping from the beasts," the man said.

Berty sheathed his sword. The others followed his lead with Alvar being last.

"You speak our language?" asked Silvia.

"Yes," answered the man. "We had to learn it to survive here."

"You are not from these lands?" Silvia inquired further.

"No. We hail from Rome. We used to be a legion of fifty strong accompanying our Emperor. After his visit, we became lost in this land. Over the years, fifty whittled down to five."

"How can this be?" Berty asked. "Rome has not been an Empire for over a millennia."

"Lost to the ages until you follow another Emperor. That is what the seer said. We have looked for another," said the man, "but none have been found."

Berty glanced at Silvia who nodded.

"I am the Emperor of all that surrounds us," said Berty. "If you wish to leave this place, then I will grant you that chance.

You must swear to follow my orders directly or through the Captain of my guard." Berty nodded his head towards Alvar. "Know that if you do come with us, we will be going to our home, the Land of Sages." He looked at the five of them. "What will it be?"

The man who had been doing all the talking studied Berty and the others. "I am Gnaeus, my Lord," he said as he fell on one knee.

Another followed suit, saying, "I am Manius, my Lord."

"Vitus, my Lord."

"Otho, my Lord."

"I am Tacitus, my Lord."

All five Romans knelt in front of Berty. "Very good," said Berty. "Come."

As the men stood, Sean and Silvia escorted Estelle through them. She continued to lead with the Romans following behind. When they stopped for the evening, Estelle informed everyone, "We will be crossing the valley tomorrow."

Sitting around the fire, Gnaeus asked Alvar, "Captain, why does the Emperor bring women?"

"He brings whom he trusts," Alvar said. He did not seem to be sure about the new additions.

Berty sat next to Silvia, then asked, "How do you know all these languages?"

With a twinkle in her brown eyes, she answered, "The ancient tongue I learned how to read from my mother. Understanding it when it is spoken is innate. I suppose it has something to do with being an elder. Latin, I learned in school. Didn't you?"

"And you remember it? I learned French," said Berty. "All I remember is bonjour and a few, select words."

Silvia laughed. "Being an elder helps the memory, too. Of course I think it helps that I actually learned Latin, unlike you and French."

Laughing, Berty conceded, "You have a point."

Spending the evening laughing with Silvia gave Berty a good feeling that he carried with him to sleep.

Morning revealed a dense fog that had settled in the valley. Before they continued their journey, Estelle checked the stars through her amulet. The knowledge that they were going to cross the valley caused tenseness through the group, especially after the Romans told their stories the night before.

After walking for a while, Estelle announced, "We cross here."

"But there is no path," said Sean.

"Precisely," Estelle replied. Sean did not look assured. Looking away from Sean, she continued, "The fog will be thick. You may want to place your hand on the shoulder of the person in front of you. Ellri, if you will walk behind me with your walking stick."

Opening her hand, the stick fell from Silvia's palm. She placed a hand on Estelle's shoulder. Berty quickly followed suit behind her. Behind Berty, Delyth, Alvar, Sean, and the five Romans formed a line.

With the amulet in front of her one eye, Estelle led them down the side of the mountain towards the dense fog. They descended quietly. The only noise was the gentle, rhythmic thud of Silvia's staff touching the ground.

Reaching the edge of the fog more quickly than Berty had anticipated, his heart pounded loudly, adding an off beat to Silvia's staff. Watching Estelle disappear into the white caused his heart to beat faster.

The white enveloped Silvia's light blue body, too. He only knew that she was still in front of him because his hand could still feel her shoulder.

As he entered the white fog, he immediately panicked. All his senses felt as though they were deceiving him. He saw nothing but a dull white cloud. The thumping of Silvia's staff sounded muffled as if he had cotton stuffed in his ears. He was not sure if he could still feel Silvia's shoulder in front of him, but he could feel Delyth gripping his shoulder more tightly.

The fast beating of his heart thumped in his eardrums. Berty was not sure if his feet were still touching the ground. Each step made him unsure of walking. He did not know if he even remembered how to walk.

Dark shapes loosely formed, then unformed around him. All he could smell was a uniform, musty dampness. He thought that mythological beasts would smell more distinctive if they came near.

Every now and then, Berty's hand would squeeze Silvia's shoulder just to make sure that she was still in front of him. Eventually, his feet felt a change in the ground. He thought that the ground began to level, but he was not sure. Berty wondered how long they would travel along the valley floor.

Suddenly, he felt as if he were walking. The soft ground changed to what Berty thought could have been wood. His ears discerned the muffled sound of water rushing. Pretending that his senses were not deceiving him, he thought that they were crossing the river at the bottom of the valley.

He tried to feel relieved because crossing the river meant that they were halfway through the fog, but he could no longer push away his anxiety with pretending. Ominous splashes reached through his muffled ears. Berty swallowed hard, hoping the bridge was secure.

As the substance under Berty's feet changed again, a soft whimpering cut through the fog. All his muscles tensed. He could not discern if someone or something was hurt, lost, or finally succumbing to the power of the fog.

After he pretended that they were climbing out of the valley, he thought the whimpering began to wane. Berty figured his eyes were playing tricks on him as the dullness of the white looked to be getting brighter.

Breathing eased while he thought he could see patches of dark red. Escaping from the clutches of the dense white cloud, he saw Estelle still leading the way.

"Do not let go of each other," she repeated until the last man emerged from the fog.

On the mountain path, Berty looked down at the valley that they had just crossed. The dense fog was beginning to evaporate. Taking a deep breath, he looked away.

Allowing everyone to remove their hands from one another, Estelle led them further along the mountain. As they walked, the trees became sparse. The path led them to a clearing filled with spring grass.

Contrasting with the light green grass, a dark yurt sat in the middle of the field. The yurt's felt covering was decorated in blues and whites. Even as they approached, Berty could not tell if the felt resembled the night sky or the ocean.

"This is it," declared Estelle.

From behind a hanging panel, a small man wearing multicolored garb walked out of the yurt. Looking at them, he said, "Only one may enter Veleda's Hollow." He pointed to the tiny dirt path that led into a small valley. "Choose well."

Berty watched the man return to the inside of his yurt. "It is my duty as Emperor to go," he said.

"We will wait here for you, my Lord," said Alvar.

Silvia stared at the grass borders of the dirt path. "Expect to be tested."

Looking at his group, Berty realized that he did not know how far he had to travel to find Veleda. "Will Sean be okay being away from both me and the Empire Tree?"

With a smile, Silvia answered, "I carry the Empire Tree with me. As long as Sean does not stray from me, he will be fine."

"Emperor," said Estelle in a serious tone, "stick to the path. Do not stray from this path for any reason, good or bad." She pierced her words into him with her sharp, light blue eyes.

"You have enough supplies, my Lord?" asked Sean.

Checking his bags quickly, Berty answered, "Yes."

"My Lord, before you go," said Delyth as she approached, "take this, just in case." She pressed a small, purple velvet drawstring bag into his hand. "A pinch is all you will need."

He looked at the bag, then back at the Fairy. "Delyth, I—"

"I can give a gift of Fairy Dust to a non-Fairy only once," said Delyth. "Use it well. Use it wisely."

"Thank you," Berty said, placing the small bag inside his cloak. "See you soon." Turning to face the path, he felt ten pairs of eyes follow him as he stepped onto the path to Veleda.

As he walked, light green shoots and buds told him that the valley would be lush come summer. Budding trees became more common along the path. Eventually, Berty found himself walking in a dense forest. The numerous branches filtered most of the light. He could not judge how much daylight was left.

Never a stranger to being alone, Berty found his new solitude a tad unnerving. The majority of his new life as Emperor had been spent with at least one other person. He rarely left the Empire Tree without some sort of escort. Until the moment that he was walking alone on a path through an unfamiliar forest, he never realized how much he relied upon the others. His entourage made him feel safe. Walking through the enclosing forest, Berty felt exposed and vulnerable. Silvia's words, *expect to be tested*, reverberated in his mind, reminding him to keep his senses sharp.

When nighttime finally pushed away the day, Berty concocted a sphere of light that hovered beside his head. The light illuminated the path and surrounding trees. Berty kept walking, not worrying about eating or sleeping. When he felt too tired to keep going, he expanded the sphere until it encompassed him. Stretching his bedroll on the path, he slept inside his protective sphere.

Berty awoke to rumbling in his stomach. Collapsing his sphere into his solar plexus, he magically heated some food, then ate it as he walked. Not long after his breakfast, a man in tattered clothes joined Berty on the path.

"I'm Ollie," the man said. His deep lined face showed signs of working long days in the sun. "What brings you here?"

"I'm searching," Berty began.

"One of those quest types," Ollie interrupted. "Plough's broke. Can't fix it no more. Gotta get a new one now," said Ollie, scratching his head. "Don't know how to get one before it gets too late to plant. Gotta plant to feed my family."

"You are asking a seer for a new plough?"

"Not exactly. Just need to know how to get one," Ollie

answered. "What's that?" He pointed to a large, mangled, dark mass strewn across the path.

The shape moved, but not well. "I don't know," said Berty.

When the two men got close enough to see it, Ollie said, "It's an injured bird. Let's eat it."

Berty glanced at Ollie with disbelief. "That is not just a bird. It is an eagle. People do not eat eagles," said Berty.

"You do when you're hungry," Ollie said while rubbing his stomach.

Reaching inside his food parcel, Berty pulled out some food. "Here, eat this instead," he said. Half wanting to be rid of the man, Berty collected two gold coins, then pressed them into the man's other hand.

Looking down at the food in his one hand and the gold coins in the other, Ollie's eyes began to well. "Thank you," he said to Berty. "This means so much to my family. How am I ever gonna repay you? I don't even know your name."

Calling himself the Emperor flittered through his mind, then he said, "My name is Berty. It is a gift."

Wiping his face, Ollie said, "I need to get home to my family. You'll be all right?"

"Go. I will be fine," said Berty.

After Ollie disappeared into the forest, Berty crouched next to the injured eagle. "I'm not going to hurt you," he told the panicked bird, as calmly as he could.

Glancing over the bird, he saw feathers sticking out in different directions. The bird squawked and writhed in pain. "What hurts?" he asked it, not knowing why he was talking to a bird.

As if the bird understood Berty, it used its beak to point at its left wing. Berty ran his hand over the bird's wing while willing it to be healed. He kept repeating his motion and thoughts until the bird composed itself.

The eagle stood calmly in the path, looking at Berty. "Can you fly?" asked Berty.

It opened its wings, wincing.

"It may be sore for a while," Berty said. Seeing the eagle's sharp talons, he put a glove on his hand. Extending the gloved hand, he said, "Do you want to come with me? When you can fly again, you can go wherever you want."

With a soft coo-like noise, the eagle hopped onto Berty's gloved hand.

"Just be mindful of your talons. They could hurt." When Berty stood, the bird carefully climbed up his arm, resting on his shoulder. Berty grimaced, waiting for the pain in his shoulder, but the bird's claws did not dig into him. Surprised, but pleased, Berty continued walking on the path.

A soft rain began to fall making Berty raise his hood. He felt like a pirate cliché, traipsing around with a bird on his shoulder. Chuckling, he thought that his life had a normalcy of strangeness.

Retrieving some food from his bag, he shared it with the eagle. As he walked, the path took him out of the dense section of the forest. The rain fell harder as the wind began to howl. Berty watched the sky grow darker. No shelter from the elements presented itself along the path. Wanting to protect the healing eagle on his shoulder, he magically constructed a shielding bubble to act like a see-through umbrella. With it working well, Berty continued to follow the path.

When he walked out of the storm, Berty removed his magic. The forest thinned to reveal patches of thawing grassland. A woman approached the path from the grassland. The wind blew her flowing, pale pink dress and long, red hair making it look as though she were aflame. Her one arm embraced a jug while a basket handle rested on her other arm. Not curious about her, Berty kept walking.

"Traveler," the woman called. "I bring food and water. Surely, you would like to have some."

Something seemed off to Berty about the woman though he could not figure out what it was. He replied, "No thank you, I am fine," and kept walking.

"I offer more than just sustenance," she said seductively. "I can guarantee you safe passage, not only to the seer, but home as well."

The eagle began to flutter on Berty's shoulder. "I am going to decline," said Berty, not stopping. "I will manage."

She walked alongside Berty, staring at him. "A kiss for luck, perhaps?" she breathed.

Berty began to feel strange like he desired to kiss her, yet he had no intention of doing so. His walking slowed. The eagle squawked loudly in his ear. Blinking, he said, "Sorry, I must keep going."

As he left her standing beside the path, he began to feel like himself again. "Thanks," Berty said to the bird, then gave it a piece of food.

Leaving the grassland, the path began to wind. Berty could not see where it led until he rounded the bends. With each turn, the path became steeper as he ascended out of the valley.

The last turn revealed a narrow strip of rocky path that hugged an otherwise sheer cliff. Trepidatiously, Berty's hand reached for the cliff wall as his feet traversed the uneven rocks of the path. When the path narrowed, Berty stretched his body against the cliff, inching along with duck feet.

A strong gust of wind loosened rocks off the cliff. Berty stopped to let the rocks slide. Hastening his pace, he slithered past the falling rocks. The uneven rock path gave way to stone steps carved into the side of the mountain.

On all fours, he climbed up the steep steps. Breathing became difficult the higher Berty climbed. He barely straightened himself on the windy mountain summit when the eagle shrieked, jumping off his shoulder. Looking around, Berty ducked as the blade of a battleaxe nearly missed his head.

Quickly checking the ground, he realized that the path had ended. He had reached his destination and it wished to behead him. Panic swept through his body. Hearing a man's grunt, his nose drew in the cold mountain air. The chill sharpened his senses. Remembering a training room far from the mountain summit on which he stood, he unsheathed his sword. The cold metal hilt warmed quickly in his hand. Raising the sword while turning towards the source of the noise, Berty blocked the man's blow.

The man wasted no time swinging his axe again and again. Berty blocked every attempt. Pushing the man back a few feet, Berty was able to see the man clearly. A strong gust made the man's mane look more wild than Berty had remembered. In the brief sunlight, Berty could see remnants of red in his otherwise long gray hair and beard.

Recognizing him immediately, Berty shouted, "Leif! What are you doing here?"

Leif answered by swinging his battleaxe with all his might. When Berty dodged his strike, Leif raged, "Fight me! No outsider waltzes through the portal and steals the Empire from me!"

Blocking another swing of his axe, Berty said, "I stole nothing! We can talk about this."

Leif laughed maniacally before saying, "Time to face the consequences, Hubert." He swung again, but Berty quickly leapt out of the way.

An unhinged, wild look took residence in Leif's eyes. Remembering the adage, *the best defense is a good offense*, Berty changed his strategy. Gripping the hilt of his sword more tightly, he planted his feet on the ground, ready to spring.

Leif lifted the battleaxe over his head. When the sun shone on the sharpened edge, Berty sprinted towards Leif. As Leif swung downward, Berty sliced across and upward. The battleaxe slid out of Leif's hands, falling over the side of the mountain.

Surprised, Leif stared at the sword pointed at his chest. "You win," he said. Falling to his knees, he pleaded, "Kill me. End it now."

Berty looked at the fallen former scholar. "No," he answered. Taking a step backwards, he asked, "What do you know about the Staff of Lightning?"

"Kill me!" Leif's shouts echoed off the mountains.

"Death may come, but not by my hand," Berty told him as he sheathed his sword. "Where is the Staff of Lightning?"

Leif hung his head. "Knowledge over glory," he said softly. "Impressive." Little bright dots began to form around Leif, causing Berty to take a small step backwards. Without warning, they converged on Leif, engulfing him in light.

The old man melted away to reveal a woman. As she raised her head, her long golden blonde hair parted, exposing her very pale skin to the sunlight. "Forgive the tests, Emperor, but wisdom does not come without its price." Berty watched her hair rise off the ground, falling to her knees as she stood. The tall, slender woman walked towards him. Her white Grecianesque gown fluttered around her, exposing her silver and gold sandals.

"You are Veleda?" Berty asked her.

Matching his height, she looked at him with her light brown eyes before answering, "I am." Walking past him, she said, "Come and have a seat. I will divulge the information for which you came all this way."

The eagle returned to his shoulder while he followed her along the ridge of the mountain. He walked through a Roman colonnade, which surrounded a mosaic tiled floor. Approaching a cozy seating area on the other side of the colonnade, he studied the mosaic picture. The tiny tiles resembled the universe with the Empire Tree at the very center. Before he reached the low table covered with food and drink, Berty looked over his shoulder at the mosaic floor again. What looked like the universe at first glance, became the largest Sages' Seal he had ever seen.

Turning from the floor, he sat on one of the large, low cushioned sofas. He noticed that Veleda already had her feet up on another white sofa. She propped her elbow on a round pillow.

Before Berty could say anything, Veleda said, "In all my years, and they have been many, I have never had a visitor like you, Emperor. They all sought knowledge of one form or another, but no matter what they called themselves—King, Queen, Emperor, Empress, Chief, Priest, Caesar—," she gave a short laugh through her nose, "they all wanted for themselves." She looked directly into his eyes. "But, not you. You seek true wisdom, Emperor. That, I will gladly give." Smiling, she took a fig from the table. She studied him while she took a bite.

"Quick fixes and ignorance led to its disappearance," said Veleda. "Even when set in stone, things are not always as they appear. Answers lead to further questions. Creating your own destiny is laid out before you, if you know where to look. Keep your heart pure and you will always know the way." Veleda looked out at the white columns.

"For you, an extra piece," Veleda said as she looked at Berty again. "The Bow of the Moon should be kept near. Its rightful place is in service to the Empire." She smiled, then said, "Please, have something from the table."

Berty did not realize how thirsty he was until he surveyed the feast of fruits, cheese and bread in front of him. Picking up a goblet off the table, he paused before bringing the wine to his lips. "What is the Bow of the Moon?" he asked.

"Drink," she answered, "you will find out soon enough."

Berty took a drink of his wine. As soon as he swallowed, the bright white colonnade around him disappeared, being replaced by toppled gray columns in ruins. Looking around, it was as if time, earthquakes, plundering, and war took their toll on the beautiful, tranquil scene of which he had just encountered. The soft ground replaced the cushioned sofa on which he was sitting. Tuffs of grass dotting the dirt replaced the mosaic tiles.

Standing, Berty realized the eagle still stood on his shoulder. "How am I going to find my way back to the group?" he asked the bird. Closing his eyes, he saw Silvia sitting around a fire with the others.

"How did you get lost here?" Delyth asked the Romans.

"The one who brought us here," answered Otho, "bartered us in exchange for guaranteed safe passage."

"We were camped on this very field," said Manius. "A woman in red came to tell us."

"Even had red hair to match," Vitus added.

"Regardless, we waited," said Otho. "He never showed. Lost to the ages indeed."

Berty opened his eyes. He felt a gentle pressure on his shoulder as the eagle flew into the sky. The eagle made a wide circle rather low to the ground. When the eagle returned, it squawked at Berty. He followed it down the sloping mountain instinctively.

The sun had begun to fall below the mountains. Through the scarlet darkness, Berty saw a fire below where he walked. The eagle circled the fire, then flew back to Berty. Walking towards the camp, the bird landed on Berty's shoulder.

Yards from the tents, a slender figure walked towards the edge of the camp. Knowing that Silvia waited to greet him made him smile.

When he reached the campsite, Silvia reached out her hand for his. He placed his hand in hers, relishing in her soft touch. She pulled him inside the campsite boundary. "Welcome back, Berty," she said. Looking at the bird resting on his shoulder, she continued, "I see you have made a new friend. Are you hungry?"

"Famished," Berty answered. She gazed into his brown eyes before dropping his hand.

When they joined the others around the fire, Alvar said, "My Lord, how did it go?"

"Well, I think," Berty said.

Silvia handed him a plate of food while Delyth asked, "What did she say?"

Staring at his plate, Berty tried to remember what Veleda had said. Being in Veleda's Hollow seemed like a vision. Only the eagle resting on his shoulder reminded him that it was real. "Vague riddles mostly," answered Berty. "Except... except about keeping the Bow of the Moon near. Whatever that is."

"It is a legendary weapon that has been out of commission for over two hundred years," Alvar explained.

"I thought we came here about the Staff of Lightning," whined Sean.

"We did," replied Delyth.

74

"The Staff of Lightning passes from generation to generation," Alvar said. "The Bow of the Moon chooses its archer."

"How does that help find the staff?" asked Sean with his arms crossed.

"I don't know," Berty said. "Perhaps it will be clear in the morning. I am exhausted." Giving the eagle the rest of his food, he walked towards the tents. Before he entered, the eagle flew off his shoulder, perching on the top of the tent.

Berty woke early to find Silvia heating root infusion over the fire. The dawn painted the sky pink and orange as he sat next to her.

Handing him a warm cup, she said, "I thought you would wake early."

He magically changed the contents of his cup to coffee. Taking a sip, his mind focused. In-between sips of coffee, he told her exactly what Veleda had told him on the sofa. Silvia said nothing, only listened. "Veleda's words could pertain to anything. The only thing about which she was specific was the Bow of the Moon. I am really at a loss about where to begin." He ran a hand through his dark hair, which was beginning to curl around his ears. "Silvia, this is a mess. And to top things off, I need to get home. Emperor or not, my mom will still kill me if I miss Easter dinner."

Smiling her warm smile, Silvia placed a calming hand on Berty's arm. Her touch always made him feel better. "Being Emperor is never easy. And complications only make life that much more fun. You have good instincts, Berty. Trust them."

He loved it when she used his nickname. As he gazed into Silvia's warm, brown eyes, they told him that he would figure it out. All he wanted to do in that moment was to hold her close. Nestled in his arms, he was sure that she would melt the uncertainty that surrounded him.

After seeing Veleda, Berty was no closer to thwarting Leif's plans to procure the Staff of Lightning. He wondered why she told him about the Bow of the Moon. It was just another object he had to find before Leif did. When the others began to stir, Berty abandoned his thoughts, not wanting to let anyone else know his concerns.

They were packing their campsite when the small man dressed in his colorful garb walked out of his yurt. Everyone watched him approach Estelle.

"The Seven west leads you home," he said to her. He looked at no one else before returning to his yurt.

Understanding his vague reference, Estelle faced westward and looked through her starburst amulet. She searched the sky. Finally focusing on something beyond what Berty could see, she said, "Let's go."

With one eye on the sky, Estelle quickly led them on a scenic path through the mountains. The fully healed eagle soared above the trees, following their trailblazing path. They traversed fallen trees and dense thickets at a maddening pace. As the sun descended towards the horizon, Estelle began to lead them down a steep mountain slope. Nobody could spare enough breath to question her methods.

When the ground had leveled, Berty had no idea where they were until a familiar voice said in the growing darkness, "Emperor, I have been awaiting your return."

Chapter Six
A Meeting of Hearts

"Tong," said Berty, "how is your friend?"

"She is recovering well," Tong answered, still not showing himself. "Thank you again, Princess."

"You are very welcome, Tong," replied Delyth.

Their Roman companions looked uneasily into the dark forest until Alvar whispered, "Relax. Tong is a friend."

When the eagle landed on Berty's shoulder, Tong appeared on the ground in front of them. "The First Dragons' Council is set to meet soon," Tong said. "It is probably best that your large party get through the Dragonlands as quickly as possible. Allow me to aid you once again."

Berty did not argue or complain. The sooner he returned home, the better, as far as he was concerned. With the eagle still on his shoulder, Berty climbed upon Tong's back. The others followed with the Romans being trepidatious.

As Berty felt his stomach drop, Tong jetted into the blackening night sky. The cool night air whipped through Berty's hair while his eyes saw nothing but darkness.

Tong landed at the border. Everyone quickly dismounted. After Berty thanked him, the black Dragon quickly disappeared into the black night.

Fixing his cloak around his shoulders, Sean complained, "I am tired and hungry."

"It has been a long day," said Berty also tired and hungry.

"We will make camp in the Land of Sages."

Not long after crossing the border into the Land of Sages, they found a place to camp.

Berty woke to find Silvia and Estelle having a serious, private conversation during breakfast. When the campsite was packed, Silvia walked over to Berty.

"It is time to part ways again," Silvia said.

"So soon?" asked Berty who was getting used to being around Silvia again.

"I have done all that I needed to do," she continued. Her hand beckoned Estelle to join them as her brown eyes gazed into Berty's. "She is ready."

Caught off guard, Berty asked, "Estelle?"

"Yes." Estelle joined Silvia's side as Silvia said, "To become what she was born to be."

"The Empire Astrologer," said Berty.

"There is nothing more I can teach her," she said. Part of her looked sad, knowing that she will be wandering alone again, while the rest of her was proud of Estelle. "You have done so much in so little time," she said to her.

"Thank you, Ellri," said Estelle.

Berty looked at Estelle who had morphed from a lost, scared girl into a confident woman. He knew what he needed to ask. "Estelle, will you sit at my Roundtable as the Empire's Astrologer?"

"It will be an honor, Emperor," Estelle replied with a smile.

Returning her smile, he shook her hand, saying, "Welcome."

Silvia beamed with sadness in her warm eyes. Berty knew that she would miss Estelle.

Estelle and Silvia hugged. The blonde hair next to the dark red hair made Berty think of a yin yang. "I will miss you, Ellri," Estelle said tearfully. "Thank you again for everything."

"I'll miss you, too," said Silvia, "but I know you will be just fine." She paused to smile at Estelle before taking a step backwards. Breathing deeply, Silvia looked at everyone before saying good-bye.

Watching Silvia walk away into the budding forest, Berty wished that they had more to say. He could not keep her with him, no matter how much he wanted her or needed her. She had to go. Tearing his gaze away from her light blue cloak disappearing into the trees, he said, "Let's make it home before nightfall, shall we?"

Looking through her amulet, Estelle guided them through the forest. Berty felt somewhat empty as they crossed the perimeter road. He tried to focus on his weary looking group.

After walking awhile, Sean cautiously approached Estelle. He asked, "What does that thing do?"

Estelle did not look at the inquiring Sean. "Makes what would normally obstruct my view of the stars transparent," she answered. "It affords my one eye focus and clarity while keeping my other eye aware of the obstacles."

"Which allowed you to see through that fog," said Sean, walking closer to her.

"Yes."

He walked in stride with Estelle. Leaning towards her, he said, "What did you see?"

"The right path to take," Estelle answered cryptically.

Misstepping, Sean scrunched his face in frustration. Knowing how much Sean hated anything less than simple and direct, Berty waited for his verbal outcry. To his surprise, Sean allowed Estelle to walk in front of him while he continued to walk in silence.

Smiling to himself, Berty thought about how Declan and Edwin would appreciate Sean's silent phase. He wondered how they were doing.

"My Lord," Alvar interrupted Berty's thoughts, "I have been thinking about our new found friends."

Berty knew that Alvar meant the Roman warriors.

"I will give them lodging in the barracks tonight," Alvar continued. "Tomorrow, I would like to offer them a place in the Empire Guard and allow them to prove themselves in order to establish rank."

Glancing at the Romans marching through his forest, Berty said, "They are in your charge, Alvar."

After walking most of the day, the treed wall, which surrounded the Sages' Grove, began to peek through the trees. Emerging into the clearing between the forest and the Sages' Grove, Berty saw a large party also approaching the gates. From the height of the people, he knew it had to be Edwin's wedding party.

Reaching the gates, both groups met each other. Edwin and Lark wore crowns of spring flowers as Irmingard Warriors surrounded them. Berty saw Declan leading the group of Elves.

Seeing Berty, Declan stopped. Bowing, he said, "My Lord, please enter before us." The Elves followed Declan's lead and bowed as well.

"Thank you, Declan," said Berty. Stepping aside, he allowed his group to enter the gates before him. When Berty caught up with the slow walking Delyth and Estelle, he said to them, "There is no need to wait with me. I am going to greet Edwin's parents and bride." They nodded their heads, then strolled up the path to the Empire Tree.

Edwin said something to Declan, which Berty could not hear. Declan then shook the hands of Edwin's parents. After saying goodbye to Lark, he tried to catch up to his peers before they entered the Empire Tree.

Smiling, Edwin approached Berty with his family. "My Lord," he said, "may I present my parents, Ryker and Femke."

"Emperor, it is an honor," said Ryker, bowing his head, "for both of us." Femke bowed her braided head as well.

"The honor is mine," Berty said looking into the man's steely blue eyes. "You have raised a fine son." He looked at Femke, who smiled proudly.

"And my bride, Lark," added Edwin.

"How could I forget," Berty said with a smile. "I hope your family is well."

"Very well, my Lord," answered Lark.

Turning his attention to Ryker and Femke, Berty said, "I am

aware that it is customary for the family to stay in Empire Guard housing in order to be close to their son. However, Edwin no longer resides in the Lieutenant's quarters. Your son is now a resident of the Empire Tree. Please, honor us by staying in the tree."

"Thank you, my Lord," said Femke. "That is very generous."

A tall woman carrying a lantern approached from the barracks. Alvar walked beside her. "My wife, Hedda, will collect Lark," Alvar said. "Irmingard Warriors, you may proceed to the barracks." Hedda smiled warmly at Lark who walked over to her. Alvar bowed to Berty before returning to the barracks for the evening.

Entering the Empire Tree, Berty led the wedding party up the stairs to the Reception Room. He was pleased to see dinner waiting for them. Inviting them to eat, Berty approached Alfred as he entered the room

"Welcome home, my Lord," Alfred greeted.

"Any news?" Berty asked quietly.

"None."

Nodding his head in relief, Berty allowed Alfred to join the table while he called for Theodore. The Dwarf appeared in the doorway greeting Berty warmly.

"Sean has returned to his quarters?" Berty asked.

"Without complaint, my Lord."

"Good. I am sure you are aware of our newest member of the Advisory Council?"

"Yes," Theodore said. "Hers and the Elves' rooms will be ready after dinner."

Berty thanked Theodore, then sat at the table. Famished, he said nothing whilst he ate. As conversation flowed around him, his mind wandered to Silvia. He missed eating with her. His mind's eye saw her short dark red hair and her soft lips he longed to kiss. Laughter from the table dissolved the picture. Finishing his meal, he wondered where she was going.

When dinner ended, Tenders showed Edwin's parents to their chambers while Theodore took Estelle to hers. Berty ran up his private staircase and across his bridge. Once in his study, he found his dual pocket watch. Opening it, the watch face told him that it was still before Easter. With a sigh of relief, Berty climbed his spiral staircase, then climbed into his warm, welcoming bed.

In the morning, Berty called an after breakfast Advisory Council meeting. Sitting around the Roundtable, he formally welcomed Estelle to the Advisory Council.

"Nothing has been out of the ordinary, my Lord," Hatcher said after Berty asked for a report.

Berty's finger ran down his lips to rest on of the edge of his chin. "Something feels wrong," he said. "Alvar, increase patrols and have them watch for Fairy Dust."

"Very well, my Lord," Alvar said. His eyes rested on the Fairy. "Delyth, do you think you can teach my men about Fairy Dust? I never would have suspected that Fairy Ring in the forest."

Looking surprised, she answered, "Of course. We are dealing with at least one insolent Fairy." Changing her gaze from Alvar to Berty, she said, "I have informed my parents about the unorthodox use of Fairy Dust. They will be looking into it."

"Good," said Berty before turning to the next order of business. "Veleda essentially said that the Staff of Lightning will be found through selfless means."

"What does that mean?" Colvin asked.

"Seers are never straightforward," answered Hatcher. Colvin still did not seem satisfied with that answer either.

"Except when she spoke of the Bow of the Moon," Berty continued.

"Bow of the Moon," repeated Alfred. He removed his glasses to shine them with a cloth. Placing them on his nose, he said, "Many Elves think that this legendary weapon belongs to the Elves, but it does not. The Elves have been its steward for a very long time. So long, in fact, that we have forgotten from where we obtained it. Legend states that it is a powerful, magical weapon in the right hands—hands the bow chooses. In anyone else's hands, it is a simply another bow."

"Do the Elves still have it?" Berty asked him.

"I do not believe so. Only the Dominatrix truly knows," said Alfred. "You would have to speak to her to be certain. Would you like me to ask her?"

Biting his lower lip for a moment, Declan said, "She passed it on a long time ago." When all eyes turned to a very uncomfortable Declan, he added, "We had a long talk while I was in Irmingard."

Alvar raised his eyebrows. "You spoke with the Dominatrix?"

Berty could feel Declan's discomfort emitting from him. Before Declan could answer, Berty asked Alvar, "What is happening with Edwin?"

Switching his focus onto Berty, Alvar said, "It is customary for the bride to spend a few days with the groom's family before the actual nuptials. I believe Femke is with Hedda as they introduce Lark to life as a guard's wife."

"It is a tradition that stems from keeping the groom honest about whom he proclaimed to be," explained Alfred. "Not usually necessary with Empire Guards or Irmingard Warriors, but sometimes the woman does not like living that kind of life."

"Edwin resumed his duties today," Alvar said. "He is determining the placement of those men we rescued."

Nodding, Berty said, "If there is nothing else, then we are done here for today."

While the Advisory Council rose out of their chairs, Berty heard Alvar asking Delyth to meet him by the guard's training area. Before Berty decided what to do next, the room had almost emptied. Staying behind was Declan.

Once Hatcher and Colvin finally left, bickering all the way down the steps, Declan asked Berty, "My Lord, did you hear my conversation with the Dominatrix?"

Berty tried to remember before his conversation with Veleda. "You talked about your grandfather."

"Yes, but I meant the conversation where she came to find me before we left Irmingard," Declan said.

"I did not."

After taking a deep breath, Declan continued, "She told me

the story of the Bow of the Moon. It was crafted by a lost people called the Lunatics. They imbued the bow with a secret magic, which gives an unlimited amount of arrows and the string never needs replacing. The Lunatics no longer walk among us as a different people. Their only enduring legacy is the Bow of the Moon. Many have studied and copied it, but not even the Dominatrix fully understands its magical powers. What she did understand was that it needed an archer. She went on a quest to find one."

"Did she?"

"No. She gave the bow to a young craftsman who lived deep in the woods. It became his job to give it to the chosen archer."

"And?"

"She did not say anything further about the Bow of the Moon. I do not think she knows."

Berty had no more answers, only more questions. "Thank you for telling me, Declan. But why not mention it in front of the rest of the Advisory Council?"

"Sometimes," said Declan, "less is best."

Agreeing with his Advisor, Berty nodded. He watched Declan leave the Roundtable Room as his words reverberated in his ears. His thoughts wandered back to Silvia. She did not know about the Bow of the Moon. Were Leif and Millicent looking for the bow as well? Deciding not to indulge his ponderings, Berty headed outside to the Sages' Grove market where he could be distracted.

The open-air market teamed with life as people finally emerged from their winter hovels. Berty watched as people buzzed from stall to stall buying what they needed. Meandering through the market, he gazed upon brightly colored eggs and figurines of spring animals. He wondered what he should bring Hope for her Easter basket.

Every Easter, Berty would bring Hope a small assortment of candy, saying that the Easter Bunny left it in his apartment. His parents always bought the one pound chocolate covered candy eggs in every flavor. Teresa's parents cornered the giant chocolate bunny market. Jon had a hankering for white chocolate that ever since childhood Berty never understood.

Berty lost focus on the stalls when he heard a quiet, "My Lord." Turning his head, he saw Declan standing beside him.

"Look over there," Declan said, nodding his head in the direction of a brown cloaked man hiding behind a wooden stall.

Berty recognized the cloaked man after spending the previous week with him. Following his line of sight, Berty saw a young woman whose bright blonde hair rested against her dark blue cloak. He sighed deeply, then looked at Declan in disbelief. Walking over, they stood behind him.

"Sean," said Declan, delighting in watching the brown cloak jump, "are you spying on an Advisor?"

Panic set in his gray eyes. "No," Sean said hastily.

"Then why are you hiding behind this stall while watching Estelle?" asked Declan.

Sean looked from Declan to Berty. "I don't want her to see me," he said.

Raising an eyebrow, Berty said, "Technically, that's called spying."

"I'm not spying," Sean whined.

Berty hated it when Sean whined. Sean's voice was annoying enough to his ears. "You find Estelle attractive?" he asked Sean.

Sean's beady eyes widened as he held his breath.

"I'll take that as a yes," said Berty. Sean's eyes quickly flickered in Estelle's direction. "Let me give you a word of advice. When you like someone, don't stalk. Women tend to find it creepy."

Declan turned his head away for a moment. Focusing on Berty as if he were internalizing what Berty had just said, Sean said nothing.

"This is a warning, Sean," Berty said. "Next time, there will be consequences."

Sean shuffled away from his hiding place. Berty and Declan watched him walk away from the market.

"Should we tell her?" Declan asked.

Watching a smiling Estelle glide from one stall to another, Berty said, "Not here. Inside."

They approached Estelle while Berty asked, "Enjoying the day?"

She smiled brightly as she looked at Berty and Declan. "Very much," she said. "This is the spring market of my childhood imagination." Estelle blinked away a budding tear. "So many things I... if things were different." Her smile returned as she glanced at the array of pastel colors arranged on the cart.

Seeing Estelle's child-like nature swimming in her light blue eyes, Berty asked, "Would you like to help me pick out something for my niece? I am at a loss."

"I would be honored, my Lord," Estelle said breathlessly.

As they strolled through the stalls, Declan kept an eye out for Sean.

Picking out candy eggs, Estelle mentioned, "Starjen have told me about her." Candy chicks and rabbits joined the eggs. "The return could save us all."

Exchanging looks with Declan, Berty paid for his candy. They walked away from the market stalls in silence. As they approached the barracks, Declan asked her, "Save us all from what?"

Berty saw Delyth talking with Alvar and Edwin whilst Declan stared at Estelle, waiting for an answer.

"Annihilation, of course," said Estelle, placing a hand on Declan's arm as if it was the most obvious thing in the world. Turning to Berty, she said, "I hope she likes them. Thank you for allowing me to be a part of it, my Lord." Smiling, she walked towards the Empire Tree.

Both Berty and Declan stared after her as she almost skipped down the dirt path. They followed in silent confusion.

Ascending into the Reception Room, Declan asked Berty, "Should we?"

Hearing Delyth's dainty feet climbing the steps behind them, Berty answered, "Yes and no."

Berty and Declan followed Estelle through the Reception

Room and up the second flight of stairs. While Berty headed into the Roundtable Room, Declan called, "Estelle, a word please."

Before she walked out onto the bridge, she glided past Declan into the room. Out of the corner of his eye, Berty saw Delyth watch Declan close the door.

"Is there a problem, my Lord?" Estelle asked, standing between the door and table.

With a hand on the top of his chair, Berty said, "I have a concern. Do you remember Sean?"

"Yes."

"He," Berty rubbed the finial of his chair while he tried to choose his words, "followed you in the market."

Her smile returned before she said, "Sean is harmless."

Declan looked at Estelle as if she were crazy.

"If he, or anyone, gives you any trouble," Berty said with his hand finally off his chair, "I do not want you to hesitate to come to any of us."

"I will," she said. "Thank you, my Lord."

Opening the door, Declan watched her leave the room. He turned to look at Berty in disbelief.

"It's all we can do," Berty answered Declan's unasked question. "I need to go. I'll return for Edwin's ceremony."

Declan gave Berty a sharp nod before Berty disappeared through his private door. As Berty ascended his staircase, Delyth's voice carried into his ears.

"Blondes your thing?"

Berty stopped climbing.

"Sean was stalking her," answered Declan.

"And you'd rather have him stalk you?" Delyth asked.

"Why are you jealous?" asked Declan in return. "It's not like it can really work between us."

"What do you mean?" Delyth said.

"In case you haven't noticed," replied Declan, "*you* are a Fairy and *I* am not."

"So?" Berty heard indignation in her voice.

"You're not just any Fairy." Declan's voice rose. "You are *the*

Fairy Princess. I am merely a woodsman from Boudon."

"You never told me you were from Boudon," said Delyth, "a Boudonian Archer."

"It doesn't matter."

"A Boudonian Archer's skills rival the best of the Elves."

"Still doesn't matter," dismissed Declan.

"Where are you going?" Delyth demanded.

"Dinner."

"Declan, wait." Delyth paused. "I do not want us to fight."

"Then stop picking fights with me," Declan countered.

"It's just that," Delyth's voice sounded small and Berty thought that she might start crying, "I do not know what to do when it comes to us."

"You have my heart," Declan said. "Do what you want."

Hearing footsteps, Berty thought Declan had walked out of the Roundtable Room. He returned to climbing his private staircase.

Declan was in love with Delyth. At least he got to see her on a daily basis unlike Berty and Silvia. As Berty crossed the bridge, he considered the thought that he had it better than Declan. Not seeing the woman he loved, but could do nothing about was actually the better way. The pain of constant closeness must be excruciating, thought Berty. Picking fights with Declan was how Delyth dealt with her pain. Declan simply shot his arrows.

Berty walked into his study, then packed his bag. Candy in hand, Berty crossed the portal. Walking into a dark house made him check his dual pocket watch. Nine o'clock Saturday night, it said. Hungry, he magically fixed himself some food before retiring for the evening.

While drinking his morning coffee, Berty checked his phone. A text from his brother reminded him of the time that he had to be at his parent's house. With Hope's Easter candy in the car, he drove away from his house.

Twenty minutes later, Berty found himself on a route he knew well. From the car, he glanced at the houses he knew since childhood. He used to ride his bike on the streets on which he drove. He used to play in the backyards of the houses he passed. The houses, which were built in the sixties and seventies, looked so much smaller to him as an adult.

Rounding the bend, he parked in front of the two-story brick house that he knew well. The red brick was speckled with black and beige bricks. He stood on the small covered porch with Hope's candy as he rang the doorbell. When his father answered the door, the warm, smoky aroma of ham baking escaped onto the porch. Inhaling deeply, Berty stepped inside.

After hugging his son, George said, "Your mom wants all the candy in the living room."

Walking into the living room, Berty placed his candy on the coffee table next to the large chocolate eggs and a two foot chocolate bunny. Berty's candy was the only non-chocolate candy on the table, but chocolate was well represented. After taking one last good look at the array of dark, milk and white chocolate, Berty followed his father down the short hall into the kitchen.

His parents' kitchen permeated with smells that Berty loved. He walked next to Kate stirring the liquid contents of a pot on the stove. "Hey mom," he said. "Whatcha makin'?"

Kate kissed her son on the cheek, then answered, "Gravy for the mashed potatoes." Rapidly stirring, she poured a thin, white liquid into the pot.

"Berty, give us a hand with these glasses," said George. He and Robert were plucking stemware from a wooden cabinet.

Crossing the kitchen, Berty relieved his father of glasses and followed Robert into the dining room. On the table sat his mother's favorite floral plates. The buffet held baskets full of plastic green Easter grass in which Lillian arranged the candy from the living room.

"Hope is going to love these chicks and bunnies, Berty," said Lillian as she nestled them into the grass. "You have such an eye."

Smiling slightly, Berty said, "I had help."

"From a lady friend?" asked Lillian.

Knowing that she meant Silvia, Berty reluctantly answered, "Yes."

Glancing out the window, Robert said, "The kids just pulled up. Do you need help finishing that Lill?"

Lillian stood back to admire her work. "No, it's done," she answered, turning a figurine slightly.

"You tell Mom; I'll get the door," George said to Berty.

Walking back into the kitchen, Kate said, "I heard Robert. Can you lift the ham onto that platter for me?"

"Absolutely." Grabbing two forks, Berty sunk them into the mahogany hued meat.

After he placed the ham on the large white platter, Kate asked, "Where is Silvia spending Easter?"

With a wave of panic washing over him, Berty quickly closed his eyes. Focusing on her dark red hair, he quickly saw her sitting at a table with six small children and a young woman with her brown hair hastily pinned back. The children passed food around the table while the woman took a moment to catch her breath.

Opening his eyes, he said, "She is having dinner on a farm. The farmer broke his ankle and Silvia is helping him and his wife with one child especially."

"She sounds like a lovely woman. I hope we get to meet her sometime," said Kate, pouring gravy into a large gravy boat.

Jon and Teresa entered the kitchen, distracting Kate. Berty dumped peas into a bowl as he watched his family interact. His mind escaped to Silvia sitting around the table. He wondered why he said anything about a farm or a broken ankle. Kate corralling her children into the dining room brought Berty's mind back to the confines of his parents' kitchen.

In the dining room, Hope said, "Ooh, look at all that candy. How come the Easter Bunny brought so much here?"

"He didn't," Kate answered sweetly. "Some he left here, some was left at your other grandparents' and some he left at your Uncle Berty's."

During dinner, conversation mainly focused around George's

business, which Jon recently inherited.

"If we can get this account, it would be a huge boom for us, Dad," said Jon. "It would give us a strong international presence."

"You've been working on it for some time. When do you think they will make their decision?" asked George.

"Next month, hopefully," Jon answered. "We're not the only ones vying for their business."

Berty lost track of the rest of the conversation when Hope asked, "Uncle Berty, do they eat ham in the Land of Sages?"

Smiling warmly, Lillian breathed, "She's been reading your column."

"Of course they do," Berty replied. "Ham, peas, mash with gravy, all of it."

Hope nodded sharply with a smile before shoveling a forkful of mashed potatoes in her mouth.

Throughout dinner, Hope did not ask any more questions about the Land of Sages, but Berty suspected that she had been thinking about it. After the plates from dinner had been cleared, George sliced fruit and nut, peanut butter and coconut eggs while Robert poured Irish Cream in etched cordial glasses.

The filling Easter meal did not make Berty forget about what he saw Silvia doing. Snatching his chance after coffee, he crept upstairs. Opening the first door on his right, he entered a bedroom lost in time.

Old college textbooks lazily filled a shelf. Awards with the name Hubert Chase hung proudly on the walls. The twin bed displayed his post-college blue plaid comforter.

Berty sat on his old bed and closed his eyes. Silvia sat at the same table, although alone. The sound of shuffled footsteps proceeded a woman placing a tray on the table.

"How is he?" Silvia asked.

"Doing so well," the woman answered. "I do not know what we would have done if you did not show, Elder." Sitting, she took a breath.

Silvia smiled. "I am happy to help. He is going to have to stay off that ankle for awhile to allow the fracture to heal."

"The kids and I can do his work until he is better," answered the woman. "At least the fields are planted."

"Now that your husband is resting," Silvia said as she rose from the table, "I am going to take a walk with Tait around the farm. After the children go to bed, we will talk about my evaluation."

Berty's body bounced slightly. When he opened his eyes, little, brown eyes stared up at him.

"Hi, Hope," he said.

"I want to meet a Fairy," Hope mentioned. "And an Elf."

Still looking in her bright, brown eyes, he said nothing.

"I have no school tomorrow," she said. "Take me with you."

"Now is not the time," said Berty.

Her whole body deflated. "I still have to wait," she said in a small voice.

Nodding, Berty said, "Sorry."

Without another word, Hope slid off the bed. Berty looked after her as she dragged out of his room with her head down. Feeling awful, his finger traced the plaid lines on his comforter.

"It isn't easy," said a female voice from the open doorway.

When Berty looked up, Teresa walked towards him. "What isn't easy?" he asked.

Teresa leaned against his bed, saying, "She believes in the Land of Sages more than she believes in the Easter Bunny. Though I am not quite sure where Santa lies on that scale." She looked at her feet. "I don't know how she is going to take it when she finds out it isn't real."

He had a feeling that Teresa at least partly blamed him for Hope's enthusiasm about the Land of Sages. "Teresa, perhaps if you let Hope stay with me for a few days or so in the summer, we will explore the forest I frequent."

Teresa's eyes lit up as she smiled. "Then she'll discover that the Land of Sages is a creation of your imagination. Berty, thank you."

Smiling, Berty watched Teresa leave the room. When he

stepped off his bed, a drawer of his desk caught his eye. Opening it, he found folded pieces of paper pushed in the back.

Grabbing a paper, he unfolded it. He read, "It was a dark and stormy night. The sounds of the storm kept him awake through the night." Laughing at his early attempts at writing, Berty placed the paper on the top of his desk.

Opening a second paper, he slid into a chair as he read. Words flew off the page taking his breath away. His eyes registered the words, *sages*, *magic* and *scepter*, written in his young handwriting.

Standing, his hands folded the paper. Placing the paper in his pocket, he walked out of his old room, closing the door. By the time he rejoined his family downstairs, it was time to leave.

Arriving home, Berty immediately stepped through the portal. In his study, he extracted the folded piece of paper from his pocket. He slipped it into an empty box on his shelf without taking a second look at it. Sitting down at his desk, he spent the evening penning more chapters of the *Adventures of Leigh and Marcus*.

When Berty stepped outside his chambers in the morning, the sweet smell of spring tickled his nose. The day could not have been more perfect for Edwin's nuptials, Berty thought as he made his way to the Reception Room for breakfast.

Chapter Seven
Bonds

Sitting at the table in the morning lit Reception Room, Berty received a cheery greeting from everyone except Declan who randomly placed food into his mouth.

"Is there a problem, Declan?" Berty asked quietly.

Placing his fork on his plate, Declan swallowed his food. He looked around the room quickly, then barely above a whisper said, "They are trying to muscle me out of the Watchers' Guild, saying that I am no longer useful to the Guild. I was actually told that if I had any decency, I would leave of my own accord. They know that they could never convince the Guild Master to eject me so they resort to bullying and intimidation."

"Who are they?"

"They call themselves the Cavern," said Declan through gritted teeth. Breathing heavily through his nose, he continued, "They are a corrupt group within the Guild. How dare they use that name." Declan's hand tightened around his fork. "How dare they besmirch us."

Berty's eyebrows scrunched briefly. "I don't understand the connection."

Leaning in close, Declan breathed, "Predates the Guild."

Declan said nothing further, so Berty continued with breakfast as if they had not had that conversation. When they finished eating, Declan gave Berty a poignant look. Without a word, Berty followed Declan up the stairs and across the bridge to Council Circle.

"Thank you for coming," said Declan as he stopped in front of a bundle of light green branches. "Please, come in."

Declan led Berty into an unassuming round room with only a table and a handful of chairs. Books did not grace the curved shelves. Berty saw boxes of different shapes and sizes. On the other side of the room rested Declan's gracefully curved bow and leather quiver full of arrows.

Motioning for Berty to sit, Declan began, "I am sorry about the secrecy, but it is what must be." Declan took a seat across from Berty. "Before the Watchers' Guild was established, there was the Fellowship of the Cavern. This is *the* Cavern from where that group takes their name. The Cavern is a home of limitless magic. It is said that both the crystal and the white metal staff of the scepter came from the Cavern.

"As Watchers became more numerous, the Fellowship morphed into a guild. The Guild is more than just a place for Watchers to meet. We discuss, we learn, and we take refuge in the Guild. Within the Guild, there are three orders to which a Watcher can attain: the Fellowers, the Seekers and the Keepers. The Fellowers deal with Watcher relations. The Seekers deal with the wands. The Order of the Keepers of the Cavern are secretive and exclusive.

"From the Cavern came a mass of gold out of which five gold lockets were crafted. You, my Lord, have one. I, another. Possession of these lockets is entrusted only to Keepers. There can only be five Keepers at any one time."

Berty wanted to interrupt, but Declan kept explaining.

"Unbeknownst to you, when the Guild Master gave you the locket, he made you an honorary Keeper. A Keeper's job is to keep magic safe; protect it; revere it. That's why I went undercover in Sean's army. I finally had a sense of purpose as a Keeper."

"Do all Watchers know about the Cavern?" asked Berty.

"No. The Cavern is a mere whisper in the Fellowers and a full-blown myth in the Seekers. Only Keepers know that it is real."

"You have been to this Cavern?"

"No," said Declan as he rose from his seat. Extracting his wand, he walked over to a box on a shelf. After tapping the box three times with his wand, Berty heard a click. Flipping open the lid, he extracted a rolled piece a paper.

Declan stretched it open onto his table to reveal the symbol of the Watchers—a six pointed star with an open eye in the center. Placing a finger on the upper left point of the star, Declan said, "Only when the wand," his finger moved across to the upper right point, "the sword," his finger slid to the bottom point, "and the bow unite with," his finger shifted to the lower left point, "the past," his finger glided to the top point, "the present," his finger slid to the lower right point, "and the future, will the key," Declan's finger landed on the eye, "unlock the Cavern."

Berty looked briefly at the paper. Raising his eyes to Declan's, he asked, "What does that mean?"

Shaking his head, Declan answered, "When the time is right, the quest will reveal itself to a worthy Keeper."

The glimmer in Declan's eyes told Berty that he wanted to be that worthy Keeper. "What are you going to do about the corruption?" Berty asked him.

"It doesn't seem to phase the Guild Master," said Declan. "I'll come up with a plan to deal with them." With a flick of his wand, the paper rolled itself while flying back into the box.

"I think it is time to head down to the barracks," Berty said.

With a nod, Declan walked with Berty through the Empire Tree.

Outside, Alvar greeted them at the Barracks. Berty and Declan followed the Elf to a large table where Edwin's parents sat with the rest of the Advisory Council. Alvar disappeared inside a building as Berty and Declan took their seats. From his chair, Berty could see tables of Empire Guards and a few villagers.

The tables of people fell silent as two doors opened. Out of one door, Hedda escorted Lark who wore a flowing lavender dress and a crown of flowers with pastel ribbons cascading into her long blonde hair. Out of the other door, Alvar led a regal Edwin dressed in his finest leather armor. He, too, wore a matching crown of flowers and ribbons.

On the edge of the circular opening between the tables, Edwin and Lark faced one another. Hedda and Alvar sat at the table with Berty while Alfred rose from his chair.

"Lark of Calledin," Alfred said, "do you come here of your own free will to join in union with Lieutenant Edwin of the Empire Guard?"

"Of course, I do," said Lark breathlessly.

"Lieutenant Edwin," Alfred continued, "do you stand before us of your own free will to join in union with Lark of Calledin?"

"Absolutely," said Edwin, wearing a wide smile.

Alfred sat in his chair in silence. Without taking their eyes off of each other, Lark and Edwin met at the center of the circle. Grasping hands, they took a breath, then said in unison, "Let two become one, until days are done. To you, I pledge my everything."

The wind began to gently blow the ribbons on the crowns. Still holding hands, Lark and Edwin kissed. Once the wind entangled the ribbons, the wedding guests cheered.

With the tip of their noses still rubbing, Edwin and Lark lifted the joined crowns off their heads, then placed it on the ground where they stood. As music began to play, the newlyweds danced around their crowns.

Mead flowed into everyone's goblets. Soon after, the dance floor filled with dancing couples. After a couple of goblets of mead, Berty found his way onto the dance floor. He danced with Femke, then Hedda, Estelle and Delyth. Through his alcohol-induced haze, he noticed how Declan and Delyth tried to avoid dancing together until right before the feast.

The sun had set by the time the feast finished. Edwin and Lark's table twinkled with candles and lanterns as guests presented gifts of salt, honey and incense. While people visited their table, they deposited coins into a box to wish them well.

Signaling the official end of the wedding, Femke carried a

thin, rectangular box to the center of the circle. Tenderly, she picked up the intertwined crowns, placing them in the box. With a smile and a tear, she handed the box to her son and new daughter-in-law.

Together, Edwin and Lark placed the gifts on top of the box. Berty watched the newlyweds rise. Gifts in hand, Edwin and Lark turned, then walked away from their guests ready to begin their lives together.

As Berty walked back inside the Empire Tree with his Advisory Council, Estelle said, "That was beautiful. I am so glad to have been a part of it."

Privately, Berty agreed with Estelle. While he climbed his private staircase to his chambers, he thought about his brother's wedding. He stood to Jon's left as his best man watching Teresa, covered in white, glide down the aisle. His mother cried in the front row. At the time, Berty was glad that it was not he who was getting married.

Sitting in a club chair, his mind drifted to Silvia. Yearning to see her again, Berty closed his eyes. A light blue hooded figure walked through the forest. The moonlight faded quickly as it hid behind the clouds. Using her staff as a walking stick, Silvia followed her own path through the trees. She walked quickly without any light. Berty wondered to where she headed, but it was too dark for him to see.

Opening his eyes, he crossed his room to sit at his desk. Before retiring for the evening, Berty wrote a new chapter of *the Adventures of Leigh and Marcus*.

In the morning, Berty said good-bye to Femke and Ryker who readied for an early morning departure. Once he finally sat at the table to eat breakfast, he noticed an empty chair. "Where's Delyth?" Berty asked.

"Elrick suffered an injury whilst he and Telor were hunting," said Alfred. "Apparently she flew home last night. I found a note this morning on my door. She said that she will send word."

Declan stopped eating. "By herself?" he asked Alfred.

"She's tough," said Colvin. "She'll be fine."

Raising his eyebrows, Declan looked incredulously at the Dwarf. "This coming from the man who did not want her learning how to use a sword."

"I changed my mind," said Colvin. "I am allowed to change my mind, aren't I?"

"That depends," said Hatcher before stuffing his face with food.

Glaring at the Troll, Colvin sneered.

"Colvin's right," said Berty. "Although, I wish she would have left with guards."

"I do hope Elrick is okay," Alfred said. "The way Delyth left makes it sound serious."

When Berty saw the concern in the Elf's blue eyes, he said, "Perhaps Lida panicked."

"Yes," Alfred nodded. "She can be protective."

Breakfast was finished in silence. Climbing the stairs, Berty's mind wandered to the conversation he had with Declan about the Cavern. Reaching the end of his private staircase, he walked down the dark, narrow hallway stopping in front of a section of wall.

Stepping through the wall, he thought about light. Candles and sconces instantly illuminated the round inner room. He gathered scrolls off the shelves. Placing them on the worn wooden table, Berty sat, ready to read. The first scroll he unraveled, he could not read. Opening scroll after scroll, Berty glanced at the foreign words.

"Is everything written in an ancient language that I don't understand?" With his elbows on the table, he ran his fingers through his dark brown hair. "How do I read these?" he asked, still holding his head in his hands.

Hearing a click, he raised his head. On the shelf, a small metal box opened. Berty approached the box slowly. Inside, he found a gold ring holding a smooth, dark red gem in its bezel. Instinctively, he placed it on his left pinky.

Returning to the scrolls, he understood every word he read.

Berty learned that the Seven High Sages practiced different forms of magic. Using their magic, together, they crafted the scepter to uphold the Sorcerer's Code. During its crafting, each High Sage imparted some of his or her magic into the scepter.

By the time Berty's stomach growled for food, he had read every scroll he had found, yet there was neither mention of the Sorcerer's Code nor any mention of the Cavern. With another protest from his stomach, he stepped through the wall. As he descended the steps to the Reception Room, his mind catalogued all that he had read.

Multiple scrolls dealt with Empire history. A few talked about how the Empire Tree and the treed wall were connected. Another scroll loosely detailed the duties of the Empress. One piece of paper stuck out in Berty's mind. It looked as though it was torn from a larger scroll. The cryptic one sentence had no meaning to Berty, but gave him no comfort either. *Black recharge the veil* replayed in his mind.

"Can't be complete," Berty mumbled as he emerged from behind the Sages' Seal. After lunch, he thought, he would return to read the books. His eyes focused on Alfred's face. Berty stopped on the dais steps.

"Delyth just sent word," said Alfred. "Elrick's wounds are serious. She is not sure if he can recover."

Berty lost his appetite. "Don't they have someone in Fairyland who can help him?" he asked.

"Not anymore," answered Alfred.

"Perhaps I can," said Declan.

Berty called for Theodore. When the young Dwarf arrived, Berty said, "Declan and I are leaving for Fairyland at once. We will need provisions."

Declan stared at Berty as Theodore left.

"We should eat before we go," Berty said to him.

As Berty forced food into his mouth, Alvar said, "I will ready a half dozen men to leave with you."

"No," said Berty.

"Then at least take Edwin," Alvar implored. "I have a bad

feeling about all this."

"As do I," said Berty. "Edwin moves back into the tree tonight. The same goes for you."

"Of course my Lord," Alvar said before hurrying out of the room.

Alfred raised his eyebrows. "Fearful for our safety?"

"I fear that Elrick's condition was not the result of an accident," answered Berty. "Hopefully my precautions are unnecessary."

"Who would want to hurt the King of the Fairies?" asked Estelle.

A memory of a strawberry blonde Fairy with freckles immediately came to Berty's mind. "Millicent," he said.

Chapter Eight
An Exiled Life

With provisions and weapons, Berty and Declan stepped out of the doors of the Empire Tree. An approaching guard said, "My Lord, your horses are ready."

Near the gates stood two majestic chestnut horses shaking their brown manes as they waited for their riders.

"They'll make the trip easier," said Declan.

Berty looked at the creatures with apprehension. "Thank Captain Alvar for us," he said.

A guard held each horse while Declan mounted his horse with ease. Standing next to the horse, Berty was in awe over how big horses actually were. He wondered how he could avoid looking foolish because he did not have the faintest idea how to ride. Catching a glimpse of his red pinky ring, he knew that he would find the knowledge somehow.

Once seated in his saddle, Berty tried not to think about how far away the ground was. Reins firmly in his hand, Berty galloped with Declan through the gates of the Sages' Grove. The wide road northward allowed them to race past the trees.

Feeling the wind through his hair gave Berty a rush of excitement in his stomach. As the night grew darker, they slowed to a canter. The horses protested the fast pace when the sky began to lighten. Slowing to a pace with which the horses were comfortable, Berty turned to a weary looking Declan, saying, "I think we are almost there."

When their path had been fully illuminated, Berty and Declan pushed their horses into a full run. The forest path gave way to an expansive clearing beyond which was a border of green vegetation.

Declan reduced his speed; Berty followed suit. He mouthed, "Magic," to Berty. Cautiously, they entered the forest path on the other side of the clearing.

The ground sparkled with muted blues and purples. In the trees, brown shriveled Fairy wings hung from their gallows. A knot formed in Berty's stomach when he thought about how many Fairies had been dewinged. Trying not to look into the trees, his eyes finally found two periwinkle armored guards flanking large, curved blue metal gates. The walls surrounding the gates were covered with a flowering ivy.

No one stopped them as they slowly rode their horses through the open gates. Looking around, Berty felt as though he had stepped inside a box of exploded crayons that had been left in the sun too long. Every color imaginable dripped down the sides of every building they passed.

"When Delyth told me that Fairyland was more colorful than the Sages' Grove, this is not how I thought she meant it," said Declan.

Suppressing a laugh, Berty saw the blue turrets of the castle. They rode carefully through the colorful town until they reached the doors of the solid blue castle. Numerous guards patrolled the area both on the ground and in the sky. As they dismounted, a Fairy ran out of the castle to greet them.

"Is there something I can do for you, sirs?" he said.

"The Emperor wishes for an audience with your Queen," said Declan.

The Fairy snapped his fingers. Other Fairies instantly appeared to take the horses. After another Fairy rushed out of the castle and whispered in his ear, the first Fairy said, "This way, please."

He led them through the doorway into a large, sun-filled, golden entrance hall. "Her Majesty and Their Highnesses wish for you to join them at the table, Emperor," he said, stopping at large double doors, flanked by guards.

When the doors opened, Berty and Declan walked into a large brightly colored room with a room-filling table. Immediately, Lida stood, walking away from the head of the table to greet them.

"My Lord, Declan, so good of you to come," she said. "Please, it would be an honor for you to sit at my table." Talking to someone behind them, Lida said, "Make sure they have rooms."

The doors closed with a boom. Lida returned to her seat at the head of the table. On her right, sat Silvia dressed in her usual gold. Berty chose a seat across from Silvia, next to Delyth. Declan found a seat next to Telor.

"Elrick will be pleased to know that you have come," said Lida.

"How is he?" Berty asked.

A sad, faraway look manifested in Lida's eyes when she answered, "Resting."

Dinner was a silent affair as if mourning had already begun. As the plates were being removed, Lida said, "Come. He will want to see you."

Lida led them up stone steps. She knocked softly on a door before opening it. Berty entered to find Elrick lying in bed. Elrick's eyelids struggled to open. He looked at Berty with dull, almost vacant eyes and said, "Emperor." His voice was as weak as his smile.

"Save your strength, Elrick," said Berty.

When Declan approached Elrick to greet him, he cocked his head to the side saying, "May I look?"

"Yes," Elrick breathed.

Lifting the covers, Declan's eyes widened. Berty was not sure what he saw, but Declan's look of urgency let him know that it was not good. "I need a burner with hot coals, a small pot, a spring of thyme, and a wide spoon—bone, if you have it," said Declan.

While Telor ran from the room, Delyth asked, "What are you doing?"

"Making a honey dressing," said Declan while he cleared a table near the window.

"He had a honey dressing as soon as Telor dragged him home," said Lida.

Pulling out a small jar from his cloak pocket, Declan said, "By the state of his wounds, it was not prepared by a Witch or Wizard."

"Fairyland has not had a Wizard in a long time," said Lida. "You are not a Wizard either, Declan. I do not see how you can do anything more than our healer."

"With all due respect, Queen Lida, I know more about these things than most," said Declan. He held up the small jar saying, "Your healer did not use Ogreflower honey."

Telor ushered in Fairies carrying everything that Declan needed. While the Fairies set everything in place, Declan opened a window. As soon as the Fairies moved away from the table, Declan went to work. Placing the bowl over the coals, he spooned a measured amount of honey into the bowl. Declan then stripped the tiny leaves off the woody stem of thyme into the bowl of warm honey.

Delyth covered her nose with her hand, saying, "Oh, that's putrid."

A faint smell of tar, burnt rubber and rotting fish wafted their direction. Berty was glad that the window was open.

"Yes, but it works," said Declan while placing the stripped thyme sprig on the coals. He kept stirring and lifting the bone spoon out of the bowl, allowing the honey to cascade back into it. Finally, he took the bowl off the hot coals.

Bringing the bowl over to the bed, Declan pulled back the sheets, exposing Elrick's slashed chest. "This may sting," he said.

Elrick grimaced weakly as Declan smeared the warm honey over the wounds.

"Do you happen to have a scrap of muslin?" he asked the Fairies.

Lida nodded her head. She was only gone a minute before she handed Declan a beige cloth.

He carefully laid it over Elrick's chest. As he pulled the sheets back over him, Declan said, "It will work while you sleep. I'll check on you in the morning."

After saying goodnight to his father, Telor showed Declan and Berty to their rooms. "Thank you," he said to Declan.

"What happened?" asked Declan. "When I heard 'hunting accident,' I thought bear, but a bear did not make those marks."

Telor turned his head, looking around. "In here," he said as he opened a door. They entered a small study while Telor closed the door. Sitting in a leather chair, Telor said quietly, "We were hunting small game. It was just the two of us. Father insisted. He wanted a day with his son." His eyes moistened. "We were laying traps when this beast came out of nowhere. We tried to run, but I tripped. The forest was too dense to fly. He stood in-between me and the beast, protecting me. It attacked him. I shot some arrows at it and it retreated. I dragged father through the forest as I called for help. Everything happened so fast. I couldn't tell you what the beast looked like." His hands covered his face. Removing his hands, he said, "If you will excuse me, I really must go."

After Telor left, Berty asked, "What kind of beast could have attacked them?"

Declan shook his head, "I don't know."

Thinking about beasts, Berty asked, "What is an Ogreflower?"

"Small pale green flowers that grow around the entrances of Ogre lairs. The flowers themselves are supposed to have healing properties, but they are very difficult to procure. Ogreflower honey, however, is much easier, though it's not something sold in the marketplace," said Declan.

"Where did you get it?"

"Witch's trade," said Declan. "And, you need to know how to find that."

Berty looked at his sandy haired Advisor. "How do you know all this?"

"I learned from a Wizard, named Geraint," Declan answered. "Back when I was roaming the Empire, I became wounded. And,

I had no idea how to dress it. Of course, I didn't know much about anything then. Geraint found me and healed me." Declan smiled. "Since we were both exiled from our villages, we stuck together. He took me on as an apprentice of sorts. Taught me everything he knew."

"You were exiled?"

"For being a Watcher," Declan explained. He stared out the window at the dark sky before continuing. "I was born in the small woodland village of Boudon. My father was a woodsman. My grandfather was a woodsmith. He crafted all sorts of items from the wood my father collected. Grandfather's specialties were bows and arrows. People came from all over to buy his goods. My siblings and I spent every free moment in his workshop. We could shoot arrows before we could walk. Even my little sister knew how to use a bow, though Julie preferred crossbows. My oldest brother, Cecil, was a junior woodsman while my other brother, Vander, spent time learning woodsmithing. Grandfather was an excellent archer as well as woodsmith. He told me that I was a natural archer. To prove him right, by the time I was eight, I joined the group of archers that accompanied the woodsmen deep into the forest as protection.

"Two years later, I found my wand while on lookout high in a tree. At the time, I had no idea what it meant. No one in the village had any sort of magic and I never even heard of a Watcher. Still, I did not share my discovery with anyone. I never realized that not everyone saw what I could see. Later, I would find that to be true of Watchers as well. My wand was with me at all times—in the trees, when I slept, when I spent time with my grandfather.

"He always told me that it was important for an archer to be able to craft his own arrows. The day before my thirteenth birthday, my grandfather took me on an arrow making expedition. We scoured the forest collecting usable items. That day, he told me the story about the one bow in his workshop he would not let anyone touch, including my brothers." His eyes looked misty as if he were getting lost in nostalgia.

"He told me, 'When I was younger, a few years older than you, I was collecting materials in the woods just like we are now. An Elf maiden sat behind a tree, crying. When I asked her what was wrong, she said, "I do not want to fail my quest. I was sent into the woods with this bow and a quiver with only one arrow. The forest is supposed to give me wisdom. But here I am, cold, wet and hungry because I cannot use this bow." I told her that I could help her, so she returned with me to my workshop. There, I gave her a blanket in which she wrapped herself while her wet clothes dried near the fire. After I fed her a hearty meal, she kipped on my bed. When she woke, she dressed in her dry clothes and I asked her if she wanted some instruction for her bow. She asked if I was an archer. Of course I told her no, explaining that I needed the knowledge for crafting them. That is when I saw a light in her eyes, and she said to me, "Thank you for your generosity and your hospitality. The reason I cannot use this bow is not for lack of knowledge. That, I have. This bow will not work for me because I am not its intended. For over two centuries, this bow has not been used." She then handed me the bow and quiver with its lone arrow. "Give this bow to the one who can use it. You will know when you find this person for this is the Bow of the Moon." She walked out of my workshop and I never saw her again. It was the most beautiful bow I had ever seen. After studying it, I made a replica. Today we are making arrows for it. Tomorrow, for your birthday, you will get to use it."'

The wistful look left Declan's face. "Tomorrow never came," he said. "That evening after supper, my brothers were fooling around like usual. They knocked me to the floor, jostling my wand out of my pocket. Everyone stopped and stared. Someone said something about me being a Watcher. Everyone kept their distance from me as if they would catch some horrible disease. Everyone, except my mother. With her one hand, she grabbed my wand off the floor and my ear with the other. She left me locked in my room, alone.

"After nightfall, she returned with food and my cloak. Handing me back my wand, she whispered, 'I always knew you were special. The village elders are discussing how best to punish you. You have done nothing wrong. Take what you can carry and go. It is a moonless night. I love you. Now go.'

"I grabbed what I could and climbed out the window. Passing my grandfather's workshop, I sneaked inside to take my bow and some arrows, but he caught me. Instead of turning me in, he handed me a bag, telling me to run far away from the village. Stuffing what little I took in the bag, I ran until I did not recognize where I was. Then, I walked. When I figured I was safe, I peeked inside the bag.

"My grandfather gave me tools, a quiver full of arrows and the replica of the Bow of the Moon. When I removed an arrow, I realized that they were the ones we made that day. It did not feel right to use the bow without him, but eventually hunger made me. No other bow felt like it. I have never used another bow since."

Declan stared at the floor. "In all my years of wandering, I never returned to Boudon. If I had stayed one more day, I would have officially become a Boudonian Archer. Privy to all the secrets and prestige of that brotherhood." Looking at Berty, he continued, "All those years ago, my mother saved me from a terrible injustice. Her strength helped me find the Watchers' Guild where I finally learned how different I really am."

Declan glanced at the window. Berty did not disturb his thoughts. "We better get some rest," Declan finally said, rising from his chair.

Agreeing, Berty followed him to the door.

With his hand on the handle, Declan said, "Thank you for coming with me, my Lord."

"Anytime," replied Berty.

In the hallway, they retired to their rooms. Berty opened his door to find a spacious room. Exhaustion began to take over his body as he hung his clothes in the wardrobe. Crawling into the large bed, he fell asleep as soon as his head hit the pillow.

Chapter Nine
Beast of Burden

B erty awoke thinking about the Bow of the Moon. He was not sure why it was important or how it fit into the grand scheme of things. His deep red crystal glittered in the sunlight pouring onto his chest. "This goes beyond the crystal mystery," he muttered.

A soft knock interrupted his thoughts. "Come in," he said from the bed.

Silvia walked into the room. "Oh," she blushed. "You are still in bed."

Realizing half his torso was bare, he quickly pulled the covers up to his chin.

"I just wanted to let you know that Elrick is doing better this morning," said Silvia.

"I am so glad," Berty said.

"Well," she looked away from him, "I'll let you...." She looked at him again. "I'll see you," she pointed to the door. Giving him an embarrassed smile, Silvia left the room.

A she-likes-me chuckle escaped Berty before he leapt out of bed.

In the hallway outside his room, Berty ran into a more cheerful Delyth. "I'm sorry for leaving the way I did, my Lord," she said.

"I understand," he told her.

"Father wanted to pass his crystal to me, but Elder Hunter

arrived telling him not to," said Delyth. "She believed that the crystal was the only thing tethering him to life. Good thing she heard Telor screaming for help in the woods."

"Can I see your father?"

"Of course," she replied. "Declan is in with him right now."

Berty entered Elrick's room to find Declan replacing the muslin cloth on the Fairy's chest.

"The Ogreflower honey is doing its job," said Declan.

"Good morning, Emperor," Elrick said. Berty thought his voice sounded stronger.

Smiling, Berty replied, "Good Morning. You are looking better."

"All thanks to Declan here."

Declan pulled the covers over Elrick. "It is important that you rest, Elrick. The Ogreflower honey has more work to do."

"Yes, thank you," said Elrick.

"We will leave you to rest, and I will check on you later," said Declan.

As they walked through the castle, Berty asked Declan, "What's the matter?"

Declan looked at him with concern in his eyes saying, "I wish I knew what kind of beast attacked him."

They walked into a room where books covered every inch of wall space. Silvia and Lida sat on sofas, talking while Delyth perused a book at a table on the side.

"Declan," called Lida. "I want to apologize for my behavior last night. I have not quite been myself lately."

"Completely understandable," said Declan. "Apology accepted."

Smiling, Lida said, "Please, sit down." Once Declan and Berty sat, she continued, "Delyth tells me that you are a talented archer, Declan."

He smiled.

"I would like to ask a favor of you, as long as the Emperor consents, of course. You see, we have been changing our military tactics ever since the treacherous disease spread through our kind. The guards' focus is now on other Fairies. So, we invested in weaponry. Unfortunately, it is not going as well as we had first hoped. We are in desperate need for an expert. Will you help us with our archers?"

"Wow," said Declan. "It would be an honor." He looked at Berty."

"There is no better archer in the Empire, Lida," said Berty.

"Excellent," Lida said with a smile. Rising from the sofa, she said to Declan, "Shall we?"

Nodding, Declan followed the Fairy Queen out of the library.

"I think Delyth would prefer to be alone," said Silvia glancing at the Fairy.

Berty rose from the sofa. "Shall we go for a walk?" he asked holding out his arm. When she took his arm, he asked, "Where to?"

Berty found Silvia gazing into his brown eyes as she said, "Let's stroll through Fairyland."

As they walked down the paved lane from the castle, Silvia said, "This is my first time in Fairyland. It is a shame that sadness and uncertainty have clouded the people."

They followed winding, narrow streets that meandered through tall multicolored buildings. Berty noticed how the buildings shimmered as if the paint were made of crushed gemstones. Some of the buildings appeared vacant. Berty and Silvia rarely passed a walking Fairy. All the buildings had balconies where Fairies flew from place to place.

The narrow street finally emptied into a large square that was packed with Fairies. Hundreds of stalls sold everything a Fairy could ever have wanted or needed.

"There is more for sale here than in the Sages' Grove," remarked Berty.

"Unlike the Sages' Grove, this market is only open every four days," Silvia explained. "Some of these people have permanent shops, but still set up a stall on market day. And, I don't know if you've noticed, but most of the farmers are not Fairies."

They passed a flower stall manned by a human woman and

112

her teenage daughter. Silvia smiled, saying, "April showers bring May flowers."

"It's May?" Berty asked in a panic. He groped his pockets, finally extracting his pocket watch. Opening the watch, he said, "Day before Mother's Day."

"Get her some flowers," Silvia suggested.

"I can't exactly send them via Fairy courier," said Berty.

Silvia laughed. "Use magic," she whispered in his ear.

He stared at her in disbelief. "I can do that?"

"Why not?"

Why not indeed, thought Berty. Silvia helped him pick out and arrange the flowers. It felt natural for him to be there with her. With flowers in hand, they returned to the castle. During their return stroll, they discussed Silvia's journeys and the people she met.

Back inside, they escaped to the small study where Declan had told Berty his life story the previous evening. Finding some paper, Berty wrote a little note to his mother, wishing her a happy Mother's Day.

"You have to have a clear idea of where you want them to go," instructed Silvia.

"And they'll just appear at my parents' front door?" Berty asked.

"Yes."

"How do I know that someone won't be there?" said Berty. "That would be awfully strange."

"Watch the way you watch me," suggested Silvia.

Thinking about his parents, Berty closed his eyes. His father sat at the table sipping coffee while he read the newspaper. His mother perused recipes in her favorite cookbook.

"I have been thinking of making this hummingbird cake for tomorrow," Kate said.

George looked up from the paper. "Don't bake on Mother's Day, Kate."

"I was going to make it today," Kate responded. "Besides, what better joy is there than to see your granddaughter happy?"

While George laughed, Berty tried to shift his focus towards the window. The sheer curtains obstructed his view, but he could tell that no one was outside.

Opening his eyes, Berty gave Silvia a sharp nod. Concentrating on his parents' front porch, he stared at the flower arrangement. When it disappeared, he jumped. Closing his eyes again, he focused on the porch. The flowers rested right outside the front door. Seeing the doorbell, he wanted to ring it. His finger made the motion as if it were pressing an invisible button. He heard the bell ring inside the house.

His father opened the door with his reading glasses perched on the tip of his nose. Picking up the flowers, George closed the door. Berty focused on following his father through the house.

"Kate," said George placing the flowers on the table, "these came for you."

Looking up, she gasped. "They're beautiful." She reached for the note. "They are from Berty," she said, reading.

Berty opened his eyes with his mother's smile fresh in his mind. "Thank you, Silvia," he said. "She loved them."

Silvia had a strange smile on her face.

"What?" Berty asked.

"You have the Eagle Eye," she said.

"The Eagle Eye?" Berty inquired.

"It's a Watcher of a different sort," Silvia explained.

Berty glanced out the window to see Declan training the Fairy Guards.

"I am not sure if you can see anyone or just people to whom you are connected in some way," she continued. "Amulets that warded against the intrusive Eagle Eye were en vogue a very long time ago."

His ring caught the sunlight causing Berty to ask, "What is the Sorcerer's Code?"

"I have always understood it to be the laws of magic," said Silvia. "At least that is what my mother told me. You learned how to read the ancient tongue?"

"Not exactly," said Berty. He leaned towards Silvia, showing her his pinky ring. "This helps me understand it."

Taking his hand in hers, she studied the ring. "I have never seen it before," she said. "Where did you get it?"

Confused, Berty answered, "The Sorcery Room. It was in a metal box on a shelf."

"Not all the boxes opened for me when I was Empress," she said. "There is so much knowledge that has been lost to us. Only now are we rediscovering it."

For the first time, Berty saw Silvia as someone who was learning as she went—just like he was. "What do you know about the Cavern?"

Silvia's eyebrows scrunched momentarily. "I've never heard of the Cavern. I don't think it is even part of the hidden documents the Goblins protect. Did you find it in another place in the Sorcery Room?"

"No," said Berty a bit disappointed. "It was something Declan mentioned. A Watcher's myth. I thought maybe you had heard of it."

With an intake of breath, Silvia's jaw dropped and her eyes widened. "The scepter's crystal comes from a cave. The cave was then sealed so that no one else could get a hold of that type of crystal. It is said that not even the Seven High Sages could re-open that cave. Perhaps that is the same cavern about which Declan spoke."

Looking out the window, Berty could no longer see Declan. "Perhaps," he said.

The door opened. Delyth poked her head into the room. "Could both of you please come to my father's room?"

Berty and Silvia exchanged worried looks before rushing down the hall after Delyth. They entered Elrick's room to find Lida, Telor, Delyth, and Declan scattered around the room.

Elrick watched Berty and Silvia, then addressed Declan. "Now that everyone is here could you please," Elrick grimaced, "tell me what is going on."

"The Ogreflower honey worked," Declan began.

"Then why is he still in pain?" asked Lida.

"On the infected wound," Declan continued. "However, I am afraid there is another problem. The wound is also magical."

"How can that be?" asked Telor.

"From what I can see," said Declan, "it looks like some magical poison." He looked directly at Elrick. "You could have only gotten it from the beast."

Elrick closed his eyes for a moment. "What does this mean?"

"I am not a Wizard, Elrick," Declan said. "I only know how to treat physical wounds. This is the first magical wound I have ever seen. I am so sorry."

Putting a hand on Declan's arm, Elrick said, "For what you have done for me, I am eternally grateful. Take care of Delyth."

Declan nodded. Tears gushed down Lida's face.

"It is time I passed this crystal to you, Delyth," said Elrick.

Delyth stared at her father, her feet frozen to the floor.

"No," said Silvia. "We will hunt this beast. You still have time. Allow us to try to make an antidote or something."

"Very well," Elrick said as he winced from pain.

Silvia looked at the others in the room. "Meet me downstairs." With determination, she walked out of the room.

As Berty hurried towards his room, he heard Lida's voice say, "Delyth! Where do you think you are going?"

"Beast hunting," said Delyth.

"No, you are not," Lida scolded. "It is bad enough Telor is going to face it again. But, that is his duty as future king. Yours is to stay with your father."

Securing his sword and cloak, Berty met Silvia in the wide, golden entrance hall. Cloaked in light blue, she stood stoically, holding her staff rigidly in her hand. Soon, Declan and Telor arrived carrying their bows.

"Lead the way, Telor," Silvia said.

The Fairy led them through a series of side corridors. Eventually, they arrived at a heavily guarded door that led directly into the forest.

As they walked through the darkening forest, Telor asked, "Should we not wait till morning?"

"Your father might not have that long," said Declan.

"But how are we going to see the beast?" Telor said.

Looking at Berty, Silvia said, "We need some light."

Berty cupped his hands in front of him. A ball of light began to grow in his cupped hands. When the ball was the size of a small melon, he pushed it above his head. It flattened into a disk, illuminating the forest around them.

Extracting his sword, Berty said to Telor, "Keep your weapon ready."

Telor imitated Declan's stance as they walked further into the forest.

Berty heard branches cracking. Turning, he examined the dark woods. His eyes found nothing. More branches cracked. Telor's breath quickened. They stopped walking. Leaping in front of them, deer crossed their path. Continuing through the forest, Berty's senses sharpened. Every sound became ominous.

Silvia pressed forward, determined to find the mysterious magical beast. Without taking a hand off his bow, Declan touched Silvia's arm. When she stopped, Declan whispered, "Something big and magical comes."

Berty could not see anything beyond the light and heard even less. Only Declan could see into the darkness. He pulled back the string of his bow. Berty could feel Telor tremble beside him. Declan released an arrow. Quickly, he shot another, then another. A roar of pain reached Berty's ears. Declan shot two more arrows. He waited with the string of his bow touching his shoulder.

Lowering his bow, Declan declared, "It's dead and it was alone."

Cautiously, the four of them approached the fallen beast. The disc of light illuminated the trees and underbrush inch by inch. Finally, Berty saw cloven feet. As he got closer, strong, brown, hairy legs came into view like the hindquarters of a horse. The beast's torso tapered. At its waist, brown changed to gray. Its chest looked similar to a large cat's. Large cat-like claws lay still on the forest floor. As the light shone on the beast's head, Berty saw a curious melding of mountain cat and bull, complete with horns.

Telor froze. His green eyes revealed pure horror.

"Can I borrow your sword?" Silvia asked Berty.

He handed it to her while staring at the beast's flesh ripping fangs.

She returned his sword, saying, "Time to go back to the castle."

Lida waited for their return. Telor greeted his waiting mother with, "The creature is dead."

Sighing with relief, Lida asked, "Should that not heal him?"

"I am not sure," answered Silvia, "but I took its claws and a phial of blood, just in case."

Glancing at the group, Telor said, "I have seen a picture of the beast in a book once. Come, I'll show you." Leading them into the library, he continued, "Delyth has read every book in this library. She showed it to me one time." He flew to a shelf near the ceiling. Picking a large, old book, he carried it to a table. He leafed through the pages until he said, "Here."

Underneath a drawing of the beast that lay dead in the forest, Berty read, "Faematask: An ancient beast known to feast on Fairies. If its attack is not fatal, its magical poison will cement the kill. It cannot jump well, but the beast's horns are sharp and full of poison. Only known protection: It cannot break a Fairy Ring."

"What's a Fairy Ring?" asked Declan.

"An unbroken circle of Fairy Dust," Lida answered. "This would have severe ramifications on Fairyland. No non-Fairy could cross the border. I must discuss this with Elrick and the Dust Master."

"I will join you," said Telor.

"No," said Lida with a hand on her son's arm. "You are still Prince Telor. The weight of the Kingdom does not yet rest on your shoulders." With quickness in her step, the Fairy Queen left the room.

"Telor, I need to use your healer's equipment," said Silvia.

"Yes, of course," Telor said. "This way." He led Silvia out of the library.

Berty sat on a sofa. "A Fairy eating beast," he said to Declan. "With all the Fairies roaming around, I highly doubt that the beast attacking the Fairy Royal family was pure coincidence."

Before Declan could say anything, Telor ran in to the room. "Declan, Elder Hunter would like your assistance."

"I agree, my Lord," said Declan. "Excuse me."

Sitting in the library by himself made Berty feel useless. Telor did not return. Berty's eyelids became heavy as he drifted off to sleep.

"Berty."

Berty heard Silvia calling him.

"Berty."

He could hear her, but he could not find her.

"Berty, wake up."

Opening his eyes, Silvia's face faced his. Blinking a few times brought her warm, brown eyes and soft lips into focus. He could see worry in her eyes.

"What's wrong?" he asked.

"Come with me," she said.

After getting his balance, he followed her out of the dark library. She led him through a couple of poorly lit stone corridors until they arrived at a plain wood door. When she opened the door, they walked into a large room cluttered with all sorts of stuff. Most of the walls were covered with shelves full of bottles and books. Bundles of herbs hung from the ceiling. Declan sat on a wooden chair near a large wooden table, his head lolling to the side.

Lit by candles, the table held mortar and pestles grinding automatically. Liquids stirred themselves over fires. Pinches of this and that sprinkled into containers. On the side of the table, Silvia's staff leaned.

"I've ground the claw, made an infusion of claw, and a claw tincture," Silvia said. "I have used the blood alone and mixed it with the claw. I have even added all sorts of ingredients. And nothing, according to Declan, has magic." She looked at the table. "I am working with bone marrow right now. As soon as it is done," a container over the fire stopped stirring, then landed on the table. "Declan," Silvia called. All the magic on the table stopped.

"Coming," a tired Declan responded. He trudged over to the container. Looking into the receptacle, he said, "No."

"Are you sure?" she implored.

"There's nothing there," said Declan. He returned to the chair. Leaning his head back, he closed his eyes.

Placing her head in her hands, Silvia collapsed into a chair.

"Did killing the beast do anything?" Berty asked.

"Minimal," mumbled Declan.

"We've tried most of this on Elrick already," Silvia said through her hands. "Declan figures you have to fight magic with magic. They are trying Fairy Dust on him now."

Berty gazed at the golden lump on the chair, longing to help her. "We have magic," he said.

"Do you know what kind of magic to use to fight this poison?" Silvia countered, raising her head. "This is why Witches and Wizards are so essential. If the poison is not contained at all times, it can spread, possibly to others."

Looking out the window, Berty saw the severity of the situation as dawn approached. When a door opened, an exhausted looking Delyth entered the room. Declan opened his eyes.

She shook her head. "It has been decided that Fairyland will have a Fairy Ring. The announcement will be made in the Throne Room. My mother would appreciate it if you all would be there," said Delyth.

"Of course we will," said Berty.

Declan followed Delyth out of the room. Still sitting on her chair, Silvia stared at the table. Her fingers perched on her lips. Tears welled in her eyes. Leaping from her chair, she whacked her staff to the floor. "What is the purpose of wisdom without practicality?" she asked. "I can't do anything. My friend is dying and I can't help him." Tears streamed freely from her eyes as her breathing shuttered.

Watching Silvia fall apart stupefied Berty. She was the strongest person he knew. It was time he was strong for her.

Gently wrapping his arms around her, he pulled her into his strong embrace. He breathed in the berry pie fragrance as she cried into his chest. Her crying slowed. Silvia took deep breaths.

"I'm sorry," she said while her head still rested on his body.

"It's okay," he replied, then kissed the top of her head. Berty savored holding her close.

Pulling back, Silvia gazed up at him. "Thank you," she said.

He wiped her wet cheek dry with his hand. Fixated on her warm, brown eyes, he said, "I'll always be here for you."

Silvia smiled. "I had better," she circled her face with her hand. "See you in the Throne Room." Taking a step backwards, she held her hand towards her staff. The staff flew off the floor into her open hand. Without taking another look at the table, she walked out the door.

Finding his way back to the main hall, Berty was not sure where the Throne Room was located. He magically made himself presentable, then studied the series of closed wooden doors. Fairy wings were carved into almost all of the double doors. Finally, Berty saw guards open the largest pair of doors.

Berty entered a large room with purplish-blue walls that sparkled in the early morning sunlight. Two gold thrones stood on a dais. He remembered the room from watching Kayla's sentencing in front of the full Fairy Court. Thoughts of her dewinging sent chills down his spine. The empty room was beautiful—the product of a very rich and opulent past.

Servants placed extra ornate chairs on both sides of the thrones. Lida and Telor entered from a door off the dais that Berty could not see.

"Emperor," said Lida, her face grave, "please sit with us."

After Berty agreed, Lida sat on her throne while Telor sat at her side. Staff in hand, Silvia walked into the Throne Room with Delyth and Declan. Delyth sat in the chair next to her father's empty throne. Next to her sat Declan. Berty and Silvia took the two seats on the side of Telor.

Well-dressed Fairies poured through the double doors. They waited with bated breath for their Queen to speak.

"Noble Fairies of the Court," Lida addressed from her throne, "as you can see, we have with us honored guests." She extended her right arm. "The Emperor of all that surrounds us, Elder Hunter and," she extended her left arm, "the Emperor's Advisor. We are deeply honored with their support for tragedy has befallen Fairyland."

The audience of Fairies exchanged nervous glances.

Paying no attention to her audience, Lida continued, "King Elrick lies on his deathbed. He was put there by the beast we do not name."

The older Fairies gasped.

"We will not abandon our people. In two days time, a Fairy Ring will encircle Fairyland."

"Your Majesty, with all due respect, I must protest," said an older woman.

"What is your protest, Headmistress?" Lida asked.

"If non-Fairies can no longer travel to Fairyland, then how are we to survive?" the Headmistress asked.

"The Godmother Guild will survive as it always has," said Lida.

The Headmistress raised her eyebrows. "With diminishing nobility, the Godmother Guild must open its doors to whomever can pay, Your Majesty. The majority of the people who seek our services are not Fairies. You know as well as I that the selection process must take place within the walls of the Guild. There is only one exception to that rule and there has not been a direct descendant for many years. The Godmother Guild cannot survive without clients. You construct this Fairy Ring and Fairy Godmotherdom will cease to exist. I do not want to imagine the fate of the Empire if that happens."

"We have similar concerns, Your Majesty," said another Fairy. "We depend on those who dwell outside of Fairyland.

Most of our food comes from non-Fairies."

"We do a lot of trade with non-Fairies," said a Fairy from across the room. "If they cannot cross the Fairy Ring, what are we to do?"

Other Fairies started audibly agreeing.

"I have heard enough," said Lida. Her stern voice cut across the room, silencing the crowd. "Two days. That is all. You are dismissed."

Fairies filed out, speaking in hurried whispers. When the last Fairy cleared the doorway, the double wooden doors shut with a resounding finality.

"My Lord, Elder," said Lida, "you are welcome to stay until—"

"No," interjected Delyth.

Lida turned to look at her daughter.

"We cannot do this," said Delyth.

"We must protect ourselves," said Lida.

"We must not do it like this," Delyth countered.

"I do not expect you to understand," dismissed Lida. "You were not raised to be Queen."

"You are correct," said Delyth, standing. "I was raised to be more."

"Then I expect you to understand your duty." Lida looked poignantly at Delyth. "The decision has been made."

"What if," Delyth glanced at everyone before continuing, "I said no?"

Lida stood. "Do not do this, Delyth. This is neither the time nor the place."

"Fine," said Delyth. "You leave me no other choice." Stepping off the dais, she determinedly walked towards the doors.

"Where are you going?" Lida demanded.

Delyth turned sharply. "To the Tower."

"No!" shouted Lida. "I will not let you destroy the very essence of Fairydom."

"What is the point of Fairydom when they have all turned against us?" Delyth asked. "No Faemastask," Lida shuttered,

123

"has been seen is over five hundred years." She took a step forward. "It was meant to kill us. No Fairy Ring can stop Millicent. She has been trying to pick us off, one by one. I have concluded this ever since she poisoned me. What is going to stop her from coming after you or Telor next?"

Lida said nothing.

"I do not care about Fairydom. Curse Fairydom! I only care about the well being of my family. I don't need anything more than that."

As Lida gazed at her daughter, her expression softened. Opening her wings, she flew across the room to land next to her daughter. She wrapped her arms around Delyth.

Watching the two embrace, Berty barely noticed a servant entering through a side door. The servant approached Telor, then handed him a piece of paper.

After reading the paper, Telor said, "Excuse me, mother."

Lida kept one arm around her daughter while she looked at her son.

"My Lord," he said to Berty, "word has just arrived from the Empire Tree. Leif has been captured."

Berty looked at Silvia. She breathed deeply before saying, "You must go."

He nodded his head.

"I will make sure your horses are readied," said Telor standing.

"Horse," corrected Berty. "I go alone." He looked at Declan. "You are needed here."

Declan nodded as Telor left the room.

Putting a hand on Silvia's arm, he said, "I'll send word."

As he crossed the room, Lida said to him, "Thank you for coming, Emperor. Your presence here has meant a lot to us."

"You are welcome. I only wish there was more that I could do," Berty said before walking through the large doors into the main hall.

After he gathered his things from his room, he stopped in front of Elrick's door. Knocking, Berty entered. Elrick lay in his bed, propped on pillows. His eyes followed Berty as he crossed the room.

Berty knew why he was there, but the words were stuck in his throat. Deciding to take a different approach, he said, "The Empire Guard has captured Leif. I must return for his trial where he will be punished severely for his part in poisoning Delyth among other crimes against the Empire. Declan will be staying for as long as he can."

"Declan has noble soul," Elrick said with difficulty. "Shame not Fairy." He smiled weakly. "Maybe does not matter. Thank you, Emperor, Hubert."

Berty smiled widely at his dying friend. "Good-bye, Elrick," he said, putting his hand on the Fairy's arm.

Leaving Elrick's bedside, Berty walked out into the hall. He closed his eyes, then took a deep breath. No one should see the Emperor cry, he thought. When he opened his eyes, he saw Silvia standing in the hallway without her staff.

"May I walk with you?" she asked.

"Of course."

While they walked through the castle towards his waiting horse, Silvia said, "I'm speaking as the former Empress, not Elder Hunter. What Leif has done to the Empire is appalling. Personally, he has hurt me deeply with his conspiring. To knowingly hide and mislead information about a magical object to its rightful owner goes deeper than just being wrong. It violates the Sorcerer's Code most egregiously, but you know that. I know there is no excuse for what he has done. A part of me just wants to know why."

They arrived at his horse much too quickly for Berty's liking. He did not want to have to leave Silvia's side. "Hopefully, he will provide answers," he reassured. Throwing his leg over his horse, he mounted with ease.

"Be careful," Silvia said.

He gave her a sharp nod and a smile before galloping through Fairyland. As he rushed through the gates into the forest, Berty tried not to think about how hard it was saying good-bye to

Elrick. The wind tousled his hair and cloak while he raced across the clearing. Berty wondered what hand Leif played in Elrick's murder. Those thoughts made him more determined to get home, so he pushed his horse to go faster.

Chapter Ten

A Glimmer of Hope

The forest canopy began to filter the midday sun well. Thoughts of Leif made Berty realize that he could loathe someone more than Sean. For Leif, it pushed beyond loathing and well into hate. Berty could not recall ever hating anyone. There were people he had strongly disliked, but no one got him to venture into the realm of hate.

As the trees blurred in his peripheral vision, Berty felt as if he and his horse were one entity. The blurring trees came back to focus when Berty found himself no longer seated in the saddle. Realizing he was flying through the air, he thought, *soft landing*, over and over again.

He fell to the ground with a gentle thud. Getting up, Berty dusted off his clothes. When he looked around, he noticed that the horse was gone. Knowing that without a horse his journey would take longer, Berty quickly began to follow the road home.

A hooded man appeared from behind a tree. "Not so fast," he said.

Stopping, Berty saw a bluish-white swirling sphere hovering above the man's open hand.

"Now, unless you want to taste my magic again," the man said, "give me all your valuables. Starting with that ring."

"No," Berty said.

"Didn't they ever teach you that swordsmen are no match for Warlocks?" the man taunted.

Before Berty could plan how to get past him, the man hurled the swirling sphere.

With a swipe of Berty's hand, the sphere changed direction, colliding with a tree.

The man lobbed another sphere towards Berty.

Again, Berty swiped it away.

The Warlock launched spheres one after the other.

All Berty could do was deflect them. Spheres exploded in the branches of the trees.

Wishing he had learned about combative magic, Berty desperately searched for a solution. The man did not change his stance, so Berty could not trip him. He was too far from any tree for a branch to fall on top of him. Magically hurling his sword could backfire. Running out of options, Berty remembered Delyth's gift.

While his one hand deflected spheres, his other hand reached for the small pouch of Fairy Dust. Taking just a pinch, Berty threw it towards the Warlock.

Fairy Dust collided with spheres causing firework-like explosions.

The Warlock stumbled backwards.

Berty reached for another pinch.

Before Berty's hand found the pouch, a bluish stream erupted from the Warlock's outstretched palms.

Placing both hands in front of him, Berty shielded himself from the steady stream of magic.

Berty's boots dug into the dirt as he tried to push the stream back towards the Warlock. His ears barely heard some sort of incantation before the stream became stronger.

Berty's boots slid backwards a few inches. "No," he breathed. He stopped sliding.

Slowly, he could feel the stream move away. Seeing nothing but a big splash of blue, Berty focused entirely on moving it backwards.

Without warning, the blue stream of magic stopped. Berty took a step forward to stop from falling on his face. The Warlock lay unconscious on the ground. Cautiously, Berty took a step towards him.

Fairies landed on the path. Berty stopped.

"My Lord, are you all right?" asked Delyth, walking through the group of periwinkle enrobed Fairies.

"Delyth," Berty said in surprise. "What are you doing here?"

When she did not answer, he said, "Yes, I am fine."

"We were flying overhead when I saw Fairy Dust being used," said Delyth. "We came to check on it. I dusted the Warlock from above."

"Thank you," said Berty.

"After you left, another message arrived from the Empire Tree," Delyth continued. "Millicent broke Leif out of the dungeon. Apparently, she used copious amounts of Fairy Dust. Fairyland has sent Containment Units." She indicated the other Fairies. "You could be in grave danger, my Lord. We will give you a lift."

Delyth motioned for two Fairies from the group to step forward. A Fairy stepped on either side of Berty. "Lock arms with us, my Lord," one of them said.

With his elbows locked with the two Fairies, Berty braced himself to leave the ground. Delyth fluttered her wings as if she were sending a signal to the others. As soon as her feet rose off the path, the others followed suit.

Berty glided into the air. The Fairies flew smoothly. He watched the branches whiz past as they ascended. Finally, blue sky surrounded him. Treetops gave the horizon a bumpy look. Shining green raced below him.

Not long after he left the Warlock on the path, Berty and the Fairies circled around the treed wall of the Sages' Grove. They descended into the forest clearing. Gently, their feet rested on solid ground yards from the open gates of the Sages' Grove.

"Your Highness," said one of the Fairies holding what looked like a voltage meter, "Fairy Dust surrounds the gates."

"Begin containment," Delyth instructed. "My Lord," she whispered, "I must conduct the containment of the Sages' Grove.

Inside the Empire Tree you are definitely impervious to the effects of Fairy Dust. I know not if it extends beyond the confines of the tree. Testing the barriers now would be a bad idea."

"You want me to wait here?"

"Yes, but I do not want to leave you alone."

The call of the eagle caused both Berty and Delyth to look to the sky. The eagle Berty rescued in God Mountain swooped out of the sky resting on Berty's shoulders.

"Good," said Delyth. "I will return as soon as I can." Her dark purple cloak floated behind her as she approached the gates. "Hatcher," she cried.

Closing his eyes, Berty followed Delyth to Hatcher's side. The Troll lay curled in the fetal position staring into space while intermittently making goat sounds. Delyth glanced at Empire Guards lying on the ground. They each made a different strange noise. Hatcher began to gurgle. Foam bubbled out of his mouth.

"Oh, no," said Delyth. "Hatcher, stay with me." She placed her hand on his forehead while saying what sounded to Berty like, "*Ahk oom crum bythe.*" An opalescent glow encased her hand. Once the glow faded, she removed her hand. Hatcher appeared to be sleeping.

Satisfied with Hatcher, Delyth rushed to the side of an Empire Guard having a seizure. After repeating the incantation with her hand on his forehead, the guard's fit stopped.

Standing, she assessed the situation. Everywhere she looked, people were hallucinating, acting as if they had escaped from a sanitarium or on the ground staring into nowhere. Bystanders who tried to help the contaminated became affected as well.

"Please, do not try to help anyone," said Delyth, projecting her voice. "I know you want to, but there is nothing you can do. I advise you to stay back and to move as little as possible. Let the Containment Units do their jobs."

The Fairies walked through the village with contraptions that looked like dull black canister vacuums hanging from shoulder straps. Methodically, they worked their way around the Empire

Tree. Once they passed the barracks, Delyth rushed in that direction.

"Miles," she called to one of the Fairies, "check the barracks."

The Fairy entered the barracks while Delyth waited outside.

"It's clean, Princess," said Miles.

"We will be using it as a decontamination center," Delyth said.

"What can I do to help?" asked Hedda, poking her head out of the door.

Looking a bit relieved, Delyth said, "We need as many beds as possible, then I am going to have to ask that all non-Fairies stay out."

Hedda gave her a sharp nod, then said, "I will let you know when everything is ready."

Delyth met the Fairies in the marketplace.

"The Sages' Grove is decontaminated," said Miles.

"You four come with me," Delyth said indicating four of the Fairies. "The rest of you, split your duties between checking every building and every person and taking every affected person to the barracks to be decontaminated. Miles knows where."

She led the four into the Empire Tree. A chaotic scene greeted them in the Receiving Room. She waited by the door as the four cleaned the room with their vacuums. Nodding her head at two of the Fairies, she said, "After you take these people to decontamination, check upstairs."

As they began to carry people out of the tree, Delyth said to the remaining two, "Follow me."

In the back of the room, Delyth placed her hand on a Sages' Seal. A door opened. She led the Fairies down stone steps into a stone corridor. At the end of the corridor, guards were having convulsions slumped at their posts.

"Go on to the cells," instructed Delyth. She watched them round the corner. Raising off the ground, she held her open hands towards the guards.

"*Ahk oom crum bythe,*" she said. An opalescent glow

surrounded her, then pushed towards the guards. Quickly, the glow rebounded back to her. The glow disappeared by the time she returned to the ground.

As she checked each guard, one of the Fairies reported, "No more people, but traces of dust."

"Bring these guards to decontamination. I'll send others to help you," said Delyth.

The clicking of her shoes on stone echoed through the corridor as she ran back to the surface.

"Everything is clear, Your Highness," said a Fairy in the Receiving Room.

"Good. There are guards in the dungeon who need to be brought to containment," Delyth said. She made sure the door to the dungeon was open before walking into the Sages' Grove. Opening her wings, she took to the sky.

Berty opened his eyes to see Delyth flying towards him. Landing, she said, "I am sorry I took so long, my Lord. I will explain once we get inside the Empire Tree."

Berty walked with Delyth inside the gates of the Sages' Grove.

Delyth whispered to Berty, "May we close the gates until everything is situated?"

Agreeing with her, he closed the gates magically. Looking left, he saw people in lines waiting to be checked by the Fairies. To his right, other Fairies carried the affected into the barracks. Before they entered the Empire Tree, he felt the gentle pressure of the eagle leaving his shoulder.

Alfred met them in the Reception Room. "Welcome home, my Lord, Delyth," he said. "I am sorry that we could not hold Leif after we caught him trying to break into the Vault Room."

"The Vault Room?" asked Delyth.

"Yes. He attempted to pry open the outer chamber door."

Delyth's violet eyes widened. "I need to check the Vault. My Lord, it is imperative that we speak in the Roundtable Room."

"Go," said Berty. "I will wait for you there."

With a nod of thanks, she raced down the steps.

"There was no way we could have held him with Millicent

using Fairy Dust to free him," Berty told Alfred as they ascended the stairs. "I wonder what he wanted in the vault."

"We asked him, but he would not say a word," said Alfred. "Alvar's plan was to keep him in the dungeon awhile, then try again. Only he did not plan to be thwarted by Millicent."

"Where are Alvar and Edwin?" Berty asked.

"Alvar went to help Colvin in the tunnels," said Alfred. "Edwin is checking everyone inside the tree."

Berty nodded, then took his seat at the Roundtable.

"What happened with Elrick?" Alfred asked sitting beside Berty.

Berty took the opportunity to tell Alfred everything—almost everything—that happened in Fairyland.

"A Fairy eating beast?" said Alfred. "I have never even heard of those. Poor Lida. What are they going to do?"

"They talked about constructing a Fairy Ring around Fairyland," Berty answered. "But, I am not sure if that will happen or not."

"It will not," said Delyth, entering the room. "We have much bigger problems, my Lord." She threw a dark blue velvet pouch in the middle of the table.

Alfred quickly pushed himself away from the table. "Are you mad?"

"Relax. It is empty," said Delyth, sitting.

"I will not relax," Alfred huffed. "Fairy Dust should be banned. You brought it in this tree and see what has happened!"

"You're blaming me?" Delyth shouted.

"Yes! She must have sneaked into your chambers and stole your Fairy Dust!"

"Mine?" Standing, Delyth pointed at her chest. "This," she pointed violently at the bag on the table, "is not my dust!"

"How do you know?" shouted Alfred.

"Aaargh!" She collapsed in her chair.

"Enough. Both of you," Berty said calmly. "Please explain, Delyth."

The Fairy breathed deeply a few times before she was able to talk again. "I found this bag by the vaults. It had traces of the same dust she used on both Colvin and Alvar, both of whom are getting decontaminated. It is the same dust we found everywhere."

"That does not make it not your dust," remarked Alfred.

Berty gave him a reproachful look.

"Yes it does," said Delyth. "The dust she used is old. Fairy Dust should only last seven years. After seven years, Fairy Dust becomes volatile. The potency fluctuates. You cannot trust that it will perform the way you want. Sometimes it will do nothing and other times it creates the chaos that ensued here. For that reason, every seven years, all the old dust is collected and destroyed. New dust is then made and distributed."

"Then how did this dust never get collected?" Berty asked.

"Ivory containers conceal Fairy Dust so that the Containment Units cannot collect it," explained Delyth. "Ivory has been outlawed for so long that it is almost impossible to find. The only other way," her eyes opened wide as her jaw dropped. "Of course. She had to have kept it in the Historian's Vault. I will return." Hopping off her chair, she ran out of the room.

"When she comes back, you owe her an apology, Alfred," said Berty.

The Elf stared at his clothes. "Yes, I believe I do."

Edwin knocked on the open door. "My Lord, may I come in?"

"Of course," said Berty.

Entering the room, Edwin stood near the table to report, "No one above the Receiving Room has been injured or affected in any way. Also, no one saw anything. If they did, I am sure they were affected by the Fairy Dust."

"Thank you, Edwin. You have done well," Berty said.

As Edwin left the room, the sound of a doorbell resonated in the room.

"What is that?" asked Alfred.

Shocked, Berty recognized the chime. "Someone is at my door," he said. "I will be back as soon as I can. Do not let Delyth leave without talking to me first."

Jetting into his private staircase, Berty took two steps at a time. After crossing the long, narrow bridge, he passed his chambers running directly into Silvia's. His legs did not stop as he crossed through the tapestry into his bedroom. Quickly, he peeled off his cloak, then threw it on his bed. As he ran down the steps, his clothes magically lost their golden trim.

Catching his breath, he turned the brass doorknob of his stained glass front door.

"Jon, Teresa, Hope, I hope I did not keep you waiting," he said. "Come in."

"Not at all," said Jon as he allowed his wife and daughter to enter before him.

"What brings you guys over?" Berty asked, closing the door.

Teresa looked at Jon who said, "We have a favor to ask."

Seeing the serious look on both of their faces, Berty showed them into his sitting room. The three of them sat on the antique furniture while Hope examined the contents of the room.

"Well," said Jon, fidgeting with his hands, "the company just acquired a huge contract in Africa. Plus, we have the chance to add more business while we're there." He took off his glasses, fiddled with them, then placed them back on his face.

Berty knew something big was coming.

"I need to go to Africa to oversee everything. Then, I need to wine and dine for the additional contracts before I can send a more permanent person over there," Jon continued.

Berty waited for the kicker.

"Thing is, Teresa has to come too."

"And we can't bring Hope," added Teresa. "We would have no one to watch her."

Jon glanced at Teresa before saying, "We thought it would be a good idea if Hope could stay with you until we return."

"Please say yes, Uncle Berty," said Hope, sitting next to him. "We can spend the whole summer together having adventures."

"The whole summer?" said Berty. "When are you leaving?"

Jon's lips almost disappeared as he sucked them into his mouth. "We tried calling," he said.

"When, Jon?"

"Teresa thought it best to just come over."

"Jon?"

"And obviously we caught you just before you left again," Jon said.

"When?" Berty asked. His brother always beat around the bush.

Jon closed his eyes tightly. "Tomorrow."

"Tomorrow?" Berty asked. Not that he really minded, although he would have preferred it when his life was not melting into chaos.

"We are sorry about it being last minute," said Teresa, "but we just found out ourselves."

Looking into Teresa's pleading brown eyes, Berty said, "I will be happy to let Hope stay with me for the summer."

"Yay!" screamed Hope. "I'll get my stuff from the car."

"No, you will not," said Teresa. "You will wait for your father."

Hope quickly sat in a chair by the door.

"I know this sounds like a silly question, but it is still May, right?" Berty asked. "I lost track of time taking care of a sick friend. And, I really need to get back. There is no possible way that I am going to be able to take Hope back and forth to school everyday."

"Our school district is having budget problems," Teresa explained. "They are letting students out early. Since Hope is in the top of her class, her last day was Friday."

"Mom and Dad can take her for about a week," said Jon. "But, then they are off with Teresa's parents."

"Look, guys," Berty said lowering his voice, "you can leave her with me now, but I have to take her with me. I can't guarantee that you can get a hold of us at a drop of a hat. And I don't want you to worry. You have already met Declan."

"Berty," said Teresa with a reassuring smile, "we understand. We also think that going with you will be good for her."

"As long as you know," said Berty.

"Come on, Hope," said Jon as he rose out of his seat. "Let's go get your things."

Hope jumped off the chair, then ran to the front door.

Berty and Teresa followed Jon into the Foyer. "Thank you so much," Teresa said to him. "This is the first time we are going to be away from our baby." She blinked away the wetness in her eyes as she watched Jon open the trunk of their car. "Before I forget," she pulled a folded piece of paper from her purse. "I made a list of important numbers." Opening, she read, "The pediatrician, the dentist, the poison control center, numbers of trusted babysitters. I also wrote down Matt's number in Tokyo and the number of our main hotel with country codes. These are just in case of emergencies. I don't want you to incur international long distance charges. On the bottom is a list of her allergies."

Hope entered the house wearing her yellow backpack.

Taking the list from Teresa, Berty said, "Thanks." He refolded it, then placed it in his pocket.

Jon walked through the door carrying two laundry bags. "Where to?" he asked.

Closing the front door, Berty relieved his brother of one of the bags. "You have your choice of bedrooms, Hope," he said.

She grabbed her mother's hand, pulling her up the stairs. Jon and Berty followed, carrying the laundry bags. Hope passed Berty's room. Disappearing through a door, she said, "This one."

Entering her chosen room, Berty placed the bag on the floor. She picked the more child friendly room with the twin beds. Carefully hanging her backpack on a chair, she climbed on one of the beds. As her gaze drifted around the room, she smiled widely.

"Daddy and I have to get going," Teresa told her. "Let's go downstairs."

"Okay," said Hope, jumping off the bed.

Berty followed his brother's family down the steps. A niche that Berty had never noticed caught his eye. Taking a few steps towards it, he could have sworn that there was never any niche in the paneling before.

Nestled in the niche was an ornate white and brass rotary phone. Surprised, he walked over for a closer look. He clearly remembered Martin saying that the house had no telephone. Yet, one sat inside the niche. On one side of the phone was a pad of paper and a pencil. On the other side was a container holding what looked like business cards.

Picking up a business card, he read, "Chase Residence," and a ten-digit number. He brought the card over to Jon and Teresa who were immersed in hugging and kissing their daughter.

"You listen to your Uncle Berty," Teresa told Hope.

"We should be back by the third week in August," said Jon. "Just in time for Hope to start school."

"Don't worry about back to school shopping. Our parents have that covered," Teresa added.

"Before you go," said Berty holding out the card. "An alternative number. I don't know if we will always be available there either."

"Thanks, Berty," said Teresa. She dropped the card in her purse.

With one last hug and kiss, Jon and Teresa said to Hope, "Be good. We will be home before you know it."

Hope waved to her parents from the porch until she could no longer see their car. Crestfallen, she entered the house. Her sadness melted when she looked up at Berty asking, "When do I get to come with you to the Land of Sages? I brought the cloak you gave me for Christmas."

Berty breathed deeply. He dreaded this day for months. "Right now," he said.

Her brown eyes opened wide with wild glee. "Now?"

Nodding, he said, "Hurry up; go put on your cloak."

He followed her up the stairs. In his bedroom, he picked his cloak off the bed. After fastening it, he turned around to see Hope standing in the doorway wearing her maroon cloak.

"I'm ready, Uncle Berty," she said. "How do we get there?"

Holding out his hand, he told her, "You have to promise me

that you will never show or tell anyone this way. This is just our private way."

"Okay," she said as she placed her little hand in his.

Berty walked with Hope past the wing chairs. Pausing in front of the fireplace, he smiled at his niece. With a single step, he brought her into Silvia's bedroom.

"Where are we?" she whispered.

"The Empire Tree," Berty said. "Keep a hold of my hand."

Hope glanced at Berty's gold trimmed sleeve as they walked through Silvia's chambers.

"Wow," Hope breathed before they crossed the rope and plank bridge to the trunk. Berty led Hope down the private staircase. When they entered the Roundtable Room, they caught the end of Alfred and Delyth's discussion.

"I accept your apology, Alfred. Thank you," said Delyth. Seeing Berty arrive, she said, "My Lord, I found traces of Fairy Dust in my vault. Millicent did hide dust down there. Oh," she said when she noticed Hope. "Hello there," she smiled.

Hope grabbed Berty's cloak with her other hand trying to hide behind him.

"Delyth, Alfred," said Berty, "I want you to meet Hope, my niece."

"It is very nice to meet you, Hope," Alfred said warmly.

Hope gawked at the Elf and Fairy.

Berty smiled. "What do we need to do about those contaminated?"

"They need time to recover," said Delyth. "How long? I do not know. A number of the Containment Units must stay behind."

"What shall I tell Fairyland?" Alfred asked.

Hope's eyes widened.

"I'll tell Declan," said Berty. He looked at his niece. "I need my hand."

She relinquished it, substituting Berty's cloak. Earnestly, she watched Berty extract the large, gold Watcher's locket from his cloak.

Opening it, he wrote with the rod, "Leif and Millicent escaped. Lots of old Fairy Dust, but everyone will be okay."

He held the locket in his hand waiting for Declan's reply. "Hope will be staying through the summer with us," he told them.

"Then she will need to be fitted with a Fairy Godmother," said Delyth.

Hope smiled, scooching away from her uncle.

Before Berty could say anything, Declan sent a reply. He read aloud, "Tell Delyth, we will lose Elrick by morning."

Tears streamed down her fair cheeks as if the news of her father's impending death had just hit her. Wiping her cheeks with her silver trimmed sleeve, she said, "I need to be there."

"Of course you do," said Berty.

"Will you return with me?" Delyth asked. "We will bring Hope as well."

He watched the Fairy try to hold back more tears. "Yes," was all Berty managed to say.

She tried to smile, but she could not. "We will leave from the Star Gazing Platform," Delyth said. "We will meet you there." Not waiting for a response, she ran out of the room.

Alfred watched Delyth's departure with sorrow in his blue eyes. "Extend my condolences to Lida and Telor. I will arrange for a coach and Empire Guards to escort all of you home," he said.

"Thank you, Alfred," said Berty. "Stay close, Hope."

Hope held onto Berty's cloak as they ascended the stairs.

"Theodore," Berty called.

The Dwarf appeared in the hallway before the steps to the platform. "Yes, my Lord," he bowed.

"My niece, Hope, will need a room."

"Will she have a Fairy Godmother?"

"Yes."

"It will be done," Theodore said.

Leaving Theodore in the hallway, Berty and Hope climbed the steps to the platform overlooking the treetops.

"Everything is ready," said Delyth as she landed on the platform.

Four Fairies landed around her. Each one of them kept their wings open. The setting sun gave the purplish blue wings a golden sparkle.

With Hope's jaw dropped, Berty squatted next to her. "The Fairies are going to allow us to fly with them to Fairyland. I am going to go with two Fairies while you will go with two other Fairies. If you get scared, just close your eyes. Okay?" he told her.

Hope nodded.

Locking arms with the Fairies, Berty watched Hope smile as the Fairies lifted her off the platform. The sun sunk quickly beneath the horizon while they sped over the treetops. Berty could hear Hope giggling somewhere beside him. Yellowish dots appeared in the distance. The dots grew bigger the closer they got to Fairyland.

Eventually, he saw a well-lighted castle balcony. After setting Berty and Hope on the balcony, the Fairies bowed, then flew away.

Hope gazed out into the dark forest.

"My father lies two floors down," Delyth said.

"Come on, Hope," said Berty.

"What is a Fairy Eater, Uncle Berty?" Hope asked.

Berty held up a hand to stop Delyth. "Go on," he said to Hope. He wanted to know what the trees knew.

"They say the Fairy Eater was released from its prison in God Mountain," Hope relayed. "It was supposed to attack the Prince, but attacked the King instead. The one who can see the magic can free the poison."

Berty and Delyth exchanged glances. "How?" Berty asked.

Hope stood as if she were listening for a second. "Using his wand. He must deposit the poison into the severed claw and bottle of blood," she said with a grimace. "All of it must be buried beyond the magic of the trees or the poison will re-enter the King."

"Thank the trees, Hope," said Berty. "I'll message Declan. Delyth, lead the way." Opening his locket, he said, "Hurry, Hope."

They followed Delyth through the castle as Berty wrote with the rod. When they arrived at Elrick's room, everyone was waiting for them. Elrick breathed laboriously in his bed.

Wand in hand, Declan looked at Berty. "What am I to do?"

Moving towards the open window, Hope said, "Move your wand over the wounds, pulling out the poison. When you wand is full, push the poison into," she grimaced again, "the beast parts. Repeat until all the poison is gone."

Declan lifted the covers off of Elrick, exposing his torn chest. Holding his wand over the wounds, Declan looked surprised. Berty guessed that Declan could see the magic going into his wand. Silvia sat in a chair, holding the claw and phial of blood for him.

Delyth and Lida held hands while they watched Declan extract the poison. Standing in a corner, Telor watched every move Declan made.

After what felt like an eternity, Declan peered into Elrick's wounds. "All gone," he said.

"You have exactly one week to bury it," Hope added.

Elrick breathed easier. He pushed himself up on the bed.

"Not so fast," said Declan. "We need to get a salve on that. How are you feeling?"

"A bit achy. Like I fell out of the sky," Elrick admitted.

With tears in her eyes, Lida walked over to her husband's bedside. She placed a hand on Declan's arm. "You let Declan take care of you," she told her husband.

"Anything you say, my darling," Elrick said with a smile.

Delyth allowed tears to fall from her violet eyes. "Daddy," was all she could muster whilst sitting on the bed.

As Telor crept out of the corner, Declan and Silvia backed away from the bed.

"Go get that salve," Silvia said to Declan. "I will put these in a safe place." She disappeared.

Chapter Eleven
The Godmother Guild

Berty held out his hand for Hope. She grabbed it without question. As Declan cantered down the hall, Berty closed Elrick's door to give him and his family some privacy.

"The trees talk a lot here," said Hope. "Much more than they do at home."

Closing a door, Silvia joined Berty and Hope in the hallway. "You must be Hope," Silvia said with a smile. "Your Uncle Berty has told me a lot about you. My name is Silvia."

Looking at Silvia, Hope decided to say, "Hi."

"You know, I haven't had anything to eat all day. Are you hungry, Hope?" Silvia asked.

Her brown curls bounced as she nodded her head.

Smiling, Berty realized how tired and hungry he was. They strolled down the hall together.

Passing Declan on the stairs, he said to them, "Thank you, Hope."

Hope smiled.

Sitting around the table, she gawked at the servants bringing food laden silver trays.

Berty felt better with food in his stomach. Not wanting to frighten Hope, he told Silvia the edited version of his day.

"It is a shame they escaped," Silvia lamented. "I was not aware of how close Leif and Millicent really became. I had always thought of them as having an academic relationship."

She stared at the wall behind Berty for a moment. Drinking from her goblet returned her focus to the table.

Lida entered the room with Delyth and Telor behind her. Berty began to stand, but Lida said, "Do not stand on my account. Emperor, I have been told that this is your niece." She looked kindly at Hope. "An honor to have you in Fairyland, my dear. You have quite a gift."

When the door opened, all eyes found Declan. "He needs a little rest, but he should make a full recovery," he said. Declan did not sit until after the Fairies took their seats.

Telor let out a breath.

"Before we all retire for the night," said Lida, "there is something that needs to be discussed. I want to know where all this is leading. For what do we have to prepare?"

"Leif has some sort of plan," Berty answered. "Though, I do not know if we have enough dots to make a picture."

Looking at Berty, Delyth said, "Remember when we traveled to God Mountain?"

Berty nodded while Telor asked her, "You went to God Mountain?"

"Not now," she told her brother. "I had suspicions that I did not share with you, my Lord."

Silvia raised her eyebrows.

"Well, now I can confirm them. With both the Fairy Ring and the yellow Dragon, someone used old dust."

"Are you sure?" Lida asked.

Delyth nodded. "Absolutely. There was so much Fairy Dust used in the Sages' Grove that I was able to do a thorough examination. The dust had gone through at least two seven-year cycles. Its volatility was the same as the Fairy Dust we encountered on the way to God Mountain. Only more potent than normal Fairy Dust could have affected a Dragon."

"Can the potency of Fairy Dust be increased any other way?" Silvia asked.

The Fairy studied Silvia. Cocking her head to the side, Delyth answered, "I know of no other way." Glancing at Berty, she said,

144

"Unless... the scepter." She stared at a point on the table for a moment. "But, it is impossible to touch."

"Leif was disturbingly fascinated with the scepter," said Declan.

"The scepter is only a device," Silvia paused, "through which magic passes," she said. Each word was slow to leave her lips as if she realized what they meant. "I have been so naive." She jumped out of her chair.

"Where are you going?" Berty asked her.

"I need to think. I'll see you in the morning," she said. Her gold dress twinkled in the candlelight as she left the room.

Silvia's departure awoke Telor from the dumbfounded look he gave his sister. "How do you know so much about Fairy Dust?" he asked.

"I made it my business to know," said Delyth, brushing off his question. "My Lord, if Leif believes that the Staff of Lightning is similar to the scepter, then we have a major problem. I know not how much, if any, Fairy Dust is stashed in ivory boxes. But if he gets his hands on that staff, then he could potentially do dastardly things with Fairy Dust that might not be reversible."

"But why try to break into the Vault Room?" asked Berty.

Delyth shook her head.

"Maybe we missed something," Declan suggested. "Or maybe he is trying to mislead us."

"And risk getting caught?" asked Telor.

"He knew Millicent could get him out without a problem," Declan said.

"She went to the Vault Room, too," Delyth rationalized. "It could not have been misdirection."

"I don't think it hurts us to check," said Berty.

A small head fell on Berty. Looking down, he saw Hope sleeping on his cloaked arm.

Lida smiled with happy reminisces as she gazed at the sleeping child. "Her room is next to yours," she told Berty.

"Let's go to bed, Hope," he said.

"Five more minutes," Hope said sleepily.

Hope reminded Berty of his brother when they were children. Jon would always ask their parents for five more minutes at bedtime, no matter how tired he was.

"Nope; it is time to go to bed," Berty said.

"Please, Uncle Berty. Five more minutes," she yawned.

"Come on, I'll carry you," said Berty, standing. Hope raised her arms up to her uncle. He scooped her off the chair. Resting her head on his shoulder, Hope fell asleep as he carried her up the stairs.

He struggled with the doorknob whilst trying not to drop Hope. Finally opening the door, he walked into the room leaving the door open. Placing her down near the bed, she woke momentarily. He removed her magenta cloak, then hung it in the empty wardrobe. As he tried to untie her shoes, he felt a hand on his shoulder.

"Let me do this," Silvia said softly. "Wait outside while I get her into bed."

Thankful for the help, Berty placed the shoe on the floor. Silvia easily untied the other shoelace as he walked out of the room, closing the door over behind him.

Berty waited in the hall. The knowledge that Hope was the Wood Listener was no longer a secret. He wondered how it would affect Hope's life in the Land of Sages. Would people demand her to relay the knowledge of the trees? Would she be able to have a normal childhood? "Being able to communicate with trees has nothing to do with normal," mumbled Berty. He resigned to let things happen and deal with them as they came.

Opening the door, Silvia smiled at him. "She's waiting for you to tuck her in, Berty."

He loved it when she called him Berty. "Thank you," he said.

Her gold dress shimmered in the dim light as she began to walk away. Stopping, she turned. She blushed, seeing that he still watched her. "Do you think," she said taking a step towards him, "would you mind if I came with you to the Godmother Guild tomorrow?"

"Not at all." He smiled.

With a wide smile, she continued down the hall to her room.

The clicking of her heels on the stone floor stayed in his head while he entered Hope's room. She lay in the bed, wide-eyed. "Flying with the Fairies was so much fun," said Hope. "I wonder if my Fairy Godmother will be just like Cinderella's. Do you think I will be able to get a magic wand like Declan has? Do I have to wait until I'm eleven?"

Chuckling a little, he sat on Hope's bed. "Things are different here than what you have read in books. Here, only Watchers have wands. Declan is a Watcher," Berty explained.

"Can I be a Watcher?" Hope asked with a gleam in her brown eyes.

Not wanting to burst her bubble, he said, "You are a Listener, so I don't think you can be a Watcher."

"What's a Listener?"

"A person who can talk to things that others cannot," explained Berty. "You can talk to trees, and they can talk to you."

"Ooh," Hope said. "I'm a Listener." She giggled a little, knowing she was special. "Are you a Listener, too?"

"Nope. Just you."

Her face fell a little. "What are you, Uncle Berty?"

"I'm the Emperor," he said.

Her eyes opened even wider. "You're like Marcus in your story," she said.

"And you have to get some sleep," he said tapping her on the nose. "The Godmother Guild awaits."

"Okay," she said excitedly. She squeezed her eyes closed. "Goodnight, Uncle Berty."

"Goodnight, Hope." He got off her bed. Smoothing her covers, he said, "I'm right next door if you need me." He extinguished the lantern, then left her room.

As he opened the door to his room, Berty saw Declan pass with a big smile on his face. His sandy hair stuck out in every direction. Noticing his partially untucked shirt, he did not want to know. Berty entered his room, ignoring Declan. The large bed welcomed him. He fell asleep as soon as his head hit the pillow.

Berty awoke with brown hair tickling his neck. A little nose and big, brown eyes were inches from his face. "Get up, Uncle Berty," encouraged Hope. "We're going for a Fairy Godmother today."

"Not until after breakfast," Berty said. Sunlight shown through the lead glass windows, but Berty felt as though he had just fallen asleep. "Uncle Berty needs some coffee," he told her while wondering why he spoke about himself in third person.

"Good morning," said Silvia, walking into his room. "Door was open."

He nodded sleepily.

"Hope, why don't you come with me downstairs while we wait for your Uncle Berty to get ready."

"Okay," Hope said way too cheerfully for Berty's liking.

"Thank you," he mouthed to Silvia as she ushered Hope from the room. Hearing the latch click, he moped out of bed. Once dressed, he trudged into the dining room to find Hope talking to Silvia. As he found the silver carafe of hot beverage, he could not believe that anyone's mouth could move so fast so early in the morning. Tuning her out, he changed the contents of his cup into strong coffee. Chugging some while standing next to the buffet, he gave the caffeine time to enter his blood stream. He randomly placed food on his plate, then joined Silvia and Hope at the table.

Hope stopped talking when Telor entered the dining room. With a sigh, the Fairy sat at the table with his breakfast.

"Everything all right, Telor?" asked Berty.

Telor looked at him wearily. "Archery is getting the best of me, I'm afraid," he said. "Before Declan killed that beast with his bow, I would have told you that the weapon was useless. Seems as though it only holds true in my hands."

"Tell Declan your concerns," suggested Berty. "His grandfather used to craft bows and arrows. He is very knowledgeable."

Nodding, Telor pushed his food around the plate. "What if I

am not cut out to use weapons? Who would have respect for me as King? What kind of woman would want to marry me then?" He stabbed his food with his fork.

The doors opened. Delyth cheerfully entered. "Mother is having breakfast with father this morning," she said. "He is doing so well."

"Do you know how to use a bow as well?" Telor accused. Leaving his food on the table, he stormed out of the dining room.

Puzzled, Delyth stared after her brother. She shrugged her shoulders, then sat next to Berty with her breakfast. "I will take you to the Godmother Guild as soon as we are done here," she said.

Hope giggled quietly while they finished eating. The giggling continued as they donned their cloaks.

While Delyth led them through the maze of streets, Hope's giggles subsided. Berty delighted in seeing his niece's look of wonderment as she gazed at the multicolored buildings and Fairies flying overhead. Their path took them to a large building that reminded Berty of a Russian church. Colors dripped from the domes that topped the building down the walls in a sparkling cascade of colored chaos. They stopped in front of double iron doors that Berty thought would better suit a fortress.

"This is it," said Delyth. Turing to Hope, she asked, "Would you like to knock?"

Letting go of Berty's hand, Hope confidently stepped forward. She balled her little fist inches from the door. On the foreboding metal, she knocked delicately.

Both doors opened wide. A sweet, grandmotherly voice said, "Please, come in."

Berty followed his niece through the opened iron doors. The inside of the Godmother Guild surprised him. Beige stone walls starkly contrasted with the rest of colorful Fairyland. A small vestibule opened into a cathedral like room. Expansive beige nothingness occupied where the pews should have been. A lone multiple candle wrought iron chandelier hung from the arched stone ceiling.

"Welcome to the Godmother Guild, Emperor," said an older woman, standing off to one side of the room. He recognized the woman whose silver hair matched her silver dress. "I am the Headmistress. It is an honor to fit your niece with a Fairy Godmother. Your Highness, if you and Elder Hunter would take a few steps back, please. The child must step into the circle."

Delyth and Silvia walked over to a beige stone pillar behind them while Hope stepped forward. She stopped apparently inside a circle that Berty could not see.

"Good. Let the process begin," said the Headmistress. The Fairy began to walk in a wide circle around Hope. Her face showed no emotion. "What is your name, child?"

"Hope Katherine Chase."

"Your favorite color?"

"Yellow."

"Your preferred playtime activity?"

"Pretending."

"If a train left Fairyland at eight thirty-five in the morning and was traveling at seventy-five miles an hour, then at what time would it arrive in Irmingard?"

Berty thought the question to be too advanced for a child who had just finished the first grade. With only a view of the back of Hope's head, he wished that he could see her expression.

After the Headmistress walked a quarter circle, Hope answered, "Where is the train in Fairyland?"

The Headmistress stopped walking. "We do not answer questions with a question."

Berty smiled.

"I'll have you know that the answer is never. There are no trains in the Land of Sages." The Fairy focused her gaze towards where the church altar would be as if she heard something. "A Fairy Godmother has been chosen," she stated.

She stared, waiting. Berty stared too, hoping to see something other than beige stone.

His eyes finally saw a Fairy walking towards them. Her bright red blouse and dark brown flowing pants shone against the beige. She stopped between Hope and the Headmistress. When she turned her head to look at the older Fairy, Berty could see her brown hair swept back in a chignon.

The Headmistress smiled, then said, "Hope, I would like to introduce you to Freesia. She will be your Fairy Godmother until you become of the age where you no longer need her."

"Hello, Hope," said Freesia. Her voice was clear, yet kind. "You have done well. Will you do the honors of introducing me to your uncle?"

Hope's curls bounced as she nodded. Turning around, she led Freesia towards him. He could see her delight in having her very own Fairy Godmother.

"Uncle Berty, this is Freesia, my Fairy Godmother," said Hope. Turning to Freesia, she said, "My uncle, the Emperor."

"My Lord," Freesia said with a bow of her head. "It is truly an honor to have been fitted with your niece. This is the time where a Fairy Godmother usually asks personal questions. I wish not to offend you, my Lord."

"Please, ask your questions," said Berty.

Freesia smiled. "Where are Hope's parents?"

"They have taken a trip and will be gone through the summer," answered Berty.

"Do you know if Hope possesses any special skills or burgeoning magic?"

"She is a Wood Listener."

Freesia's eyebrows raised quickly. "It is my job to educate Hope and help her discover the woman she will become. I will encourage her to develop her magical skill and indulge her interests. She will be given ample time to play and make friends. Do you approve, my Lord?"

"I do," Berty said.

The beige burned away, revealing beautiful multicolored designs that covered the walls, pillars, ceiling and floor. Overwhelmed, Berty did not know which way to look first. Before he could focus on any one place, teenage Fairies, who looked to be Godmothers-in-training, descended upon Freesia.

They helped her fasten her soft pink cloak and handed her a matching pink satchel.

The Headmistress accompanied them to the iron doors of the Godmother Guild. "I look forward to the time when you need us again, Emperor," she said. "You too, Princess."

Delyth blushed. The Headmistress gave a final nod to Freesia before the iron doors closed behind them.

On the way back to the castle, Freesia engaged Hope with a multitude of questions. Berty thought he heard some tidbits about the Empire from Freesia. He smiled, knowing that Hope was beginning her education without realizing it.

"So?" Berty asked Silvia.

"I never had to go," said Silvia. "What a fascinating process. Did you go through something similar, Delyth?"

"I was asked many more questions," Delyth answered with a giggle. "Headmistress did not approve of my attitude during questioning." She smiled wryly. "My first Godmother thought I was a handful."

"You had more than one?" Berty asked.

"Yes. My first fitting was at the age of one. For my second, I was three," said Delyth. "I had an insatiable appetite for knowledge which my second Godmother fed well. I would not be Historian without her."

Halfway up the steps to the castle doors, Berty heard the thundering of horse hooves on pavement. Turning around, he saw a dozen green cloaked men on horseback. They surrounded a dark green carriage. As they got closer, Berty noticed Edwin leading the pack.

When they stopped in front of the castle doors, Edwin dismounted. Running up the steps, he said, "My Lord, we are here to escort you home."

"I did not expect you so soon," said Berty. "We will not be leaving just yet."

Delyth summoned a servant and spoke to him quietly. "Excuse me, my Lord," she said softly, "Fairyland castle is equipped with guard lodging as well as a covered area to keep the carriage."

"Good." Addressing the guards, he said, "Get some rest men. Lieutenant, come with me."

The servant grabbed Edwin's horse by the bit, leading the Empire Guards down an alley on the side of the castle. Edwin followed Berty inside the castle's entrance hall.

Chapter Twelve
The Elder's Curse

When the doors closed, Delyth said, "Freesia, since you will be staying with us for a few more days, we have prepared a room. Cassandra will take you." She indicated a servant standing off to the side.

"That was very kind, Your Highness," said Freesia.

"We will be on the castle grounds," Berty said with a smile.

With a bow of her head, Freesia followed the servant up the stairs.

While Delyth led them through the castle, Berty asked Edwin, "How are things in the Sages' Grove?"

"The recovery process is slow," said Edwin. "Hatcher has regained consciousness, but his coordination is off."

"That is to be expected. Nothing that some rest cannot cure," interjected Delyth.

"Colvin?" Berty asked.

"Complaining. The Containment Units are keeping him another day. He, of course, has no idea why. According to him, he is perfectly fine."

Silvia chuckled. "Temper as fiery as his beard."

"Alvar?" Berty asked.

Edwin's face turned solemn. "His wife has taken to sleeping on a chair next to his bed. He has yet to open his eyes."

"It will take him longer to recover," consoled Delyth. "Bigger men have bigger falls."

Berty stopped in the middle of the stone corridor causing Hope to walk into him. "Who is in charge of security in the Sages' Grove?" he asked in almost a whisper.

"Lieutenant Noll," answered Edwin. "He reports directly to Alfred."

"Why are you not overseeing the Sages' Grove?" asked Berty.

"Priority, my Lord. Alfred agrees that Leif and Millicent would not try to return while there are Containment Units stationed in the Sages' Grove."

Silently agreeing with Edwin, Berty started walking. "Hope," he said, "when we get outside, I want you to ask the trees how long it would take us to reach beyond the magic of the trees."

Hope smiled at Berty.

Throwing Berty a puzzled look, Edwin asked, "What is beyond the magic of the trees?"

"Elrick's life," Berty replied.

The dark corridor spit them out onto a grassy field. Declan helped the Fairy Guards with their archery skills. Freesia landed in the grass near Hope. Letting go of Hope's hand, he watched her run towards the trees with Freesia following closely behind.

"This is horse dung!" someone shouted.

Berty turned his attention to where the guards were training. Telor threw down his bow. While he stormed towards them, Declan picked his bow off the ground. Curiously, Declan examined it, then watched the others struggle with theirs.

"Telor, what's wrong?" Delyth asked, running to him.

He stomped past, completely ignoring his sister.

"Telor! Talk to me." She ran after him.

He stopped. "Talk to you?" he said. "Princess Delyth the Great to the rescue! Maybe I don't want little Princess Perfect rescuing me. *I* am going to be King."

Mouth hanging open, Delyth stood dumbfounded.

"I am capable of making my own decisions," he said. "I do not need *your* help."

"What do you mean?" she asked in a small voice. Her bottom lip quivered.

"Do not play dumb, Delyth." Contempt filled his words. "We need to talk to Delyth," Telor mocked. "Let's ask Delyth what she thinks. After all, Delyth knows everything there is to know about anything. We consult Delyth all the time, even after she moves to the Empire Tree." His voice began to rise. "Delyth's been through the Dragonlands. Delyth's gone to God Mountain. Delyth has ridden a Dragon. Delyth had a custom sword made. Delyth practices on a live dummy. Delyth does everything." His chest heaved with each sharp intake of breath. "We listen to everything Delyth says. We cannot make a move without Delyth. We cannot die without Delyth!"

She stumbled backwards. "I never knew you hated me so much," she managed. Her violet eyes reached into his green ones until he turned.

Telor disappeared into the stone corridor.

Closing her eyes, tears streamed down her cheeks. Her body shuddered.

Silvia walked over to her. Putting a hand on her shoulder, she said, "Delyth? Do you want to go for a walk?"

Lifting her eyelids, she nodded softly. Behind her violet eyes, Berty saw the shadow of a little girl, who used to admire her big brother reverently, in a panic while her world shattered around her.

Through her tears, she said to Silvia, "I knew that I would never be Queen. I just wanted to be able to be somebody, too. Somebody who was more than just a princess." Instead of words, her mouth released mournful cries.

With an arm around Delyth, Silvia steered her through deserted castle grounds.

Berty felt a gentle tugging on his sleeve. Looking down, he saw Hope staring up at him.

"Four days on foot, if we go the way they tell us," she said.

"Then we leave first thing in the morning," Berty said. He looked from the trees to Hope. "You are going to have to come, too, Hope."

"Where Hope goes, I go, my Lord," said Freesia.

Nodding, Berty said, "Edwin, bring two men with us. The rest can take over for Declan." He looked over at Declan to see him talking with the Empire Guards while still holding Telor's bow.

When Edwin left, Berty watched Hope having fun with Freesia. He was glad that she had Freesia. For six years, he has been 'fun Uncle Berty' who would bring her gifts, play with her, then go home. The thought about having to do all the 'other stuff' scared him a little. Could he be a good disciplinarian? Could he nurture? Could he teach? Would he be able to raise a well-adjusted child who had a lot more respect and a good sense of personal responsibility than the other children he saw in the world? Jon and Teresa were doing a good job, he thought. He felt that perhaps he could, too, with the right person.

Silvia and a dry-eyed Delyth returned. Delyth hugged Silvia before running into the castle alone. A part of Berty wanted to know what they discussed. Another part did not want to ruin the mystery.

"Hope is adjusting well to having a Fairy Godmother," Silvia mentioned.

"She has been asking me to bring her here ever since I gave her that doll," said Berty. "Come to think of it, I don't think she brought it." He gazed into Silvia's brown eyes. "How is Delyth?"

"Hurt more deeply than she wants to admit. Time eventually heals all, but an apology works wonders," Silvia said.

"She may not get one for awhile. We leave at first light."

"We should tell Lida."

Hearing Hope's laughter made Berty turn his head. Smiling, he watched his niece pick wildflowers. "You go," he said.

Silvia placed a hand on his forearm. When she squeezed, a warm tingle ran through his body. Glancing at her, he had an impulse to put his free arm around her. He had a deep desire to pull her into a close embrace. Instead, he simply placed his hand on top of hers. Her hand was so soft under his. He wanted to hold her delicate slender fingers forever. After a moment's relish, her hand slid out from under his. Sighing, he watched her walk towards the castle.

Her light blue cloak shone softly in the late daylight. The Elder's Curse, he thought. It was the only thing keeping them apart. Yet, they were connected by a magic he did not fully understand. Hope's infectious laughter made him tear his eyes away from Silvia. "Not that I understand the tree thing either," he muttered. Looking back at the dark castle corridor, he remembered her telling him to give her time. He ran to catch her.

Slowing to walk by her side, he asked, "What are you doing?"

She threw him a puzzled look. "Walking."

"About the curse," he clarified.

"Oh." She studied the dim shadows of the corridor. "It is probably best that you do not know."

Berty's stomach dropped to his toes. "Silvia, I—"

Stopping, she turned to face him. "Berty, you can't save me from this."

"Help me understand what this is."

She started walking again, causing Berty to catch up with her. "Being an Elder comes with conditions. Wisdom is not free. When I give, I must take. A balance must always be maintained. If an Elder skews too far one way or another, then there are consequences." Lowering her voice, she continued, "Taking more than you give, turns you into a monster who feeds on others. Giving more than you take, causes you to waste away to nothing more than a shell of yourself."

He looked at his feet, then at her face. His eyes followed the slight upward curve of her nose as he asked, "What is happening to you?"

"Neither one of those," Silvia answered with a quick glance in his direction.

Reaching for her arm, he said, "Then what?"

Stopping again, she sighed. "Please Berty, I need to figure this out on my own."

Taking a moment to internalize what she said, he allowed her to walk ahead of him. "Wait," he said, catching up to her. "You don't know?"

158

"It's a unique situation," she said without breaking her stride. "An Empress has never become an Elder before."

"So?"

Her hand reached for her chest as she said, "The connection to the Empire Tree." Her fingers touched where her blue crystal lay beneath her gold dress.

"How does that make it different?" he asked while they entered the main hall.

Looking at him, she said, "I'm working on it." She entered the dining hall.

Following Silvia, Berty found Lida sitting with Telor. Telor looked agitated from his riff with his sister. As servants placed food on the table, Telor furiously tore a chunk of bread.

Ignoring her son's mood, Lida said, "I will be leaving you in a moment to have dinner with Elrick. A carriage arrived today. Are you leaving soon?"

"Yes, but not by carriage," said Berty, standing at the end of the long table. "Once we do what we need to do, we will return for the carriage."

"Very well. Who is going?"

"Elder Hunter," said Berty as Silvia took a seat at the table, "my niece, her Godmother, some Empire Guards, Declan and Delyth."

Standing, Lida said, "Have a safe and swift journey. We will await your return." She placed her hand on Berty's arm in gratitude before she left the room.

Berty sat next to Silvia. While he ate his dinner, he could not overlook Telor stabbing the food on his plate. He figured that the fact that Delyth was joining them further fueled Telor's anger. Although he felt badly for him, Berty could not risk taking him. Telor had yet to master a weapon.

"I know how to use Fairy Dust, too," said Telor like a child, finally breaking his moody silence.

Berty said nothing.

"I want to go," Telor said. He sounded like a toddler on the verge of a temper tantrum. "What does Delyth have that I do not?" Looking squarely at Berty, he waited for an answer.

Reluctantly, Berty said, "The title of Advisor to the Emperor."

"How does a title make anyone qualified?"

"That depends on for what one wishes to be qualified," replied Berty. "Besides, she has mastered a weapon."

Telor's eyes narrowed. "What of the child and her Fairy Godmother? Both of them can use weapons?"

"Show some respect for your Emperor!" Delyth exclaimed. She stood in the doorway with a look of sheer horror on her face.

"Tell me, Telor, how many men do I have to bring to protect you?" Berty asked calmly. "How many attempts on a Crown Prince's life can be thwarted until one hits its mark? How many men's lives are you willing to sacrifice to save yours?"

Berty paid no attention to Telor's widening eyes.

"As much as I hate to crash your solo pity party, Telor, I am going to remind you that your father was willing to give his life for yours," continued Berty. "A parent's sacrifice for his child is always selfless. Expecting your men to defend you never is." In disgust, Berty rose from the table. All eyes followed him as he left the room.

Berty walked through the dimly lit stone corridors until he reached a large hall adorned with plain plank tables and benches. At one table, Declan and Edwin sat with a mixture of Fairy and Empire Guards.

When Berty approached, everyone stood. "Sit, please," said Berty. "Do you mind if I join you?"

Declan glanced at the guards' faces, then said, "An honor, my Lord." He scooched over, making room on the bench.

Berty sat on the bench next to Declan. He noticed a bow resting on the table with a knife. "How goes the training?" he asked.

"As well as it can go," Declan answered.

Berty raised his eyebrows.

Declan continued, "I would really like to know from whom they bought these bows."

"Shoddy craftsmanship?" asked Berty.

"No," said Declan. "In fact, they are made very well. It's just... seems as though someone sold them whatever bows they had on hand to fill the order, instead of making sure that each bow was right for each archer." He looked at the bow on the table. "It is what my grandfather did. Some of the problems were fixed by exchanging bows. The rest need to be either reworked or remade. I've called for a woodsmith. Edwin has suggested the Empire Bowsmith."

"Excuse me, Declan sir," said a Fairy running into the hall. "The woodsmith is here."

"Tell him that I'll be with him in a moment," said Declan. After the Fairy left, he asked, "My Lord, what is your recommendation?"

The guards around the table watched the exchange between Berty and Declan with wide eyes. Knowing that he was being watched carefully, Berty chose his words wisely. "It is your call, Declan. We will be gone for over a week. If you do decide to summon the Bowsmith, then he will need an escort of guards."

"Thank you, my Lord," said Declan. "If you will excuse me." He climbed over the bench with his knife in one hand and the bow in the other.

While Declan met with a woodsmith, Berty figured that he should make a better use of his time. "I will see you in the morning, Lieutenant," he said before returning to the corridors.

Berty retraced his steps not knowing how to spend his evening. Realizing that he was in the main hall, he had no desire to return to the dining room. Instead, he opened a large wooden door, then stepped into the book crammed library.

Grabbing a lantern off a table, it lit at his touch. He approached the wall of books, lifting the lantern to see the titles embossed on the leather spines.

"Can I help you find something, my Lord?" Delyth's voice asked him from the doorway.

Berty turned to see her walking towards him. He was hoping to find something about Elders, but he said, "The magic of the trees."

"I had been searching for that as well," Delyth said. "I was trying to find a book or something that I have not read." Lighting another lantern, she continued, "The only book that has ever mentioned magic and trees talked about how magic pulsated in the trees."

"Yes, I remember reading that as well," said Berty. He still tried to peek at shelved titles.

"I have yet to come across something that tells of what lies beyond the trees," Delyth said. She followed the shelves to the back of the room. "It only took me about ten years to read all these books."

"You've read every book in this library?" asked Berty, following her while glancing at the books.

"Yes, and then some." Stopping, she stared at Berty in the lantern light. "My Lord," she said, "what if that knowledge predates everything in here?"

He waited for her to continue.

"Mother and Father most likely would not approve," Delyth continued, "but you *are* the Emperor." Although he had no idea about what she spoke, he allowed her to take his lantern. "Come with me," she whispered.

Extinguishing the lanterns, Delyth led him across the library. She stopped in front of a section of bookshelves. Touching the shelf with her hand, she said, "Tome dym."

The section of books turned transparent. She grabbed his hand, then pulled him through the books. The darkness on the other side reminded him of when Silvia pulled him into the Sorcery Room that was hidden in the center of the Empire Tree.

A pale lavender glow illuminated dark stone. His eyes darted around the cramped corridor, searching for the source of light. When he found it, he whispered, "Delyth, your wings."

"Not all Fairy wings glow," she said quietly. "It is a secret I keep, even from my family."

Berty nodded his head, understanding secret keeping all too well.

"These are the ruins of the ancient Fairy stronghold upon

which Fairyland Castle was built," she explained as her glowing wings led Berty down well-worn stone steps. "While most of the old stronghold has crumbled into ruins, the fortifications still hold strong." She opened a rickety wooden door. "This is the original library."

While Delyth found some candles, Berty asked, "How long did it take you to read everything in here?"

"I haven't... yet," she said, placing fat candles on a central table. As she reached for a flint, Berty waved his hand, lighting all the candles.

The candlelight offered a glimpse of the book-covered walls. Approaching the shelves, he could not read the words on the spines.

"All these tomes are written in the language of the ancient Fairies," said Delyth. "None of these books can be taken from this room. How I've tried." She perused the old leather spines. "A book on magic!" she exclaimed.

Her little hands delicately removed the thick book from the shelf. Placing it on the candle lit table, she skimmed its pages.

"Fairy Dust, wings," she muttered as she turned the large pages. "The forest," she said, stopping to read the hand written words. After her eyes darted down the page, she looked disappointed. "It talks about the different magical creatures one can encounter and how to interact with them. Some of these are creatures no one has ever seen. Others are not even in our tales. Nowhere does it tell what lies beyond the trees."

"What does that mean?" Berty asked.

"Either no one ever ventured beyond the trees or they did not think it important enough to write about it." Closing the book, she added, "At least not in Fairyland. Perhaps somewhere in the Empire Tree there is a writing. Or, that knowledge has been procured by the Goblins. Not that it matters. Goblins will not step foot in Fairyland."

"Why not?"

"A tale best told another time," Delyth said as she picked up the book. After returning it to its shelf, she strolled around the room. "I don't think that these books will tell us what we yearn to know tonight."

When she returned to the center table where Berty waited, she said, "I am sorry for wasting your time, my Lord."

"It has not been wasted," he assured her.

Her lips flashed a faint smile. "I want to apologize for my brother as well," she said. "He has never acted like this."

"Stress affects people differently," he told her. "I can imagine that he's been under a great deal of stress lately."

She nodded her head slowly. "We should go."

Extinguishing the candles, Berty followed the Fairy's glowing wings through the dark ruins. After climbing the worn stone steps, Delyth stopped in front of a section of stone. Her hand reached for the stone. Gasping, she retracted her hand. Berty thought she saw some sort of insect.

"The library is occupied," she whispered. "This way."

In a lavender diffused darkness, he followed the Fairy down a long, narrow, stone corridor. After they turned a corner, Delyth said, "Our safest exit is down here."

She stopped in front of a stretch of dark wall. Cautiously, she placed her hand on the stone. Grabbing Berty's hand, she pulled him through the wall.

The glow from her wings dimmed while she said, "We are in the Throne Room." By the time they reached the door, her wings had returned to normal. As they stepped into the main hall, she said, "Thank you again, my Lord. I will see you in the morning."

Delyth left Berty in the hall as Hope ran to his side. "Uncle Berty, I had the best day!" she said with a wide smile.

"That's wonderful," he said to his tired looking niece. Out of the corner of his eye, he saw Freesia standing back. She gazed warmly at the scene. Squatting to be eye level with Hope, he said, "How about you let Freesia help you get ready for bed and I will be in soon to tuck you in?"

"Okay," she said. She gave Berty a hug, then ran up the stairs ahead of Freesia.

The secret room and passageways within the castle made

Berty miss the Empire Tree. Climbing the stairs, he thought the only concession was Silvia. She made Fairyland a great place to be. He knew that he would have to return to the Sages' Grove without her, but not yet. They still had more time together. Finding himself in front of Elrick's door, Berty knocked.

"Come in," said Elrick. His voice was the strongest Berty had heard it in days.

Berty entered the room to find Elrick sitting up in his bed.

"Emperor, to what do I owe the pleasure?" Elrick said.

"How are you feeling, Elrick?"

"Better, though my muscles are a bit weak," the Fairy said with a smile.

"Good to hear," said Berty. "I wanted to see how you were before leaving."

"An Emperor should not have to do errands such as this," Elrick said. "Those of noble soul will always do what is right regardless of immediate outside consequences or judgement." He paused before saying, "Lida told me who was going with you. I know of no better men to trust with my life. Safe journey, Emperor. I know you will take good care of all that was mine."

"I will see you soon, Elrick," said Berty. Leaving Elrick's room, he walked through the empty hall, pausing only to knock on his niece's open door.

Freesia sprang off a chair next to Hope's bed. "My Lord, she is waiting for you."

Hope lay in her bed with her covers up to her neck and her eyes wide open.

"Thank you, Freesia."

"This is the best place ever," Hope yawned.

Berty smiled at his niece before saying, "Tomorrow, we are going to be venturing to places unknown—going where none of us have gone before." Not wanting to scare her before bed, he said, "I expect we will be walking a lot. Stay near Freesia in case she gets tired. Okay?"

"Okay, Uncle Berty," she said.

"Goodnight, Hope," he said as he kissed her on the forehead.

Closing her eyes, she said, "Night."

Berty extinguished the light, then closed Hope's door. Returning to his room, he packed his bag and readied his sword before climbing into bed.

Chapter Thirteen
Into the Woods

The dark morning greeted Berty when he opened his eyes. Magically igniting lanterns, he cringed at the darkness through the window. Although he knew that the earliness was imperative, every fiber of his being protested waking before the sun had a chance to push away the dark blanket of night. After securing his sword, he left the room as he had found it.

When he reached the dining room, it was empty. Even though he had no appetite that early in the morning, he forced food into his system.

Supplies waited for them in the Fairy Guard's hall where Edwin oversaw their distribution. "Good morning, my Lord," Edwin said with a bow of his head. "Otho and Tacitus will be joining us."

Berty was pleased to see the two Romans that they rescued on God Mountain wearing the Empire Guard's leather armor instead of the breastplates of their former Roman legion. When they glanced at the door, he turned to watch Hope enter with Silvia, Delyth and Freesia.

Seeing the surprised look on the guards' faces, Berty said, "You disapprove?"

"No, my Lord," Tacitus said quickly.

"The child is very young," said Otho. "It sounded as though she were older."

"All the more reason she needs your protection," Berty said.

"Of course, my Lord," said Otho.

"My Lord," said Tacitus, "we will follow you and fight for your Empire to the ends of the Earth."

"Good," said Berty as he noticed Declan enter the room, "because that is where we might be headed."

Grabbing supplies from Edwin, Declan said, "The sky is lightening."

"Are we all ready?" Berty asked.

The collective, "Yes," was drowned out by Telor saying, "My Lord, wait."

Wearing his dark purple cloak, Telor approached. He carried a bag as if he were going on a long journey. "Please accept my apology for my actions yesterday and allow me to join your party," he said.

Berty saw someone wanting to prove himself standing in front of him. "I accept your apology." Remembering Elrick's words, *those of noble soul will always do what is right*, he searched the Fairy's green eyes. He found the same determination he had seen in Delyth, then asked, "You have a weapon?"

"Fairy Dust," said Telor patting his belt.

"He also has this," said Declan with a bow in his hands.

Telor stared at the bow. "What is this? That is not the same bow I have been using."

"I reworked it for you," said Declan.

As Telor took the bow from Declan, Berty said, "Gather your quiver, then meet us outside."

With a smile flashing across his face, Telor ran into the weapon store.

They walked out into the cool, early morning air. Light blue edged the mostly dark sky. Once Telor joined them with his bow and quiver, Berty said to Hope, "Lead the way."

Hope took a few steps forward. After a moment, she said, "This way."

The sun continued to change the hue of blue as Hope blazed a trail through the woods north of Fairyland. Distant Dragon calls told Berty that they had entered the Dragonlands.

Thick underbrush and fallen trees slowed their progress. The forest canopy filtered the morning sun well, despite not reaching maximum leafy fullness. Berty kept an eye on Hope who stayed a few steps ahead of the group.

Walking beside Berty, Declan said, "We have been walking through the Dragonlands for hours. Why have we yet to see a Dragon?" His eyes scanned the trees and sky.

"The Pygmy Dragons are afraid of bipeds," answered Hope. Climbing over a log, she looked at Berty, asking, "What's a biped?"

"I have never heard of a Pygmy Dragon," said Telor.

"We are bipeds," explained Berty. "A biped is anything that walks on two feet."

"That's because no one has ever seen one," Delyth said to her brother.

Telor opened his mouth to retort, but one look from Silvia shut it.

After a few more hours of trekking, Berty suggested to take a break. Sitting on logs or rocks, everyone ate while looking into the surrounding forest.

"Hey!" yelled Tacitus, holding the back of his neck.

"What's wrong?" Edwin asked him.

Glaring at the tree behind him, Tacitus said, "Stupid chipmunk keeps throwing things at me." He put a hand up to block something. "Stop it," he said before saying something in Latin.

"That's no chipmunk," said Edwin as he approached the tree. "That's a Knownot."

"How do you know?" asked Delyth.

"They have a green cast. Only Elves can see it," Edwin answered. Staring directly at the chipmunk, he said, "Have you no respect for the Empire Tree?"

The chipmunk darted angrily down the trunk. As it leapt towards Edwin, the chipmunk shed its reddish brown fur, morphing into a three-inch tall green skinned creature. It hovered in front of Edwin's face flapping translucent greenish wings while shaking a tiny fist.

"She's a scout," said Edwin, who obviously understood the squeaks of the Knownot. "We seem to be near a Knownot commune. She was trying to keep us from trampling on it." The Knownot bobbed in front of Edwin's face with its arms crossed. "Don't worry," he told the creature, "we are just passing through."

After emitting a series of squeaks, the Knownot returned to the tree. It leaned against the trunk with its arms still crossed and tapping its foot while it scowled at the group. Cocking her head to the side, Hope studied the Knownot. Freesia leaned towards her to explain Knownots.

Not wanting to stay too long, Berty asked Hope, "Ready?"

With an eager nod of her head, she led them on the path only she knew.

Hours of walking only brought them further into the thick, desolate, pathless forest. As the sun fell towards the horizon, Hope's walking slowed. Berty watched her begin to stumble over the uneven terrain.

"We should find a place to camp," he suggested.

"Just a little further," Hope said.

Nodding, he allowed the trees to guide her. The forest darkened before Hope pointed to a clearing that was surrounded by a circle of tall trees. "There," she said.

Inside the circle, tents were being raised. Silvia stood in the center with her staff.

"No need to tap the ground, Elder," Hope said to her. "The trees will protect us. 'Reserve your magic,' they say."

"Thank you," Silvia said more to the trees than to Hope. She sat on a nearby rock while others collected firewood. As she gazed past the surrounding circles of trees, Berty saw a shadow of regality cast by the former Empress.

After the fire was built, Berty lit the logs with magic. Hope's eyes widened, seeing him use magic for the first time. Smiling at her, he sat next to Silvia.

"Care to share?" he asked.

Breaking her gaze, she looked at him pensively. "It's amazing to see your niece's gift in action," she said.

He waited for her to say something more, but she did not oblige.

Conversation flowed around the fire as they ate. Silvia, however, kept her thoughts to herself.

"Ready to try that bow?" Declan asked Telor.

"Now?" asked Telor.

Declan raised an eyebrow.

Looking uncomfortable, Telor got off the ground to fetch his weapon from inside the tent.

With a momentary glance at Delyth, Declan pulled a cloth target out of his bag, placing it on the ground near the edge of the campsite. He leaned against a tree whilst watching Telor take aim. After multiple shots, Declan finally walked over to Telor. Declan's lips moved, but he spoke so low that Berty could not hear his voice over the crackle of the fire. Taking his stance, Declan released an arrow. It effortlessly hit the center of the target. Moving his eyes away from Declan and Telor, Berty noticed Hope watching them with great interest.

She gaped at Telor and Declan hitting the target until Freesia told her, "Time to go to bed." As Freesia ushered her towards the tent, Hope kept craning her neck to watch them.

Berty waited a few minutes before he approached his niece's tent. "May I come in?" he asked.

"Of course, my Lord," answered Freesia's voice.

Entering the tent, he saw Hope lying awake on her cot while Freesia put her clothes away. He noticed that she did not ask Freesia for an extra five minutes. Leaning over her cot, he adjusted her blanket. "Good night, Hope. Sleep well," he said before kissing her forehead. He smiled at her, hoping that Teresa was not frantic about not being able to reach them via phone.

"Good night, Uncle Berty," Hope said. As he stepped towards the tent flap, she asked, "Can I do that?"

Turning to face her, he asked, "Do what?"

"With the bows and arrows."

"We'll see. Get some sleep," he said, then left the tent.

Declan and Telor rejoined the group around the campfire. Sipping from a metal cup, Telor looked pleased with himself. Silvia sat pensively. She did not acknowledge Berty when he sat next to her. After finishing her drink, she briefly placed her hand on his arm, then said, "See you in the morning." Her brown eyes met his before she left his side.

He wanted to plead for her to stay on the log with him. Instead, he watched her walk away in the firelight. Rising from her seat, Delyth cast a shadow onto Silvia's light blue cloak.

"Delyth, wait," Telor called to her.

The fire imparted an orange glow onto Delyth's otherwise pale skin. She watched him approach. Her orange complexion made it difficult for Berty to read her expression.

"Forgive me?" Telor pleaded. The Prince stood with his back to the fire. His shoulders slumped.

Pulling on her long, dark curls, Delyth led her brother beyond the tents. Their mouths moved in relative privacy.

When Declan's light eyes found Berty, he realized that he was not the only one keeping an eye on the Fairies. He said quietly to Berty, "Hope has an interest."

"In?" Berty asked, glancing at him.

"Archery," said Declan. "Can see it in her eyes."

After watching Telor and Delyth hug, Berty turned his attention to Declan. "She asked me about it tonight," he said.

"Do I have your permission to make her a child's training bow?"

Berty wondered if it was too much at once for Hope or if she was too young to learn. Then he remembered that Declan had learned at a young age. "You do," he said. Only after the words escaped his mouth did he think that Jon and Teresa might not approve of their daughter learning archery at six years old.

Trying to sleep, he felt badly about making decisions behind his brother's back. He hoped that he was making the right ones.

Chapter Fourteen

The Boudonian Archer

The determination to help keep Elrick healthy made Berty push himself to trudge through a barely lit forest. Glancing at the group around him, he noticed that he was not the only one struggling with the morning. Silvia looked as though she had spent all night with her thoughts. He wondered if Declan and Delyth spent some of the night with each other. By contrast, Hope had an energy Berty had never seen.

They followed an exuberant Hope while Declan collected sticks and other material from the forest floor. Walking in relative silence, the sounds of the forest kept them company. Every now and then, Hope would reach out to touch a tree trunk or branch. Not just in passing as some children do, but a deliberate touch as if it were a form of communication. Hope's abilities intrigued Berty. He wondered why he had not seen it before. Perhaps it had to blossom, he thought. Being within the portaled Empire, her gift could be nurtured.

With another touch of a leafy branch, she stopped. Turning, she faced Berty. "People," she told him.

"Up ahead?" he asked tenderly.

Her somewhat wild, brown hair bounced when she nodded.

"Are we still walking this way?"

"Yeah," she said in a small voice.

Berty heard her fear. "Walk with me," he said to her as he

held out his hand.

Frozen in place, she waited for him to reach her.

With one glance at Edwin, the Elf took point with a hand on the hilt of his sword. As Berty grabbed Hope's hand, he saw Declan clutch his bow under his cloak.

They continued on their path as a close protective group. Quick eyes detected every minute movement. Fingertips grazed weapons ready to grasp at any second.

Large raindrops fell through the branches. Their free hands raised their hoods. Muddied debris clung to the sides of their boots. The wet new growth on the forest floor was akin to stepping on patches of ice. Choosing their steps carefully, elongated drops pounded their cloaks.

The rain carried men's voices to Berty's ears. His body tensed. Squeezing Hope's hand, he tried not to let her feel his apprehension. Although he could not discern what the voices said, he could tell that there were at least four different males speaking.

Out of the corner of his eye, he saw Declan drop behind the group with his bow uncloaked. Otho and Tacitus formed a front line with Edwin.

Beyond the sounds of their feet sloshing in the muddy undergrowth was laughter. Berty saw only the dark green cloaks of his men. The laughter abruptly stopped when he heard the familiar ringing of Edwin withdrawing his sword.

Metal swiftly sliced wood. In tree branches, a young man sat holding a bow. Berty saw the shock melt off his face as he drew another arrow from his quiver.

"Hold your fire," Edwin began to shout.

A shower of arrows cut off Edwin's words.

Unsheathing his sword, Berty pushed Hope into Freesia's protection. She pulled her away from the fray. Silvia and Delyth surrounded Hope as well.

He waited to slice arrows out of the sky. In his peripheral vision, Declan sent one arrow flying. Arrows fell to the ground in a wave of dull thunks just short of the Empire Guards.

"I believe the Lieutenant said to hold your fire," Declan said coldly.

"We don't think this is any of your business," said one of the men. "Fancy bow don't make it so."

A man with long blonde hair escaping from his brown hood pushed his way towards Declan. "Well, well, well," he said, "looks like we found our thief, Cecil."

A second man parted the crowd. "Vander, what nonsense are you speaking?" Cecil had the same sandy shade of hair peeking from under his hood as Declan's.

Lowering his bow a few inches, Declan turned pale.

"Grandpa's old bow," said Vander. "The one that none of us were ever permitted to touch. Stolen all those years ago and here it is, before our very eyes, like magic." Vander's voice sounded cold, hard and hateful.

Cecil surveyed Declan through the hard rain. His blue eyes widened as his eyebrows raised. "Always wondered if we would run into you one of these days," he told Declan. "Mom cried for a month." His tone was full of anger. "Dad carried on as though you never existed."

"So did we," added Vander. "Who wanted a freak for a brother anyway? Especially one who ran from his punishment and stole Grandpa's prize possession."

Declan's light eyes switched focus between Cecil and Vander. He said nothing.

"I really am surprised at you, Declan," Vander continued to taunt. "I thought you were above stealing. Especially from Grandpa. But then again, you are a Watcher. That wand of yours doesn't make you above reproach."

Heavy raindrops pounded Berty's hooded head as his hand clenched the hilt of his sword more tightly.

"Have nothing to say for yourself after all these years?" asked Cecil. "You missed your trial."

"And your execution," said another man who stood at Vander's side.

Declan scrutinized the dark haired man's contemptuous look.

Berty could see recognition on Declan's face, then followed by disappointment. "This is none of your business, Owen," he said.

"Sure is," Owen answered with a smirk. "Julie's my wife. That stubborn girl actually believes in your innocence. After today, I can go back and knock some sense into her." He snickered.

"Disrespect my sister again and she'll be a widow," Declan said through gritted teeth.

"Is that a threat?" Owen asked.

"No. It's a promise," said Declan. Turning his attention towards the group, he said, "I owe you people nothing. The two of you were more interested in seeing me punished than being my brothers. And you, Owen, some best friend you were. Did you not think that I couldn't hear all of you talking about me? How you could use me for target practice before and after I was hung. You want to believe that I stole this bow and nothing I would say will change your minds."

"I don't have a problem with justice coming later," said Vander, raising his bow.

Murmurs of agreement escaped from behind him.

"I wouldn't do that if I were you," Edwin warned.

"Mind your business, Elf," dismissed Vander.

Taking a quick step forward, Edwin held his blade to Vander's neck. "This is my business," Edwin threatened.

Bows raised. Before arrows could be set, Berty walked between Tacitus and Declan. "Men of Boudon," he said, "you are impeding official Empire business. According to Empire law, wounding an Advisor or a Lieutenant to the Emperor results in immediate branding as an enemy of the Empire. Yes, Declan is an Advisor to the Emperor. You have two choices, either let us pass or die where you stand. Now, which will it be?"

Cecil's light eyes scanned the group before resting on Berty. The Boudonians had the advantage of numbers, but with three Fairies the scales tipped in Berty's favor. Shifting his glance to Declan, then Vander, Cecil gave a small nod. He lowered his bow. When the others followed, Edwin retracted his blade.

"Excellent choice," he said.

Brandishing his sword, Berty ushered Hope through the crowd of men. He heard squishing footsteps behind him. When he and Hope were far enough away from the archers, he gave Hope's hand back to Freesia. He told Delyth and Telor, "Keep walking. Protect them and do not turn back."

"My Lord?" Telor asked quietly.

"We will meet you up ahead," said Berty.

Delyth gave him a steely look of understanding before walking alongside Hope. Although reluctant, Telor gave Berty a sharp nod, then joined his sister.

Leaving his niece, he returned to the groups. He watched his men and Silvia walk through peacefully. Shortening his stride, he waited for everyone to join him. Declan walked away from his past without looking back at his brothers and former friend who watched him.

A scream cut through the forest.

Heart beating fast, Berty frantically searched for the source. Through the raindrops, trees, and men arming for a fight, a brown blob tried to restrain a light blue figure. He could make out flashes of gold as he attempted to run towards her. With each step, his feet were being sucked into the muddy ground.

Running slower than he wanted, he could only watch Silvia struggle to escape her attacker's grasp. She freed a hand. Reaching towards her fallen staff, she summoned it. Her staff flew into her outstretched hand. She forcefully knocked the man's head, then his ankles.

They both stumbled into the mud. A flying sword nearly missed Berty as Silvia pounded her staff on the ground.

The forest and almost everything it encased was still.

The mud released Berty's feet as it morphed into solid ground. Pushing stationary raindrops aside, he ran under halted arrows to Silvia. He held an arm out to help her off the forest floor.

"Silvia, are you all right?" he asked.

Grabbing tightly onto Berty's arm, she pulled out of the

frozen man's grasp. "Declan," she called, "recall your arrow."

Declan lowered his bow.

"You must recall your arrow, Declan. I cannot stop it. I am merely slowing its progress," she said. Still steadying herself, her brown eyes pleaded with him.

Taking a hand off his bow, Declan held it above his head. His blue eyes watched his arrow fly backwards, landing in his hand. Staring at it briefly, he returned it to his quiver.

"Thank you. The Bow of the Moon obeys only its archer," said Silvia. Letting go of Berty's arm, she said, "Let's get out of here before the magic wears off."

They walked out from underneath the arrow ceiling. Turning, Silvia tipped the top of her staff towards the ground. All the arrows and a sword landed with a hard thud.

Berty took one last look at the motionless scene. The ground was littered with arrows whilst the men frozen in their spots were poised to send more arrows into the air. Only Declan's brother, Cecil, was devoid of a weapon.

Walking away, Berty glanced at Declan. He had the Bow of the Moon the entire time, but did not know it. Berty wondered if he had suspected after Irmingard. A hand on his arm interrupted his thoughts.

Changing his focus to Silvia, he watched her lips say, "Thank you. I am fine. That man did not hurt me." Her hand slid off his forearm. She stayed next to him, tapping the ground hard with her staff.

Hope and the Fairies waited in a thicket. Satisfied with his niece's calmness, Berty said, "Let's keep moving."

As Hope took a protected lead, Edwin called, "Otho." He threw his sword to the Roman. Berty noticed Otho's empty scabbard. Catching the Lieutenant's sword, Otho gave Edwin a nod of thanks. Edwin kept a hand on his bow while he walked close to Hope.

Silence surrounded them. It was as if no one wanted to acknowledge what had happened. Every so often, Declan would glance over his shoulder.

Berty could only imagine his paranoia. Recalling the looks on the brothers' faces, he realized that Vander was jealous of Declan, while Cecil was filled with anger. Cecil internalized how Declan's departure affected their family. On the other hand, Vander could not hide how much he coveted Declan's bow and ability. The knowledge that Declan, the youngest brother, was the best archer of them all probably ate away at Vander with each passing year. Berty did not know if Vander would seek Declan for vengeance, but he was sure that Declan had been preparing for a confrontation with them since his night-clad exile in his youth.

Hope led them to a campsite relatively sheltered from the unending rain. Camp was set up quickly despite the silence. While eating around the campfire, words seemed to be too much effort for mouths to form. Finally Edwin broke the silence, saying, "That was almost a huge mess today. Wonder what they were doing so far from home."

If Edwin was searching for an answer from Declan, he was not obliging. Declan busied himself with his knife. Crafting a notch in a piece of wood under the shelter of branches, he said nothing.

"What I do not understand," said Telor, "was why you, my Lord, did not reveal to them your true identity."

"There was no need," answered Berty.

Telor scrunched his eyes. "But you could have thrown your might as Emperor."

"That would have accomplished nothing," said Berty. "It also could have jeopardized our mission."

"How so?"

"By making us vulnerable," Berty explained. "Sometimes less information is better." He glanced at Silvia, finally understanding her silence.

She smiled at him as if she knew his thoughts.

While Telor digested Berty's words, Edwin said to Declan, "The Commander was right after all."

Declan tore his focus away from his crafting to look at Edwin. "I guess."

"Are you sure he has the Bow of the Moon, Elder?" Edwin asked.

Delyth's violet eyes widened as she looked from Edwin to Declan, then to Silvia.

"All magic has limitations. You just need to know where," Silvia answered cryptically.

Shifting uncomfortably, Declan gave his attention to the carving in his hands.

The hard, steady rain extinguished most of the fire. Throwing mud on the smoldering embers, they retired early to their tents.

Inside the tent, Berty, Telor and Declan tried to stay warm with lanterns. Telor kept glancing from Declan to Berty seeing if either would speak. Berty watched Declan craft a rudimentary bow.

After running his fingers along the wood, Declan raised his head. "Thank you," he said to Berty. "Without you, I do not think that I could have emerged from a lone encounter with them unscathed."

"You're welcome," said Berty.

"But you have the Bow of the Moon, Declan," Telor said. "With its magic, you could have taken them all on your own."

Declan shook his head. "I only just learned what this bow is. I will not pretend to understand any of its magic. Even if I did, you do not seem to understand. Magic does not forgo skill. In the melee you missed, I launched an arrow only intended for Elder Hunter's attacker. As much as they wanted to do it to me, I could not raise a bow against my own brothers. Guess that makes me weak. But then again, I am not a warrior, only a man."

"We are all only men, defined by our choices," said Berty. "Just so you know, Cecil did not raise his bow either."

Declan raised his eyebrows briefly before wrapping a string around one end of the bow. When he was sure that it was secure, he glanced at Telor, then looked at Berty.

Berty understood his look to ask if he thought whether or not Delyth would accept him. Without hesitation, he closed his eyes, focusing on Silvia.

Silvia sat on her cot watching Freesia put Hope to bed.

"Was the Lieutenant right? Does Declan really possess the Bow of the Moon?" Delyth asked Silvia.

"Since he left his village, it seems," Silvia answered. Her eyes still watched Hope.

"Wonder how he actually procured it," said Delyth with a curious look he had often seen in her violet eyes.

Silvia turned her dark red head towards Delyth. "You don't believe he stole it?" she shrewdly asked.

"No," said Delyth, insulted by the question. "He said that he did not and I believe him."

Silvia smiled.

Opening his eyes, he saw Declan watching him curiously. With a quick glance at Telor, Berty gave Declan a you-have-nothing-to-worry-about smile.

Declan gave him a slight nod, then placed the bow in his bag.

They awoke to a rainless, foggy morning. The overnight fog did not want to lift, causing them to move slowly through the forest.

"How are you?" Delyth quietly asked Declan.

Ducking under a branch, he said, "Fine."

She put a hand on his arm. "If you want to talk, I'm here." Giving him a small smile, her hand slipped off his arm.

He stared at where she had touched him.

As the sun rose in the sky, visibility increased. When the fog had finally lifted, Berty thought about taking a break, but quickly pushed the thought aside. They had lost too much time. Elrick was counting on them.

"Oh, you have got to be kidding," Telor said with disdain. He stopped a few feet away from the edge of a gorge.

"Don't worry, Your Highness, there is a bridge," said Tacitus.

Chapter Fifteen
Fairy Mysterious

Berty's eyes found the narrow bits of rope and planks stretching across the gorge. The dilapidated bridge reminded him of something he had seen in movies. The rope frayed and was thin in more spots than not. What remained of the planks were either broken, looked rotten or otherwise questionable.

Edwin surveyed the bridge. "This can't be the only way across," he said.

"It is the quickest and most direct," said Hope. "The only other way is to climb into the gorge, then back up on the other side." Berty knew that she regurgitated what the trees told her.

"That's insane," Telor said. His voice was raised a couple of octaves. Pacing near Berty, he began to hyperventilate.

"Telor, focus," said Delyth, reaching into her cloak. Her pinched thumb and forefinger emerged from the depths of a velvet bag. As her arm crossed her body, her fingers opened, releasing a sparkly substance.

Glittering blues and purples flew through the air. Inhaling, the Fairy Dust entered Telor's system. With an exhale he was immediately calmed.

"Delyth!" shrieked Silvia. "You could have hit the Emperor!"

"No, I could not have. That would have been impossible," answered Delyth calmly.

A much more focused Telor stared at the bridge. "This bridge is impassable. We will have to fly."

Studying the area, Delyth stood next to her brother. "You and I will have to take," she stopped talking. Approaching an old wooden sign, she said, "We can't."

"What do you mean?" asked Berty.

"Of course we can," Telor said.

"This sign is written in the language of the ancient Fairies," Delyth explained. "It says, 'Show not wings.' There is more, but I cannot make out the word."

Looking at the concern on Delyth's face to the poor excuse for a bridge, Berty said, "Then, we must cross." Without hesitation, he ordered, "Hope, Freesia and Silvia will cross first, then Delyth and Telor. The rest of us will follow."

Hope approached the bridge entrance with Freesia closely following. Per Freesia's instructions, she stretched to grab the frayed ropes on either side. Watching her little foot step on the first plank, Berty could feel his heart beat rapidly. He dared not look away from her; he did not want to see his cloak move with his heartbeats. With each step she took, the bridge groaned in protest. Freesia walked behind her, encouraging her to reach the other side. He did not breathe until she was safely on solid ground.

With a look at Berty, Silvia stepped towards the bridge. She held her staff horizontally while cautiously watching her stride as if she were on a tight rope. Once she had crossed the bridge, Delyth took her turn. Her light footsteps caused the bridge to creak. Passing the halfway point, she started to canter. Telor watched his sister join Silvia on the other side before he grabbed the ropes. Little snaps found Berty's ears. With conviction, the Fairy kept placing one foot in front of the other.

Declan stood next to Berty. In a low voice, he told him, "That doesn't sound good. I don't think that bridge is going to hold much longer. Unfortunately, the bridge looks to be impervious to magic."

Watching Telor finish crossing the bridge, Berty knew where Declan was heading.

"Either some of us stay behind by choice," Declan continued, "or we all cross together and take our chances."

With a nod of his head, Berty looked at the others. Meeting Edwin's blue eyes, he did not have to ask.

"I am all for taking chances," said Edwin.

Otho sternly nodded his head while Tacitus answered, "Let's go."

"My Lord, after you," said Declan.

Berty's eyes followed the badly spaced planks to their end. "Declan, you're first," he said.

Declan knew better than to argue. Arms outstretched, he grabbed the rope sides. After he had taken a few steps, Berty followed. Berty could feel the bridge sag when Edwin and the others joined him on the bridge.

Carefully avoiding broken and weak planks, they crawled across the gorge. Berty did not like moving so slowly, although crossing too quickly would have placed undue stress on the rope. Reaching the halfway point, he became aware of his breathing. Through his hands, he could feel the rope's tension shifting with every step.

A howling gust caused them to pause. His ears filled with an angry whoosh. His hands felt vibrations as if the tension slacked.

Declan turned to look behind him. "Run!" his voice faintly shouted.

Still clutching the ropes, they sprinted towards the other side. While Berty's eyes could peek past Declan to see the edge of a cliff where the bridge ended, his hands felt the tension relax. The frayed ropes finally snapped free of their twists. Gravity reclaimed the bridge.

Berty could no longer feel his stomach. His section of the bridge was still attached. A sheer cliff waited for them. Glancing behind him, he shouted, "Brace yourselves!"

Tacitus leapt from a free falling bit of bridge onto theirs. He grasped the last plank still attached.

Wrapping the ropes around his arms, Berty crouched. Screams reached his ears. He waited for impact as he tried not to see past the brown blur.

Wood and bodies slammed into the rock with a series of thuds. Hearing a loud crack, Berty looked down. Holding onto a broken wood plank, Tacitus was falling into the gorge. When he disappeared into the fog, Berty's insides sank. He closed his eyes.

"Telor!" screamed Delyth.

Berty opened his eyes to see something sparkly-blue streak into the crevasse.

"Climb past me, my Lord," said Declan who perched on the side of the dangling bridge with his legs entwined in its ropes. His hands kept an arrow ready.

Untangling his arms, Berty climbed. Some of the wood cracked under the weight of his feet. He only hoped that Edwin and Otho could successfully climb behind him. As he passed Declan, an arrow shot into the fog. Running out of wood and rope, he grabbed earth and grass.

"Berty, grab my hand," Silvia said.

Raising his head, he saw Silvia's hand stretching for his. He extended his arm. Delyth's joined Silvia in helping him climb over the edge.

Free from the broken bridge's clutches, Berty locked eyes with Hope. Freesia held her at a safe distance from the cliff's edge. "Thanks," he said.

Kneeling on the ground, he assisted Edwin to the surface. Declan kept firing arrows into the depths of the gorge. Once Otho was safely off the bridge, Edwin called to Declan.

"This bridge isn't going to hold much longer," he said.

Ignoring Edwin, Declan released another arrow.

Telor geysered out of the gorge while holding Tacitus across his torso.

Shooting a final arrow, Declan shouted, "Coming up!"

Edwin and Otho pulled Declan to safety. Landing, Telor released Tacitus.

The Roman fell on one knee at the Fairy's feet. "I owe you my life, Your Highness," he said. His right fist struck his leather armor over his heart before rising to his feet.

"Magical net like things," said Declan as he made sure his bow was secured to his back. "Probably designed for catching Fairies."

Tears rushed down Delyth's cheeks. She made no attempt to wipe them away.

Putting a comforting hand on his sister, Telor said, "No more death."

Delyth nodded, wiping her face.

Taking Hope's hand, Berty allowed her to lead them away from the crevasse. They followed a seemingly ancient path. No one said a word as they kept pace with the young girl.

As the sun crept lower in the sky, they approached an outcropping of dilapidated black rock mingled with forest.

"We must take shelter in the ruins before nightfall," said Hope, conveying the trees' message. "Their lingering magic will protect us from what lurks in the dark in this section of the forest."

Their pace quickened as they hastened towards the ruins. The path led them to a wall of dull black.

Telor examined how the path continued through the black stone. "If there was an entrance here at one time, there is not one now," he said.

"Should we search for another way in?" Edwin asked.

Investigating the dull black stone, Delyth said, "This *is* the way inside."

The dull stone sparkled from within when Delyth's hand touched it. Moving her hand around the stone, her touch revealed a worn carving of half a Fairy wing.

"Telor," she said excitedly, "find the other part of this wing. Should lead to an opening."

At the inside edge of the found wing half, Telor touched the rock. He walked along the dull stone dragging his hand, which caused the black to sparkle. Ten feet from his sister, he yelled, "I found it!"

"Do you see a strange symbol inside the wing?" Delyth asked

him.

Telor used both hands to scour the wall. "I think so," he said finally.

"I'm guessing that we have to press at the same time," said Delyth. "Ready?"

Telor's hand mimicked Delyth's over a carved symbol Berty could not see. "Ready," Telor told her.

"Press!" she instructed.

When their hands simultaneously touched the stone, a silvery-gold current began to run through the dull, black stone. It illuminated carvings that looked to be a mixture of runes and some sort of hieroglyphs. Emitting from where the Fairies touched the stone, the current met in the middle of an arch between where the siblings were standing. The arch glowed brightly before faint rumbling could be heard. Slowly, the black stone rose into itself, revealing an arched entrance.

Both Telor and Delyth stared into the archway. Looking at each other, Delyth gave her brother a little nod. Telor took a deep breath, then motioned for the group to follow him. Holding Hope's hand, Berty walked behind Silvia through the arched entryway.

The arch opened into a corridor that sliced through ruined stone concentric circles. Copious amounts of black granite showed varied deterioration. Parts of the ruins were covered with rotting plant debris. The structure reeked of neglect and birds. They kept walking until they found the innermost circle.

The stone wrapped circle was more of an overgrown courtyard. Fresh air welcomed them. Different colored stone pillars dotted the courtyard leaning every which way. Berty figured that the pillars stood erect at one time. Ivy masked carvings. Long grass and weeds hid the original floor. The setting sun gave the weathered stone an orange sparkle.

When Delyth and Edwin joined the group, she said, "The door closed behind us." Her mouth opened as if she were going to say more, but no words escaped. Her eyes scrutinized the sparkling stone.

Berty, too, watched the stone. The sparkling intensified as the sun sank below the horizon. He thought his eyes tricked him. The sparkles began to concentrate into shapes. Springing from the stone, the shapes materialized into translucent Fairies.

Five translucent Fairies examined the group. One spoke in a language Berty could not understand, but believed he had heard. He looked to Silvia for a translation. She merely shook her head.

Delyth cautiously stepped towards them. After listening for a minute, she said, "They are the Guardian Spirits of this place. Telor's and my touch awoke them. We are their descendants."

"Descendants," Telor repeated. "They are the original Circle of Fairies, who united the five tribes into modern Fairydom." He gazed upon the spirits with awe.

Another spoke. Delyth translated, "We welcome the wearers of the Sage Stones, the Keeper, the Listener, and those who protect them. Their alignment with Fairies brings much honor. The Elf, however, brings dishonor. As long as the Elf stays within our walls, we cannot protect you from... from the Night Golems."

"What? Why?" protested Telor. "What does an Elf have to do with anything? And what are Night Golems?"

Raising a hand, Delyth silenced her brother. She talked to the Fairy spirits in their language.

When one spoke, she translated. "Elves and Fairies are natural enemies."

Delyth took another step towards where the spirits had gathered. When she spoke their language, she sounded as if she were pleading and rationalizing with them.

The spirits listened to Delyth. She gestured to Telor, then to Berty. One spirit looked as if she had seen the ruins for the very first time.

Breaking away from the other four, the female spirit walked around the courtyard. She gazed upon the tilted pillars and the weathered stone. Sadness showed on her translucent face when she spoke to Delyth.

Delyth answered matter-of-factly.

As the spirit rejoined her brethren, Delyth said, "I gave them

188

a brief history of what has happened since the Circle of Fairies. She wanted to know why this place had fallen into such disrepair. She also asked why it took us so long to return. I told her that we did not know this existed until now."

One of the spirits, who spoke prior, glared at Delyth and Telor. Speaking, he sounded as if he were scolding them. Berty had no idea what was said, but his tone cut.

Telor took a step back. Delyth did not cower. She retorted, throwing his tone back at him.

The spirit backed away from Delyth. Telor's jaw dropped slightly.

Another spirit, who had stayed quiet, reprimanded the spirit with the cutting tone. When the shamed spirit respectfully bowed his head, the other spirit turned his attention to Delyth. He spoke to her kindly, as an equal.

She gave him a one-word answer.

"I have agreed to a gesture of good faith—an offering of sorts," Delyth told the group. "In exchange, Edwin can stay and we get their protection."

"What are you giving?" asked Telor.

Berty knew the answer before Delyth replied, "Fairy Dust." Looking at the non-Fairies, she said, "I would advise everyone to stand back."

Delyth took a few steps forward whilst everyone else took a few steps backwards. Using their language, she almost chanted, which reminded Berty of watching her work with the old Fairy Dust in the Sages' Grove. She threw her hands high above her head. Releasing Fairy Dust, the blue sparkling dust sprinkled over the Guardian Fairy Spirits. They danced under the sparkly shower with their palms open as if they were trying to catch the dust.

Once the dust had settled under the overgrown grass, the spirits bowed to Delyth and Telor before being absorbed back into the surrounding black stone. The exodus of the Guardian Spirits plunged them into darkness.

Immediately, Berty conjured a few spheres of light. They

erected the tents and made a meager fire out of what wood they could find.

Staying in the center of the ruins, they ate while Telor asked his sister, "What language was that?"

"The language of the ancient Fairies," she answered. "Same as the sign."

He scrunched his eyebrows. "I thought their language was lost to us. How do you know it?" he asked.

Lowering her plate, she cocked her head to one side. "How can you carry a man by yourself at full flying speed?" she asked him in return.

Telor laughed a little. "I have always been able to carry more than my wings should allow. Mother and Father told me never to tell anyone."

Shaking her head, Delyth muttered, "All these secrets."

"Why not tell anyone about your gifts?" asked Edwin.

Telor explained, "Because of our ability to fly, Fairy bones are less dense than those of the other peoples. Our wings are only designed to carry one and a half times our weight. It may take two or more Fairies to carry a non-Fairy. Even then, a Fairy carrying another cannot fly at full speed. Usually, those of royal blood have special gifts. In addition to flying at high speeds, I can carry heavy loads. It seems as though my sister's gift is to understand dead languages. Being Historian makes perfect sense."

Delyth gave her brother a little smile. Her gaze returned to her plate.

Berty saw Declan gaze at her dark curls that danced in the gentle breeze. He asked her, "Why did they not know Elder Hunter as an Elder if they knew me as a Keeper, which is my order within the Watchers' Guild, and Hope as a Listener?"

Her violet eyes searched into his. "I do not know," she said. Glancing at Silvia, she said, "Maybe the crystals supercede everything."

"Or maybe they had no knowledge of Elders," Silvia suggested. "After all, Fairies and Elves being enemies predates the formation of the Empire."

Delyth nodded her head in agreement. "They knew nothing of the Empire Treaty or of how the Seven High Sages got the peoples to work together. Sure, prejudices may still exist, but we respect each other."

Sitting with Otho and Tacitus, Edwin said to her, "Thank you for defending me."

"You are welcome," she said, giving him a warm smile. "It is imperative that we stick together. If we do not, we will be destroyed, one at a time."

A deep, prolonged groan reverberated off the surrounding stone.

Keeping still, only Berty's eyes moved. He noticed that no one moved.

More groans joined the first one.

Freesia pulled Hope closer to her. Berty and Declan exchanged glances before visually checking the stone surrounding them.

"Night Golems?" asked Telor.

An orchestra playing a symphony of sadness stalked the black stone ruins.

"We're safe in here," reassured Delyth.

"Time for bed, Hope," said Freesia, obviously trying to ignore the mournful moans.

Hope shook her head adamantly. "I don't wanna go," she said quietly.

Knowing how fearful his niece must have felt, he said, "You can stay here until we all retire tonight."

Somewhat relieved, Hope brought her knees to her nose. She wrapped her arms around her legs, then stared into the flames.

The ground beneath Berty's feet vibrated. Clomping noises mixed with the moans as the Night Golems stampeded around the ruins. Pairs of eyes nervously glanced at the protective stone. Even the flames shook in fear.

Trying to distract from the rumbles, Berty said, "Do you think they are working alone?"

"The Night Golems?" asked Telor.

"Leif and Millicent," Silvia clarified. "I don't know. I often wonder about that."

"Sean may no longer be rallying the troops, but an anti-magic sentiment still persists. They could tap into that," suggested Declan.

"Mother and Father have done a good job of cleansing Fairyland of the treacherous," Telor added.

"But?" asked Berty.

Telor focused his green eyes on him. "Something does not feel right. I wish I knew what."

Looking at Hope sleeping with her head on her knees, Silvia said, "We should try to sleep. Tomorrow will come. We do not want to be unprepared."

Berty scooped Hope off the ground. She woke briefly as he placed her on the cot. After kissing her goodnight on her forehead, he retired to his tent. Declan extinguished the lantern. The woeful wails of the Night Golems serenaded them as they attempted to sleep.

Grogginess greeted Berty. He knew he did not sleep well. Attempting to rise from his cot, he felt so drained of energy that he was not sure if coffee alone would help. Sitting on the edge of the cot, he saw Declan rubbing his head that hung almost to his knees.

Carefully raising his head, Declan said, "I feel like I finished an entire cask of mead last night."

"Rough night with those noises," said Telor who was nowhere near as groggy as either Berty or Declan.

"Uncle Berty!" screamed Hope.

Adrenaline pumped through his veins. Running out of the tent, he called, "Hope? Where are you?"

"In here!" she said from inside the women's tent.

Pushing away the flap, he said, "Are you hurt?"

"Something's wrong with Silvia," Hope pointed.

Berty's eyes followed Hope's finger. Silvia sat at the edge of her cot with her head slightly tilted towards the ground.

192

"Silvia?" he asked as he approached.

She did not answer.

Crouching, he noticed that her open brown eyes stared into nowhere. He placed his fingers on her wrist, trying to feel for a pulse. Nothing. He slid his fingers to a new spot. Still nothing. His heart dropped to his stomach.

A blade shone under Silvia's nose. The shining blade barely fogged with her breath.

Relieved, he looked at Delyth who held the blade. "She's catatonic," he told her. "We need to get her out of here."

Without saying a word, Delyth left the tent.

He was not sure why he thought that removing Silvia from the ruins would help. It was just the thing that made the most sense. Placing his one arm behind her knees and the other around her lower back, he lifted her off the cot.

In the courtyard, Delyth gave orders. "Freesia, help Telor pack everything. Edwin, take Hope's hand. Leave the rest," she said to Otho and Tacitus. "Follow me out of here." While she led them to the arched entrance, she said, "There is something wrong with this place." She opened the wall with a touch of her hand. "Telor, Freesia and I will gather everything. We should not be too long."

When Berty stepped out of the ruins with Silvia, he felt as though he were breathing for the first time. He found a soft bit of ground on which to set her. Leaning her against a tree, he gazed into her vacant brown eyes.

"Snap out of it, Silvia," he pleaded. Grazing her cheek with his hand, he whispered, "Come back to me."

Sitting with her, he glanced at the others. Declan lay in the grass allowing the morning sun to fall on his upper body. Next to him sat Otho with his fingers buried in his dark curly hair. Tacitus rested on a log while Edwin leaned against a tree with Hope. Each looked as exhausted and drained as Berty felt.

"She will be all right," said a young voice in his ear.

Turning his head, Berty saw Hope plop on the grass next to him.

"She'll just take longer to recover," Hope continued.

Berty knew that the trees spoke through his niece. "Why?" he asked.

"Because she's an Elder."

"I don't understand," said Berty. What does being an Elder have to do with it?"

"Let me worry about that," Silvia breathed.

"Silvia," said Berty as he placed a hand on hers, "how are you feeling?"

"Been better. Weak." Her voice was as pale as her cheeks.

Gently squeezing her hand, he said, "If there is anything I can do."

The corners of her mouth barely turned upwards. "Rest. Good," was all she could manage to say.

Telor, Delyth and Freesia emerged from the ruins, dragging the stuff everyone left behind. As the arched entrance sealed, they sat with everyone.

"I'm sorry," Delyth said.

"For what?" asked Declan perched on his elbows.

Her violet eyes brimmed with wetness. "I should have explored when we first got there. I never thought," she glanced at Silvia as a tear escaped from her eye. "It could have been much worse."

"Do not blame yourself," said Telor, tenderly placing his arm around her. "It is not your fault."

"I could have prevented," Delyth began. Tears freely cascaded down her cheeks. Her breathing shuddered.

"Delyth, there is no way you could have known that this was going to happen," Telor reasoned.

When the Fairy regained her breathing, she wiped her cheeks. "It was a Sethbravin."

"What was?" asked Telor.

"The ruins," she answered.

Telor stared at his sister.

"But it was wrong," she continued.

"How do you know?" Telor asked.

"Wait a minute," said Declan. "Back up. What *is* a Sethbravin?"

"An ancient legend," Telor answered.

"Loosely translated, Sethbravin means magic breaker or curse breaker," explained Delyth. "It referred to both a device and a person. According to the ancient texts, the device, Sethbravin, were carved out of stone similar to the ones in the ruins. They were small enough to carry with you. Fairies used them to protect themselves from magical beasts. A Sethbravin was used to imprison the Faematask. A person was labeled a Sethbravin when a Fairy gave birth to a wingless baby."

"A Fairy can give birth to a non-Fairy?" said Edwin.

"Hasn't happened for hundreds of years," Delyth said. "Sethbravins are impervious to magic. Magic has no affect on them, nor can they use it. A pinch of Fairy Dust in their fingers loses all magical properties."

"What if they were to give it back to you?" asked Declan.

"I do not know the answer to that. The books never mentioned," Delyth responded.

Seeing the color slowly return to Silvia's cheeks, Berty asked Delyth, "How are these ruins a Sethbravin?"

Delyth took a breath. "After we packed, I took one last look around to make sure that nothing was forgotten. That's when I noticed how the stones resembled a Sethbravin. The entire courtyard was built like a giant curse breaker. Only, there was something off about it. Some of the stones were out of place.

"The morning sunlight made it easier to see the carvings. The walls talk about Night Golems." She closed her eyes for a moment. "Supposedly, Night Golems are the physical manifestations of restless Fairy spirits. The result of spilling innocent Fairy blood. The Fairies of the time believed that by constructing a large scale Sethbravin, it would release the spirits of their earthly bonds. However, when the Night Golems did not disappear," she glanced at Hope before continuing, "bad things happened. Within a generation, this place was deserted."

"Why did the Sethbravin not work?" asked Silvia.

"From what I could tell, they did not fully understand how a Sethbravin worked," Delyth answered.

"And you do?" asked Telor, his eyebrows raised.

"No," said Delyth. "Not yet. But I have seen one."

"Where?" Telor asked.

"It doesn't matter," dismissed Delyth. "The thing is, had I realized what it was, I would have drawn a Fairy Ring. It could have prevented the loss of energy all of you encountered."

"I didn't" said Telor.

"Of course not." Delyth sounded a bit perturbed with her brother. "*You* are a Fairy."

"No one is holding you responsible, Delyth," said Silvia. "We have rested enough. Let's not keep the far reaches of our world waiting."

Chapter Sixteen
The Unknown

Hope handed Silvia her staff as Berty held out his hand to help her off the ground. Silvia's soft hand found his. As she stood, her arm looped into his for support.

Arm in arm, they walked with the group. He noticed that she relied on him as much as she relied on her staff to walk.

"Are you okay? Do you want to wait a while?" he asked her.

"I'll admit to feeling woozy," she said quietly. "But I think that the further I get from these ruins, the better I will feel."

"If you need to stop, you let me know," he reassured.

Silvia smiled warmly. "We'll stop soon enough," she said. "Maybe you can make me some coffee when we do?"

He loved her smile. It always made him feel as if anything were possible. "Certainly," he smiled in return.

They walked for hours before stopping to eat. Berty magically made coffee for both Silvia and himself. Sitting next to her, he sipped his coffee allowing the caffeine to enter his bloodstream and relax his sore muscles. Silvia stared at Delyth over the rim of her cup.

Knowing her mind churned, Berty whispered, "Do you think it will work?"

She drank some coffee before responding just as quietly, "It is probably not a good idea, but I'd like to see it. Do you think she'd let me?"

Berty imagined that the Sethbravin Delyth had seen was

somewhere in the bowels of Fairyland Castle. "For as much as she dislikes secrets, she guards plenty," he answered.

"I'll make sure that we are very much alone when I ask," said Silvia.

Thinking about the Elder's Curse, Berty asked, "Was that part of your plan?"

"It's good to have options," Silvia said mysteriously. Her free hand automatically touched her chest where her blue crystal lay beneath her gold dress.

After a heartier than normal breakfast, Berty helped Silvia to her feet. As he held out his arm for her, she said, "Thank you, but I need to try walking on my own."

Berty gave her an understanding nod and smile.

Keeping an eye on Silvia, Berty walked behind Hope as she led them through the forest. She kept touching trees systematically every so many feet. Berty watched Hope's little hand graze a tree trunk longer than she had been doing. At the next tree, Hope stopped.

"What's coming?" Berty asked.

"We're here," said Hope.

Berty stood next to Hope. The edge of the forest ended with a line of trees. On the other side, a vast expanse of a short green carpet waited for them. Berty surmised that the short vegetation beyond the tree line was lichen—plants of the tundra.

"So that's what lies beyond the trees," said Delyth.

"A big bunch of nothing," Telor added.

"The magic of the trees does not end at the tree line," explained Hope. "We have to walk until I can no longer hear them." Turning to Edwin, she said, "Do not cross the tree line or you will not be able to return."

He looked from Hope to the tundra, then took a few steps back. "I will wait for you here," Edwin said.

"Are we ready?" asked Berty.

Hope took the first step away from the trees. Cautiously, the others followed, leaving the Elf behind. As they walked, the lichen faintly crunched under their feet. The tree line grew smaller behind them. Berty noticed how much closer the sky felt.

Once the trees had entirely disappeared from view, Hope said, "It's quiet. The trees are gone."

"Then let's start digging," said Berty.

Grabbing the shovel he had been carrying, Otho began to dig. After a few shovels of dirt, Otho said, "The ground is hard. How deep do we have to go?"

"Permafrost," mumbled Berty vaguely recalling grade school science.

Declan looked at him curiously.

"That's why the ground is hard. It's frozen," Berty explained.

"Deep enough to cover, they told me," said Hope.

"What is that?" asked Telor. He gazed further north. "The structure in the distance."

At first glance, Berty thought it was a snowcapped mountain. Staring at it longer, he noticed sheer walls and pointed turrets. The structure looked sleek as if it were made of ice.

"It can't be," said Silvia, gaping at the structure.

"What can't be?" Telor asked.

"It is supposed to be a myth," she continued.

"What's supposed to be a myth?" Telor inquired, sounding nervous.

"Rimþar Castle," Silvia answered. She turned to Otho, saying, "That's deep enough."

Berty heard fear in her voice.

Extracting the claw and phial of blood, Silvia threw them into the hole. "Back fill, quickly," she said. "In the myths, Frost Giants do not take kindly to strangers. Hopefully, we will go unnoticed."

Otho knocked dirt into the hole as quickly as he could. Tacitus started stepping on the dirt to make it level with the ground around it.

"Leave it," said Declan. "Run for the trees!"

Knowing Declan could see things everyone else could not, Berty scooped Hope off the ground. A large, shiny blue, double-headed battleaxe sliced into the frozen ground beside them.

Scattering, everyone ran for the tree line. Berty dodged flying battleaxes with Hope in his arms. After glancing over his shoulder, Hope hid her head in his chest and clutched his cloak more tightly. He willed his legs to move faster.

Out of the corner of his eye, Berty saw Declan leap over a battleaxe without breaking stride. Turning his head slightly, he was able to see Silvia holding both her staff and her gold dress in order to run. Behind her were Otho and Tacitus. Freesia kept pace with Berty while Delyth's and Telor's light bodies allowed them to sprint faster than everyone else.

With the tree line in sight, Berty glanced over his shoulder. Very pale, with a slight blue tinge, human-like creatures the size of a three-story building chased them. What they lacked in speed, their long strides overcame.

Berty could barely feel his heart beat or his legs move. He had no idea if his feet touched the ground. All he cared about was reaching the trees.

As the trees got closer, the ground shook with giant fury. The Frost Giants were almost upon them.

Telor ran past a hurling blue sword as big as he was. The sword clanged onto the hard ground as he crossed the tree line. Delyth followed unobstructed.

Berty heard a large object hacking the air. As he entered the forest, a massive blue battleaxe wedged into a passing tree. "Keep running!" he yelled.

Over his shoulder, he saw Silvia, Declan and Freesia dash into the forest. Seconds later, Otho and Tacitus crossed the tree line.

Returning to the edge of the forest, Declan said, "They're gone."

Berty placed Hope on the forest floor. "Is anyone hurt?" he asked.

After a general murmur of, "No," Berty's eyes searched the trees.

"Does anyone see Edwin?" Berty asked.

"Telor?" said Delyth. She walked around the trees. "Telor!"

she screamed.

Declan rushed to her side. Crouching, he said, "Looks like he was dragged." He followed the tracks in the ground. "Something big took him."

"Ogres," said Edwin as he jumped out of a tree. "I hit at least one with arrows. They almost knocked me out of the trees. Followed invisibly instead. They took him inside."

"If we hurry, we can get him back," said Declan.

Silvia put a hand on Berty's arm. "I'll stay with Hope," she said.

Berty nodded. Crouching in front of Hope, he said, "You stay here. I'll be back soon."

Hope said nothing.

Holding out a hand, Freesia called to Hope. As she took Hope's hand, Freesia brought her into a hug like hold. Unfolding very large wings, Freesia flew Hope high into a tree.

Berty looked from Hope to Otho. The Roman stood next to Silvia with his sword drawn.

"We'll get him," Declan told Delyth.

"I'm coming with you," she said.

"No. It's too dangerous," said Declan.

Delyth gave him a look that said, *how dare you tell me what to do.*

"I'm just trying to protect you," he said in return.

"I'm still coming. I can protect myself," she said.

"Enough arguing," said Berty. "Let's go." With a last look at Silvia, he followed Edwin on the path to Telor.

"I know you can, Delyth," Declan said quietly. "It's just," he did not finish.

"He's my brother. You can't expect me to do nothing," she said.

Declan reached into a bush. Extracting Telor's bow and quiver full of arrows, he gave them to Tacitus, who immediately strapped both to his back.

A mound of grass came into view. Edwin mouthed, "Ogre Lair."

Edwin and Declan readied their bows while Berty, Delyth and Tacitus unsheathed their swords. Creeping around the mound, Declan kept his bow drawn. He released an arrow. Berty heard a thud.

A large, lumpy looking creature had fallen to the side of a wood framed entrance. Whatever skin that was not covered with animal hides was a muddy green. The ogre easily could have blended into his surroundings.

Facing the entrance, they waited. When nothing emerged, Edwin led them inside.

Berty separated Declan from Delyth as they crept down a dimly lit tunnel. Pierced metal torches rested high on the tunnel walls. The dim light revealed thick timber supports reminiscent of a mineshaft. A dank, wet earth smell filled Berty's nostrils.

After walking a while, Declan said quietly, "No magic down here. Must be blocked. Even my bow seems to have lost it."

Nodding, Berty felt uneasy. He had begun to rely on his magic. Without it, he had to rely on the forged metal in his grip. Taking a breath, he remembered what Edwin said about using a sword—it was an extension of your arm.

The tunnel emptied into a room with many more tunnels branching from it. "Which way?" Declan whispered.

"We should split up," whispered Edwin.

Delyth took a step towards one of the tunnels. "This way," she whispered.

No one asked her how she knew. Tacitus charged ahead with Edwin close behind.

As the tunnel rounded a bend, grunting echoed off the rough stone. Tenseness filled the tunnel. Berty could feel his heart beat in the hilt of his sword. Moving forward, they anticipated Ogres with every step.

Their chosen tunnel graded sharply, plunging them deeper underground. Berty turned his feet sideways to keep himself from sliding. The others did the same.

The grunts grew louder. Listening to them, Berty thought that the grunts sounded like chanting. He did not want to know what would happen if the grunting crescendoed.

When the steep slope leveled, they had walked into a cavernous room full of Ogres. Dozens of Ogres formed a semicircle facing a waterfall. A light blue glow radiated from the small pool of water at the foot of the falls. In the center of the Ogre circle, Telor was being passed from one Ogre to another as if they were playing a game of hot potato.

The grunting stopped. Many pairs of beady eyes found the intruders. Large spiked clubs descended, scattering Berty from the others.

Sharp points swooshed inches from his body. He tried to use magic to disintegrate the club, but it did not work. His eyes saw that each one of them fought at least one Ogre. No one could help him.

The Ogre lifted his club again. Berty tilted his sword horizontally. As he stepped to the side, he swung with all his might. His blade found its target. The Ogre fell to the ground.

Without reprieve, another Ogre swiped at him. When metal sliced through wood, the club struck its owner.

Telor was still near the waterfall. Berty could not imagine losing the son to save the father. *He* permitted Telor to come. The force of his blade would not permit him to regret his decision.

While fighting his way towards the water, he caught glimpses of the others. Tacitus fought multiple Ogres at once with his sword in one hand, and a claimed club in the other. Arrows from both Edwin and Declan rained upon the Ogres. Running through the melee, Delyth viciously fought any Ogre between her and her brother.

Delyth used her small size to her advantage. She easily squeezed past confused Ogres. While their beady eyes and spiked clubs searched for the Fairy, she reached Telor next to the glowing pool.

Berty and Edwin arrived in the inner circle from opposite directions. The number of Ogres in the cavern doubled. Berty found himself fighting two Ogres with only his one sword.

Over the sound of the falling water, he heard wood being smashed. Pieces of splintered wood scattered across the ground.

Looking over, Berty watched an Ogre throw Edwin. The Elf flew into the waterfall. His body disappeared behind the water.

The Ogre fell. Tacitus stood in the void with Ogre blood on his blade.

Two Ogres began to drag Telor away from the glowing pool. Delyth stabbed one. Although bound, Telor writhered, trying to fight off the other one. An arrow pierced the Ogre. Telor fell to the ground. Hurrying to his side, Delyth cut his bonds.

Declan appeared in the center, shooting arrows as fast as he could pull them from his quiver.

The cave shook. Fighting ceased as the Ogres retreated to the edges of the cavern. The four of them surrounded Telor.

Thundering towards them was an Ogre almost as tall as a Frost Giant. Berty's eyes darted around the cave searching for something.

Telor relieved Tacitus of his bow and quiver. Standing next to Declan, they shot arrows at the beast. While the arrows slowed him, the others stood ready with their swords.

The Ogre was almost within swinging reach. Berty shifted his weight while keeping a firm grip on his hilt. A shadow in the waterfall caught his eye.

The cascade parted. Edwin's torso broke through the water. His hand clasped something black in the rock.

From the rock behind the waterfall, Edwin removed a long sword. He leapt off the wet rock. As he soared over the pool, the blue light reflected on the gold blade.

Landing between them and the Ogre, Edwin brandished the sword, readying for a battle. The giant Ogre slid to a stop. Berty shook as the Ogres stampeded from the room.

"Are you hurt, Your Highness?" Tacitus asked Telor.

"Just a little sore. Will probably have a number of bruises later," Telor answered. "They took all my Fairy Dust."

Lowering his bow, Declan asked, "What do Ogres want with Fairy Dust?"

Telor secured his bow to his back, saying, "I don't care. Let's get out of here."

"Wait," said Delyth. She peered into rock and bone containers. Kneeling, she examined the ground. "They burn it." Her fingers rubbed soot off of a stone.

"Would the fumes get them high?" Berty asked. When Delyth gave him a confused look, he clarified, "Affect their consciousness."

"Don't know," she answered as Declan helped her off the ground.

"We should go before they are no longer afraid of this sword," suggested Edwin.

Retracing their steps, Edwin led them out of the Ogre Lair. As they approached Silvia and Otho, Freesia and Hope floated to the forest floor.

Silvia walked up to Berty. Wiping dirt off his cheek, she said, "I am so glad you are all right."

Smiling, Berty said, "We may not have been if Edwin did not pull that sword from the stone."

Curiously, she glanced at the golden blade of the sword in the Elf's hand. "The Blade of the Golden Flame," she remarked.

Edwin turned the sword over in his hand. The sunlight made the gold shine brightly. "Who would have known," he said. "Wonder what it was doing in there."

"If I remember correctly," Silvia began, "legend says that the Blade of the Golden Flame was crafted ages ago by a blind Dwarf named Ezard. Ezard was an expert swordsmith. Being blind, he crafted solely by feel. During a time of many wars, a warrior commissioned a sword from the Dwarf. The wars kept the Dwarves busy smithing weapons and armor. Ezard had a difficult time finding a free anvil on which he could craft a sword. Wandering through the Dwarf mines, he stumbled upon an empty anvil. Being able to work alone, he crafted the sword in record time. He brought the finished sword to the foreman for inspection. Upon noticing its golden hue, the foreman brought both Ezard and the sword to the Dwarf Prince.

"The Prince told Ezard that he had forged the sword upon the Anvil of Darkness. The anvil imbues a weapon or piece of armor with magical properties. A long time before, the Dwarves forbade the crafting of magical items. Because Ezard's intentions were pure and he was completely unaware of his mistake, the sword was allowed to be given to the warrior.

"In battle, the sword looked to be made of golden flames. Hence its name. Supposedly, the sword is magical. Those who used the sword for their own gain became obsessed with obtaining power through any means necessary—usually ruthlessly. For that reason, the Dwarves reclaimed the sword intent on destroying it. All efforts to destroy the sword failed.

"To stop the sword from being used as a weapon of massacre, they encased it in a stone hidden in one of their abandoned mines. They guarded it with a crystal which would only permit a pure, selfless soul to wield it."

Edwin's pale face flushed.

"At least that is what the legend says," said Silvia. "Why don't we find a place to camp far from here?"

"Ready to lead us back to Fairyland, Hope?" asked Berty.

With a smile, Hope nodded. Her loose, brown curls bounced as she led them on a path of her own making.

They walked quickly trying to gain more ground before night fell. While they ate around the campfire, Tacitus told stories about the Ogre Lair. Sitting beside Berty, Hope listened with interest until she fell asleep across his lap. When Freesia took Hope to bed, Berty noticed Declan securing a string on the bow on which he had been working.

As they packed in the morning, Berty felt a bit uneasy. He looked around trying to figure out what bothered him. "Does it seem unusually quiet this morning?" he asked Declan and Telor.

Declan's eyes searched the trees. Fixating on one spot, he said, "I think we have a visitor."

Berty looked in the same direction as Declan.

"My Lord, I was waiting until you finished packing your camp," said a disembodied voice that Berty recognized.

A boxy black head with gold eyes and moustache materialized between the trees.

"Good to see you again, Tong," said Berty. "What brings you to this part of the Dragonlands?"

"You do, my Lord," said Tong as his body appeared.

Hope gasped. "A long Dragon," she breathed.

"My pigmy friends have informed me that the bridge spanning Fairy Death Gorge has collapsed. I am here to help," said Tong. "I can take you back to... in close proximity to Fairyland, my Lord."

"Fairy Death Gorge?" Telor mouthed.

"Close proximity would be very much appreciated," Berty said.

Approaching Hope, Berty was relieved to see her looking thrilled. "Are you ready to fly on the back of a Dragon?"

Her eyes grew bigger as she grinned from ear to ear.

"I'll take that as a yes," said Berty chuckling. "Freesia?"

Freesia stood frozen staring at Tong. She finally took her eyes off the Dragon to look at Berty. "Yes, my Lord?"

"You will sit with Hope," he told her. Lowering his voice, he said, "There is nothing to fear from this Dragon."

Tong laid his belly on the forest floor. While the Empire Guards helped Silvia and Delyth, Berty assisted Freesia onto the Dragon's back. Once she was secure, he handed her Hope. After checking everyone, Berty climbed onto Tong's back right behind his head.

Effortlessly, Tong soared skyward. Breaking through the canopy, Tong's black feathers glistened in the morning sunlight. Berty basked in the sunlight while he waited for the free fall feeling.

The forest was covered in a beautiful blanket of green. Wispy tendrils of fog crept above the canopy as the sun burned the water vapor back into the sky. In the distance, black billows of smoke pierced the green blanket.

Tong dove sharply. Green whizzed past in a blur. Tong's long body wove through the forest like a snake.

"I am so sorry, my Lord," Tong said quietly. "First Council deliberations are not going so well. I find it best to stay out of sight."

"Understood," said Berty.

They glided just under the forest canopy at tree blurring speed. Berty could hear Hope giggling behind him. Although the leaves hid the sun, he could still detect its movement across the sky.

Brightness escaped the forest. Nighttime eclipsed Berty's sight. Tong still slithered under the tree ceiling. When he no longer heard glimpses of giggles, he figured that Hope either fell asleep or flying lost its appeal.

The Dragon slowed whilst descending. Punctuated through the trees, Berty could see the distant lights of Fairyland. When they landed, he conjured spheres of light to help everyone dismount.

"This is as far as I can take you," said Tong. "I apologize for taking so long, but dematerializing makes me half blind. With growing Dragon on Dragon hostility, I did not want to take chances. A rebellion against Angana and the clan of Cian I believe to be imminent. It could result in a full-blown Dragon war. Tensions are mounting, my Lord, and Dragons will not hesitate to burn everything that lies in their war path."

"Thank you, Tong. Take care of yourself," said Berty.

The Dragon disappeared into the darkness.

Edwin gazed upon Fairyland in the distance. "Should we keep going?" he asked.

Looking at the group, Berty searched for signs of exhaustion.

"I will walk all night for a hot bath and a soft bed," said Telor.

Privately, Berty agreed. "Can you walk some more, Hope?" he asked.

As soon as Hope answered, "Yes," they began to walk along the path to Fairyland. Berty's spheres of light accompanied them, illuminating the path and surrounding forest.

"What's that noise?" Otho said.

"What noise?" asked Telor.

Faint woeful wails reached Berty's ears.

"It can't be," said Delyth. Fear showed in her violet eyes.

Declan stared down the path behind them. Turning to Delyth and Telor, he said, "Take Elder Hunter and Hope and fly out of here."

"We can't," said Telor grabbing his bow. "It is too dark and the forest here is too dense to fly."

The earth vibrated beneath Berty's feet. He almost wished Frost Giants were chasing them.

Thunderous beating of large feet hitting dirt approached as mournful moans haunted the surrounding forest.

Turning her back on the welcoming lights of her home, Delyth unsheathed her sword. "I'm out of Fairy Dust. We can't take a chance of the Night Golems reaching Fairyland," she said.

Berty looked at Silvia, Hope and Freesia, "Run," he said.

Glancing both ways on the path, Silvia said, "Our chances are better here."

Edwin, Otho and Tacitus drew their swords. Readying an arrow, Declan waited.

The trees around them burst into flames. Fiery orange reflected on a sleek black body flying overhead. The intense fire illuminated large brownish blue lumps galloping towards them.

"Sorcerer," Tong called to Berty. The Dragon opened his mouth. A fireball rushed towards Berty.

As his Dragon match, Berty knew exactly what to do. His arm reached into the sky. Catching the fireball in his hand, he absorbed the magical Dragonfire.

Extracting his sword, Berty gave it to Silvia. She, in turn, passed her staff into Hope's care.

Declan released his first arrow. It pierced the shell-like hide of a Night Golem. The creature kept coming. Behind the first one stampeded about a dozen more.

With his palms open towards the creatures, Berty shot Dragonfire at them. When a few caught on fire, they tried to shake it off like a dog shaking off the rain. Ablaze, they continued their crusade.

Arrows rained upon the Night Golems. None of them fell.

Edwin ran towards the charging creatures. His golden blade seemed to have caught some of the Dragonfire. With a swing of his blade, the Night Golem screamed liked a banshee, then disappeared in a puff of blue.

"One down," said Otho.

"Only twelve more to go," Tacitus said.

Both Romans ran to slow the Night Golems. Declan and Telor continued to shower the creatures with arrows. Berty focused Dragonfire on only one Night Golem. In the time it took Edwin to destroy two, Berty finally burnt one leaving nothing but blue smoke and a final scream.

Another replaced it.

"Otho!" screamed Tacitus.

The rescued Roman lay motionless on the ground. Tacitus picked up his fallen sword, using both swords to viciously attack the remaining Night Golems.

Silvia and Delyth dragged Otho to where Hope and Freesia stood.

When the last scream faded to silence, Berty and Edwin ran to Otho's side.

The Roman's dark eyes found Berty. "An honor serving you, Emperor," he labored.

All Berty could do was nod in gratitude. His voice was stuck in his throat.

Otho tried to breathe.

Falling to his knees, Tacitus said to his fellow Roman, "May your Lars accept you home."

A glowing translucent hand reached for Otho's forehead.

Berty's eyes followed the glow to see the five Guardian Fairy Spirits standing with them. They said something in their language.

"Move away from Otho," said Delyth.

The spirits formed a glowing circle around Otho. They chanted. With each repetition, their glow brightened.

Only Delyth understood their words. She wiped a tear away

from her cheek.

The glow dimmed. The spirits broke their circle. One spoke.

"He will need rest," Delyth translated. "Thank you, Elf. Without you, the Night Golems would still be trapped in their bonds. We apologize for how we treated you in Gosembreeth."

Delyth said something to them in their language.

"The Night Golems hunt those who enter their territory," the Fairy translated. "Once they were set free, so were we. You have brought much honor to Fairydom tonight."

They bowed, then faded into the forest.

Tacitus helped Otho to his feet. The trees burned around them. With a wipe of his hand, Berty extinguished the fires. His conjured spheres of light were the only source of illumination. He barely saw the char on the trunks.

A gentle hand touched his arm. "Thank you, Berty," Silvia said. She gave him his sword. "Dragonfire. No one has harnessed that power in a very long time. Perhaps that is why your color is a deep red."

"Then why is yours light blue?" he asked.

She smiled.

Returning his sword to its scabbard, he said, "Shall we continue to Fairyland?"

"Yes, I think we should," she said.

Their eyes met. Giving each other a smile, they broke their gaze.

Approaching Hope, Berty saw the remnants of fear on her face. He knelt beside her. Her little arms wrapped around him. She squeezed him so tightly that he hoped her fear had escaped her body. After giving her a warm, everything-is-okay smile, he stood, looking at everyone.

Edwin glanced at the partially scorched scene. With a hand on the hilt of his sheathed sword, he turned towards the distant lights of Fairyland.

Otho walked with the help of Tacitus. Slowly, they walked down the path.

"Delyth," said Telor, walking in sync with her. "I am so sorry.

Sorry for my tantrums and my outbursts. I behaved like a jealous brat of a brother."

She abruptly stopped, causing Declan to quickly sidestep.

"You were so amazing back in that Ogre Lair," he told her. "And I was so horrible to you before. I feel so low."

"Thanks," she said as she began to walk. "I—"

"Do not say anything yet," Telor interrupted. "I have done a lot of thinking. What I said to you days ago was not enough. When we were children, you were always more interested in reading books and consuming knowledge. That never interested me. I was fine with you knowing more than I. Becoming Empire Historian was a perfect fit for you. As your brother, I could not have been prouder. I understand why you wanted to learn how to use a weapon after being poisoned. But, then you got to travel. You went places no one has gone in recent memory. Here I was cooped up in a castle. A prisoner of my own birthright. I could not go anywhere. I could not master a weapon. With father on his deathbed, you were being asked for advice. No one asked me anything. I felt as if I were being pushed aside. My job was just to look princely because I did not have the brains to do more."

She closed her eyes. Tears streamed down her cheeks.

"Forgive me?" he asked her.

She threw her arms around her brother. "Of course I do," she said quietly. After they hugged, she said, "When we get home, I have something to show you."

The hidden old library popped into Berty's mind.

"And Declan, I am sorry for giving you a hard time, too," added Telor.

"Don't worry about it," Declan said. "Just keep practicing. If your bow is with you at all times, then you can practice whenever you have a chance."

Berty missed Telor's answer because he saw Freesia pick Hope up in one fluid motion without stopping. As he opened his mouth, gentle pressure on his arm prevented anything from escaping.

"It's her job," Silvia said softly.

Glancing at her slender fingers on his brown shirtsleeve, he slowly nodded. "Am I being over protective," he asked her.

"Just a little," she smiled.

Chapter Seventeen
Fairydom Forever

The forest began to thin. The lights from Fairyland spilled beyond its walls. Following the path, they walked through a vast expanse of grass, which separated the forest from Fairyland. Large kettles of fire punctuated the sides of the path leading to the wall.

Armed Fairy Guards protected a closed blue metal gate. As they approached, Berty extinguished his spheres of light. Telor walked in front so that the guards could see him. The gate had risen fully into the wall by the time they reached it.

Graceful metal and glass lanterns lit the streets of Fairyland. Telor took them on the most direct route to the castle.

Once inside the main hall, Telor said in hushed tones, "Thank you all for doing this for my... our father." He smiled at Delyth. "We will alert our parents that we have returned. I will have food brought to your rooms and baths drawn if you want them."

Berty trudged up the stone steps behind Freesia who carried a sleeping Hope. In the hallway, he rushed ahead of Freesia to open Hope's door for her. Before he reached the doorframe, the door opened automatically. He stepped aside to let Freesia pass.

"Fairy Godmother magic," Freesia told him. "I will get her ready for bed, then come for you, my Lord."

He gave her a tired smile. Leaving the door to his bedroom open, he threw his claret cloak on the bed.

A servant knocked on the open door. "Excuse me, my Lord," the servant said. "Would you like some food and a bath drawn?"

"Yes, please," said Berty.

A team of servants entered his room. Most of them filled a metal tub that was camouflaged behind a wooden screen. One placed a silver tray of food on the small round table while another hung his cloak in the wardrobe.

"My Lord," said Freesia from the doorway. "She is asking for you."

"Thank you," he said to everyone before leaving his room.

Sitting in the bed, Hope waited for him.

"Aren't you going to sleep?" he asked.

"Freesia says that we're leaving tomorrow," said Hope.

"Yes. It is time we return to the Empire Tree," Berty answered.

"Are we going on a Dragon?" she asked. Her eyes filled with excited anticipation.

"No Dragons."

"Oh."

He looked at her crestfallen expression, then explained, "Riding a Dragon is really rare. Not many have seen a Dragon let alone have ridden one."

She thought for a moment. "Uncle Berty? Are Ogres very scary?" she asked.

"Yes, very," he answered while nodding.

"Scarier than Frost Giants?"

"Almost as scary."

She slunk under the covers. "Will there be any of those?"

Berty smiled reassuringly. "No. We will be riding home in a carriage pulled by horses." Surrounded by Empire Guards, he thought.

"Ooh, okay," she said. The smile returned to her face. "Goodnight, Uncle Berty."

"Goodnight, Hope."

Entering his room, a tub full of warm water enticed him. He popped a piece of cheese into his mouth before getting undressed. The warm water surrounded his sore muscles. Leaning his head back, he inhaled the woodsy herb perfume that mingled with the wafting steam. His mind drifted.

Night Golems. Dragons. Ogres. Frost Giants. Myths. Silvia learned about Frost Giants as a myth. He wondered how many other myths the Land of Sages had and how many were real. Less than a year ago, he would have told anyone that Dragons, Fairies, Elves, Trolls and Goblins were myths, too. What were myths, really? Myths were stories invoked from the pieces of our distant memories.

Opening his eyes, Berty said, "The Cavern. That's what they're after."

He emerged from the tub. The cooler air stung his senses. Finding a towel, he dried his goosebumped skin. He wrapped a robe over his nightclothes. Lantern in hand, he strode into the hall.

Stopping in front of his chosen door, he knocked.

The door opened. "My Lord," said Declan in a robe.

"Is there a Watcher's Vault?" Berty asked quietly.

Declan's tired expression morphed into understanding. "Yes."

"I'll see you in the morning," said Berty.

Returning to his room, Berty took comfort in knowing that Leif and Millicent did not enter the Vault Room. He fell asleep pondering whether or not they coveted the Staff of Lightning to enter the vault or to lead them to the Cavern.

Rumbles of thunder woke him. Looking out the window, he groaned at the dark sky. He dressed for a soggy departure.

At breakfast, Declan sat next to Berty. "I've never been inside," he whispered.

Nodding, Berty watched servants move relatively unnoticed around the dining room. Freesia had Hope eating a healthy breakfast whilst engaging her in a game about the Land of Sages.

Sauntering into the room, Silvia glanced at Berty, then looked away. Sitting down with a plate of food, she smiled. "I believe Lida and Elrick want us in the Throne Room before you go," she said.

"How is Elrick?" asked Berty.

"I checked him this morning," Declan said. "His wounds are healing nicely. He is in such a great mood that he did not care when I told him that he will have scars across his chest."

The doors opened. Delyth walked to the table wearing a beautiful violet dress that matched her eyes. "If everyone would please come," she said.

As they followed Delyth to the Throne Room, Berty and Silvia dragged behind Declan, Hope and Freesia. "Did you get to see about what you were curious?" Berty asked Silvia with the Sethbravin in mind.

"This morning," she answered.

"And?"

"Interesting." She looked at Berty. "Not useful."

Entering the Throne Room, he noticed that the gray skies made the sparkle more pronounced. Elrick and Lida sat on their respective thrones. Telor stood proudly on the side. Behind Berty and Silvia walked Edwin, Otho and Tacitus.

"You are all forever friends of Fairydom," said Elrick. "I am in your debt for saving both me and my son. However, there are two of you without whom I would not be sitting before you. Hope, please approach."

Slowly, Hope climbed the few steps of the dais.

Lida held a white metal necklace with a multicolor crystal Fairy wing charm hanging from the fine chain. "For your service to the Fairy Royal family, we present to you this Fairy Pendant," Lida said. Rising from her throne, she placed it around Hope's neck. "As long as you wear this, you will be able to possess the magic of Fairy Dust without consequence. When you return to the Empire Tree, Delyth will teach you proper Fairy Dust management."

"Thank you," said Hope softly.

Lida smiled warmly. "You're welcome, dear." She gestured for Hope to go back to Freesia's side.

Once Lida sat on her throne, Elrick continued, "Declan, would you please come forward."

Declan approached the dais while both Elrick and Lida walked down a step. In Lida's hands was a wad of black cloth. "In addition to killing the beast that we do not name, you reinvigorated our archery legions with solutions and knowledge," said Lida. "You also possess a gift for healing that goes unmatched in this world. Without you, Fairydom would have faced great peril. For being a champion of Fairydom, we present you with the title of Duke of Fairyland." She handed him the black wad.

"Declan," Elrick said, "you are of noble soul. Your true nobility, although previously unrecognized, runs deeper than most. The title of Duke makes you one of the Fairy Court. The cloak allows you to display your noble rank with your own seal."

Running his fingers over the clasp, Declan's eyes misted. "I am so honored. Thank you," he said. He shook the folded cloak, revealing a purple sheen within the black material. Fairy servants freed his hands of the new cloak. Removing his brown cloak, he stuffed it gently in his bag as if he were saying good-bye.

The Fairies draped his shoulders in the purplish black cloak. Declan fastened the clasp, then glanced at Berty, Edwin and Delyth who wiped her cheek with her fingers. Descending the steps of the dais, the dark cloak floated behind him.

Telor stepped forward, saying, "To the Empire Guards, Lieutenant Edwin, Tacitus and Otho, I present the Fairyland Metal of Valour."

A servant carried a tray while Telor approached the guards. Telor carefully picked a blue ribbon off of the tray. He let the sparkling metal hang before placing it around each neck. Shaking their hands, he said, "Until we meet again."

When Telor returned to the dais, Lida said, "Freesia, a generous donation has been made in your honor to the Godmother Guild."

"Thank you, Your Majesties," said Freesia, curtsying.

"Elder Hunter," said Elrick, "how can we repay you?"

Smiling, Silvia answered, "All I ask is for your hospitality so that I may extend my stay in Fairyland."

"For as long as you would like," said Lida.

"Emperor, we did not know how to express our gratitude," Elrick said.

"But with careful thought, we have decided to allow Fairies to enlist in the Empire Guard," finished Lida.

"We never thought it necessary before to have Fairies learn weaponry and combat beyond Fairy Dust," Elrick continued. "We were wrong. The tradition which we followed was also wrong."

"The Empire Guard happily accepts all who wish to serve the Empire militarily," said Berty diplomatically.

With smiles, Elrick and Lida stepped off the dais. Elrick shook Berty's hand. "Safe journey home, my Lord. Thank you again for everything."

"Seeing you doing so well is all the thanks I need," said Berty.

Both Lida and Elrick hugged Declan before saying warm good-byes to their daughter.

Silvia walked with them to the castle entrance. "It was nice meeting you, Hope. I'm sure I will see you again soon," she said.

"Bye, Silvia," said Hope happily.

The opened castle doors revealed the large green carriage waiting at the bottom of the castle steps. The steady rains darkened all the colors of Fairyland.

"Pick your seat in the carriage. I'll be there in a minute," Berty told Hope.

Hope smiled.

"Raise your hood," Freesia told her while raising her own.

With her hood covering her head, Hope waved to Silvia before following Freesia through the rain to the carriage.

"I guess this is good-bye again," said Berty, gazing into Silvia's warm, brown eyes. He barely noticed Declan and Delyth scurrying out of the castle.

"For now," Silvia said.

His fingers grazed her cheekbone as they slid into her dark red hair. Silvia tilted her head towards his hand, then closed her eyes. Staring at her lips, he found his nose touching hers.

"We can't," Silvia breathed. Opening her eyes, she seemed reluctant to pull away.

"Just to say good-bye?" he said softly. His lips yearned to touch hers.

As she pulled her head back, her eyes came into focus.

"Berty, don't make this more difficult," she pleaded. "As an Elder, I am tethered to you. If we kiss, then you will be tethered to me. The tethering is different, but the concept is the same. To break the curse, I must sever all bonds. We would never be able to connect the same way again. Give me time. That is all I ask."

His hand slid down her arm. Caressing her hand, he said, "Whatever you need." Her skin was so soft under his fingers. "Be careful."

She smiled. "I always am. Usually."

They laughed.

He relinquished her hand. Raising his hood, he trotted down the wet stone steps. With a foot on the carriage step, he turned back towards the castle. She stood radiantly in the doorway. Her short, dark red hair framed her face. Her delicate figure was enrobed in gold. Their eyes met. She smiled. Taking a breath, he entered the carriage.

Berty sat next to Hope. As he looked across from him at Declan and Delyth trying not to sit too close to each other, he felt the carriage begin to move.

The rhythmic thunder of horses weaving through the streets echoed off of the colorful walls. Sheer curtains covered the carriage windows, allowing the dim light to enter while shrouding them from view. Berty felt the rain pounding the carriage roof as if it were pounding his heart.

His head knew that they could not be together, but his heart ached without her. He wished that she could return to the Empire Tree. She would find a way, he thought.

The echoes disappearing signaled leaving Fairyland. A flash of brightness surrounded them. He did not even count to one before he heard the crack of thunder. The carriage bounced and jolted from side to side as it moved faster. He braced himself on the bench seat while missing the rubber tires and shocks of his car.

"Why is it so bumpy?" Hope asked as she held onto the seat.

"Dirt road," said Berty.

"If we stay at this pace, we'll reach the Sages' Grove by nightfall," Declan remarked.

"Or break a wheel," added Delyth.

"I don't think that's possible," Declan said. "Magic surrounds the undercarriage."

"Uncle Berty, will Mommy and Daddy call when we get home?" Hope asked.

"Yes, definitely."

"Good. 'Cause I can't wait to tell Mommy all about riding a Dragon and stuff," said Hope a little too enthusiastically.

Looking into Hope's big, brown eyes, Berty chose his words carefully. "I wouldn't tell anyone about riding a Dragon."

"Why not?"

"Because Dragons can be temperamental."

"What does tem-per-ral mean?"

"Tem-per-a-ment-al," he repeated. "Not all Dragons are as nice as Tong. So if other people wander into the Dragonlands wanting to ride a Dragon, they could get hurt. That's why riding a Dragon is rare. Dragons don't always let you." He glanced at Declan looking for backup.

"And," added Declan, "Dragons are very secretive."

"Oh," Hope said. "I can keep a secret."

"I bet you can," said Declan with a smile.

Berty gave Declan a nod of thanks.

As they rode through the forest, the thunder began to sound distant although the rain did not want to yield. Their pace did not slow. Berty figured that the guards on horseback wanted to get dry as soon as possible. Not that he minded. He was sure his voicemail was full with messages from Jon and Teresa.

The bouncing subsided as the carriage slowed.

"We can't be there yet. It is still light out," said Delyth.

"Tree down, completely covering the path," shouted a guard's voice. "No way around. Going to have to move it."

Delyth's hand reached for the curtain. Declan quickly grabbed it. "Don't," he said. Looking at Berty, he continued, "Thieves trick."

Noticing the dark drapes, Berty whispered, "No sounds. Aim an arrow at the door. Draw closed the drapes."

When the drapes darkened the carriage, a dim ball of light escaped from Berty's palm.

"Ambush!" someone outside yelled.

Berty pointed to Delyth, then to Hope and Freesia telling her to stay and defend the carriage. Delyth nodded. Berty motioned for Declan to wait. He pointed at himself, then at the door. Declan gave him a sharp nod, keeping his arrow ready.

From inside her cloak, Delyth pulled out two velvet bags.

Freesia recoiled.

"You may need to defend," Delyth breathed.

"The Godmother Guild does not use Fairy Dust," Freesia breathily retorted.

Delyth's eyebrows raised. "You are a Fairy," she mouthed angrily. Pressing a bag into Freesia's hand, she turned her attention to Hope. She gave the other bag to Hope, then whispered in her ear.

Berty could not hear, but assumed she whispered instructions.

When Delyth returned to her seat, the fighting sounded closer. Berty placed his hand on the handle of the carriage door. With a deep breath, he opened the door.

Declan released an arrow. Jumping out of the carriage, he released another.

Sword drawn, Berty jumped as well. He quickly closed the door behind him.

Through the rain, Berty saw each Empire Guard fighting at least one man. The men wore ski mask like sacks over their heads. Declan picked off bandits with each arrow he shot.

While the guards were distracted fighting, two men weaseled

through the melee. Berty watched them make their way to the back of the carriage. Following, he waited for them to struggle with the trunk's lock.

"Having problems picking the lock?" Berty asked the men.

When they spun around, Berty pressed his blade to their throats. He could see the fear in their eyes.

"I'm going to give you two options," Berty said. "Either I kill you where you stand or you move the tree out of the path. I don't care. I just want to get to my destination. Pick one."

"We'll move the tree," said one man.

"Good choice," Berty said. He slid his sword away from the men's necks. "Move. Now."

Berty marched them at swordpoint around the carriage. Once past the carriage, they both turned, drawing blades.

One lunged.

With a swipe of his free hand, the man rose off the ground. The fighting stopped as all eyes watched the man slam into a tree, then slide to the ground unconscious.

In a rage, a bandit charged the carriage. He opened the door, then fell to the ground. Delyth and Freesia emerged from the carriage. They flew above with fists full of Fairy Dust.

Sparkles mixed with the raindrops.

"Retreat!" yelled a bandit before dropping in mid stride.

The Fairies landed as the remaining bandits disappeared into the forest.

"They'll think twice before trying that again," said Edwin, sheathing his sword. "Let's get this tree moved," he instructed the guards.

Six guards lifted the large trunk off of the path. Berty poked his head inside the carriage door to see Hope alone with the ball of light.

Smiling, she said, "I dusted a bad guy."

Berty's heart skipped a beat. "Good," was all he could manage to say. He helped Freesia and Delyth into the carriage before he jumped in with his muddy boots. Joining them, Declan closed the door.

After opening the drapes, Berty reclaimed his light ball. The carriage once again began to move.

"Good job, Hope," commended Delyth. "And Freesia, thank you."

"These are becoming increasingly more dangerous times," Freesia said. "Perhaps the Godmother Guild should rethink its practices." She looked at Hope who sat between her and Berty beaming.

"I'm surprised they attacked us," said Declan. "Did they think that they could defeat Empire Guards?"

"That wasn't their intent," Berty explained. "They had strength in numbers. Enough to distract the guards while they stole whatever valuables we had."

"Once they got the goods, they would have retreated," said Declan, nodding. "I just didn't think they would try."

"Who's richer than the Empire?" Berty asked.

"True," conceded Declan.

The constant tapping of rain lulled Berty to sleep while the constant bouncing kept waking him. As night drew near, the insides of the carriage darkened. Yellow light spilled into the windows from the exterior lanterns.

A maroon covered head rested on Berty's arm. "Are we almost there?" a tired Hope asked.

"Almost," said Berty.

"I'm hungry," whined Hope. She yawned.

"You are also tired," Berty observed. "Take a quick nap. We'll eat when we get home."

"Okay. Can I have chocolate milk?"

"We'll see."

With her head still on Berty's arm, the movement of the carriage rocked her to sleep. He leaned his head on the tufted cushion behind him. Thinking he saw Declan and Delyth touch fingers, he closed his eyes.

A slight lean of a hard turn caused him to open his eyes. The curtains drifted away from the windows long enough for him to spy the familiar treed wall. "Home at last," he breathed.

Chapter Eighteen

Lessons

Finally, the carriage came to a stop. "Wake up, Hope. We're here," Berty said. The carriage door opened as Hope separated from his arm. Hooded Tenders held lanterns, illuminating the drizzle.

Stepping out of the carriage first, Berty waited for Hope and Freesia before entering the dry Receiving Room.

Theodore met them in the Reception Room as they emerged from the staircase. "Welcome home, my Lord," he said with a bow.

"It is good to be home, Theodore," said Berty. "Is Hope's room ready?"

"Of course. Follow me."

The young Dwarf led them up the stairs. At the landing outside the Roundtable Room, Declan and Delyth exited onto the bridge. Theodore continued climbing.

Across from the door to the Scepter Room was an entrance to a bridge Berty had never noticed. He followed Theodore onto the bridge with Hope and Freesia in tow. The rope and plank bridge was wide enough for at least two people to walk side by side.

The bridge ended at a platform that rested in front of a large mass of green.

"Miss Hope," said Theodore, "if you would please grab that branch." He pointed to a branch inside the mass.

Standing next to Theodore, Hope towered over him by a head. When she touched the branch, an arched door opened.

"After you, miss," Theodore said.

Berty followed Hope through the arched opening. Lanterns flickered to life, illuminating a large room. Running right, Hope examined all the toys and games. Freesia walked around a large wooden table on the left to peruse book titles along the wall of shelves.

"Upstairs are the bedrooms, Imelda is your Tender," Theodore stated more to Freesia than to Hope. "Outside, a rope lowers a bridge that goes directly to your platform, my Lord. Both you and Godmother Freesia have unrestricted access to these chambers."

"Thank you, Theodore," Berty said.

"Let's go look at my room, Uncle Berty," said Hope while tugging his hand towards the stairs at the back on the room.

At the top of the stairs, a tapestry depicting an owl in a tree hung between two doors. Hope ran into one of the rooms. Tearing his eyes from the scene, he followed her into the room.

She flopped onto the big bed. "This is the best tree house," she said.

"Yes it is," he said, smiling at her awe. He heard wind chimes.

"What's that?" she asked.

"When you hear wind chimes, it means that someone is at your door," he explained.

"Ooh." Jumping off the bed, she scampered down the steps.

He had no idea where she got all of her energy. Taking one last glance at the tapestry, he followed his niece down the stairs.

A Tender, who Berty assumed was Imelda, placed a tray on the table. Hope hung her cloak on a tree near the door while Declan stood on the side.

Upon seeing Berty, Declan said, "I finished Hope's training bow." He showed Berty the simply curved bow. "I would like to leave it here with her—without arrows. Tomorrow, after breakfast, would be a good time to start her lessons."

"Sounds good," said Berty.

Declan rested the bow against the wall. "Bring this to breakfast with you," he told Hope.

"Okay," she said. Her eyes lit up with the excitement of a child at Christmas.

"Before you go, Declan, can you do me a favor?" asked Berty.

"Of course."

"At the top of the stairs is a tapestry. Look at it. Tell me what you see," instructed Berty.

With a nod, Declan climbed the steps.

"My Lord," said Freesia, "would you like some warm milk?"

He watched the Fairy pour a mug of steaming milk for Hope. "No, thank you. Not tonight," he said. The thought of warm milk disgusted him, but he did not want to stop Hope from drinking it.

She was pouring a second mug when Declan returned.

"Is it chocolate?" Hope asked Freesia.

"No," Freesia answered.

"It is similar to the other," said Declan.

"That's what I thought. Thank you," said Berty.

"Excuse me, Your Grace, would you like some warm milk?" Freesia asked.

Declan looked from Berty to Freesia, then pointed at himself. "Me?"

"As you are the Duke of Fairyland, I and all non-noble Fairies are to address you as Your Grace," Freesia explained.

His mouth moved as if he were going to speak, but could not find the words. He glanced at Hope who happily munched on a cookie. Finally, he said, "Thank you, Freesia. Yes, warm milk would be very nice."

She poured another mug. When she sat, Hope asked her, "Why?"

"Why what?" asked Freesia.

"Why call Declan, Your Grace?"

"Because he is a duke. Tradition dictates that dukes are addressed as Your Grace. More importantly, it is a sign of respect. Fairies have lost so much already. If we lose respect for each other, where would we be?" Freesia answered. "No place worth being."

"Should I call him that?" Hope asked.

Freesia stared at Hope for a moment, then glanced at Berty and Declan. "What makes a Fairy a Fairy is complicated," she said.

"How so?" asked Berty. Both he and Declan took seats at the table.

"Before the unification of the five tribes of Fairydom, Fairy history is sketchy at best. Fairy Dust is a mystery to all of us except the Dust Master. Officially, His Grace, is a Fairy, although not born a Fairy. When Their Majesties, the King and Queen, deem a non-Fairy a Fairy, it is said that that person can cross a Fairy Ring to enter Fairyland. I am sure the Princess knows more than I. The fact that the pendant allows Hope to use Fairy Dust in the way we can may make her a Fairy when wearing the pendant," Freesia explained. "I am sorry about the long answer Hope. Your relationship with His Grace determines how you address him, since you both may be Fairies."

Berty heard the wind chimes again.

"I'll make it easy, Hope," said Declan. "You can call me Declan."

"Come in," said Freesia.

"Okay." Hope smiled.

"What can we do for you, Your Highness?" Freesia asked.

Both Berty and Declan stood.

"I did not realize that you had company," said Delyth. "I found a lock box for Hope's Fairy Dust. We must keep it in a safe place—away from prying eyes."

"Declan and I will go outside," said Berty. "Do what you need to do."

He led Declan to a corner of the platform. "About the vault," he whispered.

"I was going to go look inside before breakfast," said Declan.

"Good. We will discuss it in my chambers," Berty said.

Before Declan could answer, Hope's door opened. Delyth

walked onto the platform. "All done," she said. Looking at Berty, she continued, "Do not worry. She will not be able to unlock that box until she has mastered Fairy Dust."

Nodding, Berty asked, "About Fairy Dust. You said that you could only give a non-Fairy Fairy Dust once, yet you gave Hope a bag of Fairy Dust. How does that work?"

"While wearing the pendant, Fairy Dust recognizes her as a Fairy," Delyth answered.

His eyebrows raised. "The dust recognizes her?"

Delyth explained, "Yes. The pendant is made from rare Fairystone. The magical natures of the stone and the dust work together. Fairy Dust's magical properties are complex and hard to explain." She paused for a breath. "Hope's Fairystone pendant will allow her to use Fairy Dust as both a weapon and a tool. Whereas you can only use Fairy Dust as a weapon and only in small quantities."

"Thank you for clarifying, Delyth. I will see you both in the morning." Berty watched them begin to cross the bridge before re-entering Hope's chambers.

The room was still. Freesia's pink satchel rested next to the stairs. He wandered into the playroom side. All sorts of games and puzzles lined the shelves. Strolling further, he saw dolls made out of everything from cloth to porcelain. Bottles full of color sitting next to containers of brushes caught his eye. Checking out a basket of balls, he heard footsteps descending.

"She is waiting for you in her bed, my Lord," Freesia said quietly.

Dropping a stitched leather ball into the basket, he smiled at the Fairy. He glanced at the other side of the room. It held enough books to counter balance the toys. Walking up the stairs, he made a beeline for Hope's room.

Hope was lying in the middle of her big bed, smiling profusely.

"This is a much bigger bed than the one you have at home. Don't get lost during the night," he teased.

"Uncle Berty," she said with a roll of her eyes. The smile

could not leave her face. "I'm going to use a bow tomorrow. Just like Declan."

"Yes, you are. Get some sleep." He kissed her on the forehead. "Goodnight."

"Night." She quickly closed her eyes.

Downstairs, Freesia had cleared the table. "I will take care of the lights, my Lord," she said.

"Breakfast is in the Reception Room. Two flights down," he told her.

She gave him a nod.

On the poorly lit platform, Berty searched for the rope Theodore mentioned. He found it next to the bundle of branches. One tug lowered a stepped bridge that curved slightly with the circumference of the trunk.

A lantern ignited when Berty stepped off the bridge. Relieved to see his leafy chamber exterior, he entered his study. He paused only to hang his cloak before heading to his own room filling bed.

Waking with the sunrise, he knew Declan would be in his vault soon. He waited for the Watcher whilst adding chapters to *the Adventures of Leigh and Marcus*.

Hearing wind chimes made him put down his pen. "Come in," he said.

Declan entered saying, "I found something." From inside his dark cloak, he extracted a small leather bound book. Placing it in front of Berty, he said, "A Watcher's journal."

Berty looked at the worn leather as Declan reported, "He talks about the Cavern. For pages, he wonders if the Cavern is the same as the caves that other traditions mention. Then, I found this." He opened the journal.

The owner of the journal drew the Watcher's symbol on a page. The words *wand*, *present*, *sword*, *future*, *bow*, and *past* were written next to their corresponding points of the star. Over the center eye was the word *key*.

An arrow from the word, *sword*, pointed to the words, *earth/stone* and *fire*. From *bow*, it said *wood* and *air*. The arrow from *wand* lead to *water* and *crystal* with a question mark.

Declan gave Berty a moment to study the drawing, then he pointed to a spot below the bottom most point that corresponded with *bow*. Circled were the words *Bow of the Moon*.

"What does it mean?" Berty asked.

"I'm not sure. I need more time with the journal," said Declan.

Picking up the journal, Berty handed it to Declan. The journal disappeared under Declan's cloak.

"I have no doubt that your vault was the target," Berty told him. Standing, he walked towards the door. "Have Theodore place extra security on your chambers."

"Why mine?"

After fastening his cloak, Berty said, "If the Bow of the Moon is one of the elements for entering the Cavern, then we must ensure its safety. You may have been unaware of having it in your possession until recently. Others, however, could have known since you left Boudon all those years ago."

"And information can be bought," Declan added with a scowl.

"Yes, but it can also innocently be passed," said Berty. "Is there anything else in your vault worth a break-in?"

"I am planning on taking a longer look later today," Declan answered.

Giving him a nod, Berty led Declan through the private passages to the Reception Room. They exited from behind the Sages' Seal to find that almost every seat was occupied around the breakfast table.

"My Lord, welcome home," said Alvar, standing. Chair legs rubbed against the wood floor as everyone stood.

"Sit, eat, please," Berty said to everyone. As he took his seat next to the Elf, he said, "How are you Alvar?"

"Doing well, thank you," answered Alvar. "In fact, everyone affected by the Fairy Dust has fully recovered."

"I am so glad to hear that," he said. He looked down the table to see Hope eating quietly. When she glanced at him, he smiled. She waved happily.

While Tenders cleared the table, Berty joined Hope and Freesia near the stairs. "Did you bring your bow?" he asked his niece.

Smiling, she showed him the bow.

"Great," said Declan, standing next to Berty. "Are you ready?"

"Yup."

"Follow me." Declan led them outside. "Alvar allows me to use targets in the Empire Guard practice area. That's where we are going today."

Walking past the barracks, Hope gawked at young recruits learning how to use their swords. Beyond the sparring area were archery targets. Declan stopped at the one at the end of the line. Hope watched guards' arrows hit their targets.

"Pay no attention to them," Declan told Hope. "They do not matter. The only place you should put your focus is on your bow."

Looking at Declan, she nodded.

"That target down there is nothing but a bundle of hay covered with colored cloth," he continued. "Now, your bow is important. You also need a quiver in which you hold your arrows." He held a cylindrical quiver by its leather strap. "This one is yours. Freesia, can you help put this on her?"

Berty held Hope's maroon cloak while Freesia buckled the leather strap across her body. Clutching onto her cloak, he watched Declan explain the different parts of the bow. Declan threw his cloak off his one shoulder to expose his quiver. In slow motion, he demonstrated how to shoot an arrow.

After his arrow hit center, Declan said, "Your turn."

Watching Declan correct her stance, Berty wondered if introducing his young niece to archery was a bad idea. How would Jon and Teresa react?

Hope released her first arrow. It sailed through the air effortlessly until it landed halfway between Hope and the target.

Crouching next to her, Declan told her things that Berty could not hear.

She nodded. Pulling another arrow from her quiver, she readied her bow.

"Aim a little higher this time," Declan told her.

When Hope raised her arm, the tip of the arrow caught the sunlight.

"Is she using real arrows?" Freesia asked.

"Yes," answered Declan. "Anything less would throw off the balance and she would learn incorrectly. She is much too old for dummy arrows."

Berty knew better than to question Declan's methods.

Hope's second attempt flew better, but still fell short of the target.

"That was much better," said Declan as he walked towards her. He adjusted her grip. "Again."

Her next arrow soared through the air over the target.

"Good! You've got the distance. I know you are going to hit the target today. Try again," Declan said.

She pulled another arrow from her quiver. Her shoulders raised as she took a deep breath. She released the arrow. It hit the target, then fell to the ground.

"Why'd it do that?" Hope asked Declan.

"Your shoulders shouldn't move when you breathe," Declan replied. "Place your bow on the ground. Stand up straight." He stood directly in front of her. "Breathe."

After watching her, he said, "Okay. I want you to breathe from here." He pointed at his stomach. "This moves as you breathe. You get deeper breaths and it doesn't change your stance."

Hope looked as if she were pushing her stomach out on purpose with each breath.

"No, no, no. Don't move your stomach," he told her. "Close your eyes and just breathe." He watched her for a moment. "Now, pick up your bow. Let one fly."

In one fluid motion, Hope extracted an arrow, set it in place, and pulled back the string. She released it without hesitation. Her arrow pierced the cloth one ring outside the center bullseye.

"I did it! Uncle Berty, did you see? I hit it!" she squealed.

"Of course I did. That was excellent," praised Berty.

"Great job! Let's do that again," Declan said.

Smiling, Hope hit the target again and again. Once she had run out of practice arrows, Declan declared that that was enough for the first day.

"Time to collect our arrows," said Declan. Walking towards the target with Hope, he made sure that no other arrows would stray their way.

Quiver full of arrows, Hope and Declan returned to Berty and Freesia. She happily fastened her cloak over her quiver.

Crouching to be eye level with Hope, Declan said, "You have a true talent for archery. It shouldn't be long before we are picking a real bow for you. Before summer is over, you will know how to string a bow and make your own arrows. When you are not with me practicing, I want you to keep your bow and quiver in your bedroom, so that you can easily get it at anytime. Okay?"

Her brown curls bounced as she nodded.

"Let's go put those away and see if your mom and dad called," said Berty.

"Okay," said Hope. Freesia grabbed her free hand before walking out of the practice area.

"She's going to be a great archer," Declan told Berty as they followed Hope and Freesia. "Could rival the Elves."

"With you teaching her," said Berty.

"I can only impart knowledge. Skill is hers and hers alone," Declan said.

Berty nodded in agreement. "Thank you for taking the time to teach her."

Smiling, Declan said, "I enjoy the challenge."

Before reaching the doors to the Empire Tree, they saw Delyth leaving a white cob house.

"She has a lot of visits to make," mentioned Declan. "The way she described the chaos from Millicent's Fairy Dust." He shook his head as if he were trying to shake her words out of his memory.

"The limited amount I saw was horrific," Berty said. "I am glad she is checking on those who were affected."

In the Receiving Room, Berty climbed the stairs behind Freesia.

"I wish to request an audience with Declan, Advisor to the Emperor," an old man said.

"Who is making the request?" asked the receptionist.

"Oberon, Senior Craftsman of Boudon," the old man proudly stated.

Declan stopped climbing. Turning, Berty watched Declan approach the old man.

"Grandpa?" Declan said to the man.

Chapter Nineteen
Gifts

"Declan?" The old man threw his arms around Declan. His cane fell to the floor as tears navigated his lined face. "It has been too long."

"I'm granting the request," Declan told the receptionist. Picking the fallen cane off the ground, he said, "Can you make it up the stairs?"

"That piece of wood is for decoration," said Oberon.

Declan stood aside to allow his grandfather up the stairs first. Without his cane, Oberon climbed the stairs with ease.

In the Reception Room, Berty told Hope, "Go ahead up. I am going to speak to Declan first."

Carrying her bow, Hope raced up the stairs.

"We do not run in the tree," Freesia said firmly as she followed.

"My Lord," called Declan, emerging from the room below, "I would like you to meet my grandfather."

Oberon bowed. "Oberon of Boudon, my Lord. What an honor."

"The honor is mine," said Berty. "Declan has spoken about you."

Oberon smiled with a tear in his eye.

"What brings you to the Sages' Grove, Grandpa?" asked Declan.

"Your brothers came home telling a story. They had just

finished selling a large order of bows in and around Fairyland. Cecil told us that you were an Advisor to the Emperor. All Vander could do is accuse you of stealing that bow. I told them I gave you that bow the night...," he looked around the room. "I gather you can use it the way it was intended?"

Declan nodded.

Not wanting to intrude on Declan's reunion with his grandfather any longer, Berty said, "It was nice meeting you, Oberon. I have a matter to which I must attend. Please do us the honor of staying in the Empire Tree for as long as you will be in the Sages' Grove."

"Thank you, my Lord," Oberon said with another bow.

As Berty ascended, he could hear Oberon saying, "Tell me about your life, Declan. I want to know everything."

He was glad that something good came out of the altercation with his brothers. The muddy mess in the woods made him think about Silvia. He wondered how she fared in Fairyland Castle. They were apart for only a day, but it might had well have been an eternity.

Finding himself in front of Hope's chambers, he mumbled, "Silvia will be fine. I should worry about me. What am I going to say to Teresa?" He decided not to worry.

When he stepped inside," he saw Hope and Freesia reading a book at the table.

Hope tore her eyes from the page to look at her uncle. "We're reading a Sage's Tale. It's about Dragons," she told him.

Laughing a little, he said, "Sounds exciting. Are you ready to go see if your parents called?"

"Ooh, yes!"

"Think you better put on your cloak." Looking at Freesia, he said, "We shouldn't be gone long. Just a quick trip through the portal."

Jumping out of her chair, Hope ran to the cloak tree. Before her little hands touched her maroon cloak, ringing filled the room. Freesia looked beside the stairs.

Berty's eyes followed her line of sight to an old-fashioned

white and brass rotary phone like the one that appeared in his house.

"Mommy! Daddy!" Hope screamed as she ran towards the phone.

"Do not touch that phone," said Berty in a more disciplinarian manner than he thought he could muster.

Hope stopped in her tracks.

Crossing the room, Berty picked up the receiver. "Hello?"

"Berty, finally," said Teresa's voice. "We tried your cell a few times, but it went straight to voicemail."

"Sorry about that, Teresa. I don't get service here. How's everything in Africa?"

"Missing Hope already. Going well, so far. It's different here, but it has only been a couple of days in a strange, new place. Glad we left Hope with you. How is she doing?"

"I'll let her tell you herself. She is right here," said Berty.

"Let me put you on speaker. Jon, come here," Teresa said. "Okay."

"Hold on," he told them. He held the phone towards Hope. "It's for you."

She ran to Berty. Holding the receiver to her ear, she squealed, "Mommy! Daddy!"

He walked away to let her speak with her parents. "I'm having the best time with Uncle Berty," he heard her say.

He sat at the table across from Freesia. As he watched Hope dance a little while she talked, he said, "I'm guessing the phone will be a permanent fixture in this room."

"That allows her to speak with her parents?" asked Freesia.

"Yes, but only when it rings," he explained. "If it rings when I am not here, then you must answer it."

"How?"

Berty never thought he would have to explain how to use a telephone. "Pick it off its base. Hold the top to your ear. The other near your mouth. All you have to say is hello and the person on the other end will tell you what they want. I can't imagine it being anyone other than Hope's parents. Unless it's her grandparents."

"Sounds simple enough," she said.

"One other thing. When speaking on the phone, refer to me as Mister Chase," he added.

"Uncle Berty," Hope called. "Mommy and Daddy want to talk to you."

"Excuse me," he said to Freesia before he walked towards Hope. Taking the phone, he said, "I'm back." He could hear Jon laughing.

"Who decided to call a nanny a Fairy Godmother?" Teresa asked.

"Her name is Freesia," said Berty. "She is very good and has been a big help."

"Jon, stop laughing. I can't hear your brother. Sorry," said Teresa. "That's good. I hear she met Silvia."

"Before mom. I don't know, Berty," Jon teased. "And the tree house... Is that because the tree in our yard growing up was too small to build anything?"

"Absolutely," Berty said with a roll of his eyes.

Jon's laughing subsided. "Thanks, Berty," he said. "Her friends have been few and far between at school. We felt that she needed to feel like she was having the adventure of a lifetime."

"And it sounds like she already is," added Teresa.

"Honey, don't cry," Jon said.

"Tears of joy. I'm happy because she's happy," said Teresa.

"We've got to get going," said Jon. "We're meeting clients for dinner."

"Thank you so much," said Teresa. "We will call again soon."

"You are very welcome," Berty said. "You guys enjoy. Talk to you soon. Bye."

"Bye," they both said.

Hanging up the phone, Berty felt better about everything. He walked to the table where Hope sat.

Freesia returned the book to the shelf whilst saying, "Put your cloak on, Hope. We are going to spend the rest of the morning outside."

Fastening her cloak, Hope asked, "Can we visit the tree Ashley came from?"

"Not today," said Berty. "You are to stay inside the walls of the Sages' Grove. There is plenty to explore."

"Are you coming outside, too?" she asked.

He looked into the big, brown eyes staring up at him. Swimming beneath the brown was apprehension and a touch of fear. "Of course I am," he told her.

Only looking partially relieved, she allowed Freesia to usher her through the tree. Outside, she asked Freesia all sorts of questions. "Why are all the houses white?" What are those?" She pointed to the market stalls. She asked about each item being sold.

Beyond the market, kids played in the clearing where the Wassail Kettlebarrel would be constructed in the fall. Hope watched the girls and boys with a longing to join them in her eyes.

"Go ahead. You can play," said Freesia.

Hope shook her head.

"Why not?" Freesia asked.

She shook her head again.

Freesia smiled warmly. "You're allowed to play."

"What if," said Hope barely above a whisper, "what if they don't like me."

"That is just not possible," Freesia told her.

Hope's eyes began to moisten.

Crouching next to Hope, Berty asked, "Hope, what's wrong?"

"The kids at school make fun of me," she admitted.

"Why do they make fun of you?" asked Berty.

Hope shrugged her shoulders.

"Well all those kids in school would be awfully jealous right now because *you* are here and *they* are not," Berty said.

Hope smiled a little.

"Don't let them stop you from having fun. Because, you know what? They're not worth an ounce of you," he encouraged.

240

"Those kids, however, are not the same as the ones from school. I say, give them a chance. If you don't like them, then we'll go back inside and finish that Sage's Tale."

Smiling brightly, Hope said, "Okay, Uncle Berty."

Freesia wiped her eyes as she and Berty watched Hope run towards the kids, saying, "Can I play?"

"Come on," said one of the girls, "you don't want to get tagged."

Berty could not help but smile while he watched Hope run around with the children of the Sages' Grove. Her laughter filled the clearing.

He and Freesia found seats on a nearby bench. "Will she be returning to this school?" Freesia asked him.

"Yes, at the end of summer."

"How should she deal with her offenders? Defend herself or ignore them?"

He stared at Hope for a moment before replying. "I am only her uncle. But, I am afraid that if she ignores them, then she will ignore the world. Personally, I believe in defending herself is the better path against those bullies. I will speak to her parents about this. They may not be aware of the extent of it."

Nodding, Freesia said, "Then until I hear otherwise, we will work on defense."

"Thank you, Freesia."

Hope ran towards the bench where they sat.

"See you later, Hope," said one of the kids.

Stopping, she waved, "Bye!" When she arrived at the bench, her eyes gleamed. "Everyone is going home to eat," she told them. "They'll be back later."

"Well, I'm hungry," said Berty.

"I'm starving," Hope exaggerated.

As they strolled into the Empire Tree, Berty asked, "How was it?"

"I had. So! Much! Fun! They are nothing like the kids at school," said Hope. "Can I go back out later?"

"As long as it is okay with Freesia," Berty said.

"I do not see why not, but we must make it back in time for your lessons with Her Highness," said Freesia.

Throughout lunch, all Hope could talk about were the games she played that morning. After they ate, Hope asked Berty, "Are you coming?"

Declan caught Berty's eye with an I-need-to-speak-with-you gaze.

"I would like to, but I can't right now," said Berty. "I need to speak with Declan. You have lots of fun and listen to Freesia."

"Okay." She gave him a hug, then jetted down the steps with Freesia.

"Can we go upstairs?" Declan asked him quietly.

With a nod, Berty and Declan left Oberon speaking with Delyth and Alfred. Once inside the Roundtable Room, Declan closed the door.

"My grandfather asked me to go for a walk with him," Declan said. His hands fidgeted.

"Where?" asked Berty, taking a seat at the table.

Declan sat partially on a chair. "To see an old friend. He promised. Wants me to meet his friend." He flashed a smile.

"What's wrong?"

"I don't know. He wants to leave this afternoon," said Declan. "I won't be able to study the journal until I get back. I'm guessing a couple of days. Do we have the time?"

"As long as that journal stays in your vault until your return," Berty told him. "My concern is for your safety. You should take some Empire Guards with you."

"Grandpa wants it to be just him and me. Like old times."

"What about the locket? If there's trouble, I can send people," suggested Berty.

"I'll wear it," Declan agreed. "But, permit me to request that only you watch."

"You have my word."

"Thank you, my Lord," said Declan, rising from his chair. He extracted his large, gold Watcher's locket from his pocket. After securing it around his neck, he tapped it twice with the tip of his wand. He tucked the locket behind his shirt. "We'll be leaving soon. Tell Hope I'll make up the lessons when I return."

"Be safe," said Berty before he accompanied Declan back to the Reception Room.

Sitting alone, Oberon smiled at his grandson. He took a sip from his goblet as Declan hurried down the steps.

"May I join you?" Berty asked Oberon.

Surprised, Oberon replied, "Of course, my Lord."

"I'm sorry you have to leave so soon, Oberon."

"Promises must be kept. My grandson is a busy man."

"Yes, he is."

Oberon smiled with pride. "I knew that one day he would be the best archer Boudon has ever seen. Even if he is no longer in Boudon. He has made a good life for himself. He has good friends. He is happy. I could not ask for more."

"Declan is a good man," said Berty.

Oberon's light eyes welled.

Declan reappeared in the room, saying, "Provisions are waiting for us downstairs."

Rising, Oberon said, "My Lord, meeting you has been such an honor."

Berty stood as well. "The honor has been mine. Safe journey."

With a smile, Oberon bowed.

Giving Berty a small nod, Declan placed his arm around his grandfather. Berty watched them descend to the room below.

He wanted to check on Hope, but did not want Declan to think that he was following him. Turning, he climbed the stairs until they reached their end. Berty opened an arched wooden door.

In the center of the curved Watching Room sat the still miniature of the Sages' Grove. He blew into the hollow trunk of the mini Empire Tree. Tiny likenesses of every person in the Sages' Grove appeared.

Declan and his grandfather, complete with cane, disappeared beyond the gates. His eyes found Freesia in her light pink cloak sitting on the same bench as earlier. In her lap was fabric held taut in a wooden circle like his grandmother used when she did her needlepoint. Every few stitches, Freesia would look over at Hope.

His niece ran around with the kids of the Sages' Grove. She seemed to spend a lot of time with one girl in particular. The girls whispered and giggled together. Berty thought Hope's new friend looked familiar, but he could not place her.

When the Sages' Grove lanterns flickered to life, the girls waved goodbye to each other. He was happy that she found a friend. Blowing into the tree once again, the people vanished.

He extracted the large gold locket from the depths of his pocket. Using the rod, he depressed the pupil of the carved Watcher's Symbol. When he opened the locket, he saw Declan lighting a fire with a flint.

"Do you love her?" asked Oberon.

Declan poked the logs to spread the fire while blowing on the flames. "With all my heart," he answered. He glanced at his grandfather who stirred a pot.

"Then what are you waiting for?" his grandfather asked.

"She's a Fairy. I'm... not." Declan grabbed the pot, then placed it next to the fire.

"Are you or are you not the Duke of Fairyland?" Oberon said.

"It's just a title, Grandpa."

"Ah," said Oberon. "The title is merely a string of words. But words are important. They convey meaning. If words didn't mean something, then there's no point in using them. And if there is no point in words, then a man's word can never be his bond. Therefore, respect, honor, loyalty, and decency would cease to exist. We would live in a chaotic, dark world where truth and lies are interchangeable and people have no trust in one another. That is not a world I want. Do you?"

Declan sighed. "No, of course not."

"Good. Stir that before it burns," his grandfather said.

Closing the locket, Berty tucked it in his pocket before leaving the Watching Room.

In the Reception Room, the inhabitants of the tree began

gathering for dinner. Berty took a seat at the table next to Hope. "Did you have fun this afternoon?" he asked her.

She smiled. "Tons. I met this girl named Alina. Me and Alina had—"

"Alina and I," corrected Berty.

"Alina and I had so much fun together. We're gonna play again tomorrow," Hope continued. "After my archery lesson."

Looking at Hope's elated face, he hated being the one to tell her. "Declan had to postpone your lessons," he said.

"Till when?" Her face dropped.

"Just for a few days. He promised to make them up," said Berty.

"Okay." She sounded so sad.

"How about you have lessons with me twice a day," suggested Delyth.

Hope's big, brown eyes found the Fairy sitting across the table. Smiling at her, Hope said more cheerfully, "Okay."

Berty accompanied Hope, Freesia and Delyth to Hope's chambers. Outside her door, he said, "Have a good lesson with Delyth. I'll be in my chambers if you need me. This bridge takes you directly to me."

"Can't you come, too?" Hope asked quietly.

"Since your uncle cannot use Fairy Dust the way you will be able to," Delyth said sweetly, "he will not be able to be present during practice. Until you have mastered it, it would be unwise to use it in front of him."

Hope nodded.

"I want to hear all about it," Berty told Hope. "So you better come up to see me later."

A smile returned to Hope's face. "I will, Uncle Berty."

He watched the trio enter Hope's chambers before crossing the bridge to his own.

Entering his study, he threw his cloak on the hook. He opened his locket, then set it on his desk. After passing his hand over the open locket, a fire-illuminated Oberon hologram sat beyond his desk.

"What do you mean a Watcher shouldn't use magic?" Oberon asked.

"It's unethical. In essence, you're stealing someone else's magic for your own use. The Watchers' Guild outlawed it. Any Watcher caught using magic for personal gain faces severe consequences. Watchers can see magic, find magic, transfer magic, and even transport it," explained Declan. "There was a time when magic flowed freely from tree to tree. That magic was free for Watchers to use. Because, once you used it, the magic returned to the trees."

"What happened? Why doesn't magic flow freely anymore?" his grandfather asked.

Declan looked at the dark branches overhead. "I don't know, Grandpa. Eirawen must not have been the only culprit."

"Who?"

"A crazed, power hungry, magic stealer," said Declan as he looked at Oberon again. "The mist lifted when she died—the magic returned to its rightful owners."

"Not all the magic is gone, right?"

"No. There is just less of it."

"Good," said Oberon. "Let's get some sleep. We have a lot of walking tomorrow."

The wind chimes rang gently in Berty's study. Closing the locket, he said, "Come in."

Hope entered his study with a huge smile. "All done, Uncle Berty." Her eyes darted around the dim study while Berty rose from behind his desk.

"Pick a chair," he said. Once they were both seated, he asked, "So? How was your first lesson in Fairy Dust?"

Exhaling loudly, she answered, "Hard." Her fingers straightened her brown curls. "It's so easy when Delyth does it."

He reached out a hand to clasp her little hand. "That's okay. It will get easier. You have another lesson with Delyth in the morning. Ask lots of questions. If there is anything you don't understand, just let her know." Giving her a warm smile, he squeezed her hand, then let go.

"There's too much to learn," she said whilst using her hand for dramatic effect.

Waving his hand in front of him, he said, "Bah! You'll know everything in no time."

A smile faintly returned to her face. The smile quickly turned into a yawn.

"I saw that," Berty teased.

Hope quickly shut her mouth with her cheeks puffed out like a chipmunk. Using his index fingers, Berty popped her chipmunk cheeks. She broke out into uncontrollable laughter. Laughing with her made him feel the child-like innocence of his youth.

When the laughing calmed to chuckling, Berty said, "Come on, let's go back to your room."

Jumping off the club chair, Hope said, "I have more books than you do."

"I bet you do," he said with a little laugh as he ushered her to her chambers.

When they entered, Freesia looked up from her needlework. "Are we ready for bed?"

Hope nodded. "Goodnight, Uncle Berty," she said giving him a big hug.

"Good night, Hope. I'll see you after your lessons," he told her.

Returning to his study, he continued writing *the Adventures of Leigh and Marcus*.

He woke with the morning sunlight streaming through his window. Before jumping into the shower, he opened the locket. Declan smothered the fire's remnants with dirt, then followed his grandfather through the woods.

As Berty walked down his spiral staircase, he heard Declan say, "You still haven't told me where we're going."

"That's right," said Oberon.

Declan stopped. "You're not taking me to Boudon, are you?"

Berty sat at his desk.

Turning, Oberon looked at Declan. "Of course not." Oberon

sounded sympathetic and reassuring. "My old friend is not a Boudonian," he explained further, "but an Elf."

"The maiden who gave you the bow?" inquired Declan.

Oberon smiled. "Yes." He continued walking.

Hearing the wind chimes, Berty contained the sound and picture back inside the locket, then hid it in his lap. "Come in," he said.

"Good morning, my Lord," said Theodore. He carried a breakfast tray to the table.

"Good morning, Theodore. How is everything?" asked Berty.

"Going very well. I have been experimenting with allowing Sean outside the Empire Tree more as a reward for good work," Theodore said. "Since I started, his performance has been improving exponentially."

"Excellent. Thank you, Theodore," he said, smiling at the young Dwarf.

With a bow, Theodore left Berty alone with his breakfast.

He passed his hand over the open locket allowing the holographic forest to fill his study. Sitting at the table, he ate while watching them trek through the lush underbrush.

Stopping, Oberon leaned on his stick. "We're here," he said.

"The middle of the forest?" Declan looked around.

"This is where I was told to come," said Oberon. "I am glad you came with me. It gave us some extra time together, no matter how short."

"Grandpa, what's going on?"

He gave his grandson a warm look. "Good-bye, Declan."

"What do you mean, good-bye? Why is this good-bye?"

"I made a promise."

"I don't understand."

Oberon looked at his grandson with the love only a grandfather could give. "Declan, I'm dying."

"What? No. You walked all this way." His voice cracked a little.

"Being able to walk here was part of the promise that I made. I am glad that I was able to see the man you have become."

"Maybe you can be healed. Please let me try," Declan pleaded.

Reaching for Declan's hand, Oberon said, "No. It's too late for that. I am so proud of you."

"Grandpa," was all Declan could manage to say.

The bottom of the hologram got wavy. Berty figured that Declan's eyes were collecting tears.

"Promise me, Declan, that you will make the trip to Boudon someday to see your mother. You could even take that lovely young lady with you," said Oberon.

The scene moved as if Declan were nodding his head.

"I don't want you to go," Declan said. The woods blurred.

All Berty could see was Declan's arms on Oberon's back. He guessed they were hugging.

"Hello again, Oberon," said a female voice.

With a wipe of his eyes and a few blinks, the scene sharpened. An old Elf woman stood about five feet in front of them. Her long, silvery-white hair glistened in the filtered sunlight as her white dress contrasted with the dark browns and greens of the forest.

"You look as beautiful as the day I met you, Zederra," said Oberon. "This is my grandson, Declan."

She blushed a little. "Declan knows me by another name," Zederra said. "We met while he was in Irmingard." She smiled. "You have chosen well, Oberon. You have kept your promise to me. Now, I will keep mine."

"Wait. What promise?" asked Declan.

"Your grandfather was to give the Bow of the Moon to its rightful archer," Zederra explained. "In return, I am to give him the Gift of the Elves."

"What good is being able to be invisible in a tree now?" Declan asked.

"Invisibility is only part of the Elf Gift," she said. "Are you ready Oberon?"

"In a moment." Turning to Declan, Oberon said, "I love you, Declan."

"I love you, too, Grandpa."

Oberon walked to Zederra's side. "I'm ready," he told her.

"After I begin the incantation, the path will illuminate for you. Walk along that path. Continue walking until you and the wind become one," she instructed.

Declan watched his grandfather smile warmly at him while Zederra spoke in a language Berty could not understand. Zederra's silvery hair and white dress fluttered as wind entered their part of the forest. Turning his head from Declan, Oberon strolled towards a section of trees. He walked away from Declan, approaching something only he could see. Zederra's words were the only sound.

Declan's eyes did not stray from his grandfather's path. He gasped softly when his grandfather disappeared.

The wind blew gently through the branches. Zederra's incantation stopped.

"Declan," she called to him.

His eyes found her.

"Do not be sad, Declan," she said. "Like great Warriors, your grandfather is not truly gone. If you listen carefully, you will be able to hear his whispers in the wind."

He did not say anything. Berty could tell that he watched her leave without really seeing.

The trees blurred as Declan wailed like a wounded animal. The lost, exiled child inside of him mourned.

Declan's cries pierced Berty's heart. After wiping his eyes, Berty brought the picture and sound back to the confines of the locket. He did not want to intrude on Declan's sorrow any longer.

Chapter Twenty
The Bow of the Moon

When Berty heard the wind chimes, he said, "Come in."

"Play time, Uncle Berty!" said Hope as she ran into his study. Stopping in front of his desk, she asked, "Are you crying?"

Gazing at the brown-eyed bundle of happiness, he said, "Just something in my eye. How did your lessons with Delyth go this morning?"

"Good," said Hope.

"Well," he corrected. "The lessons went well. Not, the lessons went good."

"Well," repeated Hope. "Fairy Dust was more fun this morning."

"Good. Are you ready to go play with your new friends?" he asked.

"Uh-huh. You coming, too, Uncle Berty?" Her eyes begged him to say yes.

Not wanting to disappoint, he said, "I will for a little while, then I need to do some work." Standing, he closed the locket, then slipped it into his pocket.

While he threw on his cloak, he asked, "Did you come up here all by yourself?"

"Today, but not last night," Hope told him as they walked to her chambers. "Freesia walked with me."

Cloaked in pink, Freesia waited on the platform. "Good

morning, my Lord."

"Good morning."

Hope skipped across the bridge into the trunk. As she galloped down the stairs, Freesia called to her. "Do not go past the Reception Room."

"I am sorry she is such a handful. Is there anything I can do?" Berty asked quietly.

"She is inquisitive and excited about everything. There is nothing wrong with a happy child," replied Freesia.

When they reached the Reception Room, Hope was on the dais studying the Sages' Seal.

"Hope, we're heading outside," Freesia called.

"That's the same design on your desk, Uncle Berty," said Hope, jumping off the dais.

"Pretty cool, huh?" Berty said.

Hope nodded with a smile as her hand found Freesia's.

Outside, Hope spotted her friends. "There's Alina. Can I go?" she asked.

Letting go of her hand, Freesia said, "Go ahead."

As he watched Hope run towards her new friends, he smiled.

People carrying gourd lanterns caught Berty's eye. They placed them along both sides of the path to a building whose door was draped in black.

"The house is in mourning," explained Freesia. "With every window and the door covered, it means someone important inside died."

"That's the Watchers' Guild," said Berty surprised. He saw the sign on the building also covered with black.

"Then their Guild Master has died," said Freesia. "The guild will be in lockdown for at least one day. At night time, the only light will come from the candles inside those gourds."

"Lockdown?"

"The guild will be in a state of flux. During that time, no one will be able to come or go from that building," Freesia explained further. "After, it will open to guild members who were locked out, then to the public."

"Why the lighted gourds?" Berty asked.

"It is a sign of support for the ones who have lost. They light the path to remind the mourners to not lose their way. Grief can make one nearly blind," she said.

Berty could feel the large Watcher's Locket press into his leg as he sat on the bench. His heart went out to Declan. He wondered if Declan needed a lighted path home.

Trying to stay filled with Hope's contagious happiness, Berty speculated how he could tell Declan of the Guild Master's death since the lockets could not be used while in watching mode.

"My Lord," said an annoying voice Berty tried hard not to despise.

"What is it, Sean?" Berty asked.

Crouched next to the bench, Sean's gray eyes darted around the courtyard. "I saw something suspicious early this morning."

"You should be alerting the Empire Guards," said Berty.

"I... it didn't seem suspicious at the time," Sean said.

Berty's patience wore thin. "What was suspicious?"

Lowering his voice, Sean said, "A group of Watchers seem to have crept out of the Watchers' Guild not long before the black cloth covered the sign."

Raising an eyebrow, he asked, "Why do you feel it suspicious?"

"They acted as though they were planning something," answered Sean. "I recognized that behavior."

"Of course you did." Berty remembered Sean's crimes all too well. "Where did they go?"

"Outside the gates."

"How many?"

"Four."

Berty felt like he had been hit with a brick. The Watchers' Guild Master was dead. Declan was in the woods somewhere alone. According to the journal Declan found, Watchers connected the Bow of the Moon with the Cavern. A group of Watchers calling themselves the Cavern had been harassing Declan.

"Freesia, tell Hope I'll be back in a day or so," said Berty. He realized what he had to do. "Sean, quietly grab your sword and meet me by the Empire Tree entrance."

Sean bowed before scurrying.

Rising from the bench, he saw that Hope noticed him. He waved with a forced smile. She waved back. Turning, he calmly power-walked inside the tree.

As he climbed the stairs to the Reception Room, he called for Theodore.

"Yes, my Lord?" said Theodore at the top.

"I need four horses, one that will follow the others without a rider, immediately," Berty stated. "Have Edwin meet me outside. Sean is accompanying us."

Theodore disappeared as quickly as he appeared. Opening the locket, Declan still sat, staring into the trees. He breathed loudly while the picture in the locket blurred slightly.

Keeping the locket easily accessible, Berty raced down the steps. Edwin and Sean waited for him next to the horses.

"My Lord?" said Edwin.

Saying nothing, Berty mounted a horse. The other two followed his lead. Before more could be said, Berty led them through the gates of the Sages' Grove.

With his free hand, he extracted the locket. "Which way?" he asked it.

The locket glowed orange. It rested in his open palm, then turned slightly. Berty directed his horse to where the locket pointed.

They raced along the path the locket took them. He pushed his horse faster. The Watchers left hours before they did.

The lush forest muffled the sound of hooves propelling them. Berty knew not how deep or shallow he breathed nor of the rate his heart beat. The trees through which he had woven a path his eyes did not see. His mind focused only on getting to Declan.

Burning hot in his hand, the locket quickly blinked glowing orange. He pulled back on the reins. When his horse stopped, he dismounted.

As he surveyed the area, he recognized it from seeing through Declan's eyes. All he saw were trees and underbrush. The locket in his hand blinked furiously.

A glint of gold sparkled under a light green carpet. Reaching for it, his fingers grasped a large oval hunk of gold. Both of his hands held Watcher's Lockets.

"Declan's," said Edwin, looking over Berty's shoulder.

Berty flipped both lockets open. Insides together, he placed his locket on top of Declan's so that the picture side of one faced the sound side of the other. Clasping his hands around the lockets, he said, "Show me."

The lockets projected a hologram of the same woods in which they stood. Berty could hear the swooshing of clothing brushing over vegetation.

Two men appeared, holding wands towards Declan. "Well, well, well," said the bigger of the two. "What have we here?"

Declan said nothing.

"Look, Nolan," the larger man continued, "it's Declan the Great with his fancy new cloak."

Nolan snickered.

"Go away," said Declan halfheartedly.

"We rather like it here. So, I think we'll stay."

From behind trees, two more men appeared, one on each side of Nolan and the nameless speaker. Both men also held their wands towards Declan.

Slowly, Declan stood. "What do you want?" he asked with a cold directness in his voice.

"Your fancy covering is inspiring," the man said. "I'll be gentlemanly and ask nicely. Give us the Bow of the Moon."

The other three men laughed.

"What makes you think I have it?" asked Declan.

"You're always carrying that bow with you," said Nolan.

"Just because I have a bow doesn't mean it's the Bow of the Moon," Declan said.

"According to my research it is," the first man said.

"Your research, Aaron?" asked Declan.

"To find the Cavern, you need to do research," Aaron responded.

"The Cavern is a myth," Declan dismissed.

"In every myth is a kernel of truth. Now, this chat grows tiresome," said Aaron.

The men flicked their wands at Declan. The underbrush started to back away from Declan as if he were being hoisted off the ground.

"The Guild Master—" Declan began.

"Won't be doing anything now," finished Aaron.

"What did you do?" Declan asked angrily. "Put me down and fight me like a man. Only cowards steal magic."

The men laughed. "Cowards? Us? What would you call a man too afraid to use the magic surrounding him?" taunted Aaron.

"None of you have any honor," said Declan. "Magic is not a toy."

"Who needs honor when we'll be richer and more powerful than the Emperor?" asked Nolan.

"Do you think you are going to rule the Land of Sages?" Declan asked.

"The world will grovel on its knees," said Aaron.

Trees pointed down while the ground hovered above their heads. Declan must have been flipped upside down. Something shiny fell into Declan's face.

"Look boys, he's wearing his locket. Can't have you communicating with someone now can we?" Aaron said. "Bring him down."

Declan crashed to the ground with a groan. The tips of three wands descended upon him. The scene disappeared.

"What happened?" Sean asked.

Separating the lockets, Berty answered, "They removed his locket."

Edwin studied the ground while Berty pocketed both lockets separately.

"He was dragged away from here recently," said Edwin.

Following the tracks, Edwin led Berty and Sean through the woods. Not too far from where they found the locket, Edwin held up a hand, signaling to stop.

"Is he tight?" a man asked.

Edwin pointed to a tree.

Understanding, Berty nodded.

As Edwin climbed the tree, he became invisible.

Berty and Sean crept closer to the source of the voice.

"This is a nice bow," another man taunted.

Hiding behind a bush, they peeked through its branches.

The large man who Declan called Aaron, leaned against a tree. Another man stood to his side, pointing his wand at Declan who was tied to a tree with a piece of cloth wrapped around his mouth. Declan's quiver lay on the ground. The man called Nolan ran his fingers along the curves of Declan's bow.

Muffled sounds came from Declan's gagged mouth.

"Destroy wands," Berty mouthed to Sean.

As Sean nodded, Berty's eyes could not find the fourth man.

"Stand up, slowly," said a man's voice from behind them. The fourth man found them.

Glancing at the man, Berty saw him pointing his wand at them like someone would threaten with a gun. Both Berty and Sean stood. Their hiding place was no longer hidden.

Aaron set an arrow in the bow, targeting them. As Aaron pulled the string to his shoulder, Berty glanced at the ropes holding Declan. Staring at Aaron's fingers, Berty waited.

Aaron's fingers opened, releasing the arrow.

Berty thought, cut.

The arrow flew through the air. Berty watched it turn away from him.

Declan caught the arrow in his newly freed hand. Removing the gag, he stepped over the fallen rope.

Aaron scrambled for another arrow.

Swords unsheathed. Leaping from the branches, Edwin landed between Berty and the three Watchers.

Spinning, Berty sliced the fourth man's wand. Sean sprinted

257

after Nolan.

"Return to me," said Declan with his arms outstretched. The Bow of the Moon escaped from Aaron's grip. Both the bow and the quiver flew into Declan's hands.

Trying to point his wand, Aaron screamed worse than a little girl. Edwin's sword chopped the wand in half.

The third man fled, dropping his wand. Retrieving it from the forest floor, Berty's blade cut through the thin piece of wood.

Declan pointed an arrow directly at Aaron. "The Bow of the Moon would never help you find the Cavern. It reserves its magic only for its chosen archer. That would be me. Consider yourselves expelled from the Watchers' Guild."

Chapter Twenty-one
Friends

After the wandless Aaron and Nolan hastily disappeared into the woods, Declan lowered his bow. "Collect the wand pieces. They need to be given to the Guild Master," he said. He secured his quiver and bow to his back before throwing his cloak over his body.

Approaching Berty, he said, "Thank you. I was so frozen that I couldn't stop them on my own."

"You're welcome," said Berty. Holding Declan's locket in his hand, he said, "I think you lost this."

Taking his locket from Berty, Declan stared at the Watcher's Symbol carved into the gold.

"About the Guild Master," Berty began.

"He's dead, isn't he?" asked Declan.

"Yes."

Declan nodded. Glancing at his locket, he placed it inside his cloak.

When all the pieces of wood had been gathered, Edwin led them to where they left the horses.

Walking with Declan, Berty said, "I'm sorry about your grandfather. How are you?"

"Thanks. I've been better," Declan admitted. "At least the group who call themselves the Cavern will be less prominent within the Watchers' Guild."

Once they reached the horses, Declan added, "Grandpa would

have liked that my friends came to rescue me."

"I'm sorry that you didn't have more time with him," said Berty before mounting his horse.

"Thank you," Declan said. Grasping the horn of the saddle, he placed his foot in the stirrup. He hoisted himself onto the saddle, saying, "Fate works in strange ways. Might not be what you want or how you want it, but it gives you what you need to make you stronger. Grandpa said, 'Only the strong fulfill their destinies.' He was strong and I will be, too."

Smiling approvingly, Berty said, "You already are." Turning his horse around, he led them through the forest.

Although the days grew long, night had commandeered the sky before they reached the Sages' Grove. The gourd luminary brightly lighted an otherwise dark Watchers' Guild. After dismounting, Declan gazed in that direction.

As they entered the Empire Tree, Declan said, "I'm going to go first thing in the morning. I'll return in time to give Hope her archery lesson."

"You don't have to," said Berty. "Hope will understand."

"Yes, I do. It is my way of honoring him."

Berty nodded to let Declan know that he understood.

In the Reception Room, Delyth and Lark sat in their robes with a pot of tea. Upon seeing the men, the women stood. Delyth said, "I couldn't sleep. When I knocked on Lark's door, she offered to keep me company."

While Declan only had eyes for Delyth, Berty said, "Sean, Edwin, thank you."

Sean bowed. Berty thought he almost saw a smile on Sean's face as he crossed the room.

"You worried about me?" Declan asked Delyth.

"Of course," she answered. "Whenever we're apart."

Declan's legs automatically brought him close to her. His one hand caressed her cheek before sliding into her long, dark curls. His other hand rested on the small of her back, pulling her towards him. Their foreheads met. Her hands clutched his dark cloak as his lips found hers.

Smiling, Lark guided her husband onto the bridge that led to their chambers.

Berty disappeared behind the Sages' Seal. Climbing his private staircase, he wondered if Declan and Delyth's public kiss would change anything.

He wished his relationship with Silvia could change. Every step made him miss her even more. Closing his eyes, he saw the dancing reflection of lantern light in dark red hair. A delicate hand lifted a porcelain cup. As Silvia sipped, her other hand turned a large, yellowed page. She sat alone in the Fairyland Castle library, pouring over old tomes. Berty knew that she searched for answers in the vast knowledge pool procured by the Fairies.

When he opened his eyes, he entered the Scepter Room. The scepter glowed a bright claret. He glanced at it as he crossed the room. Within the crystal's many facets he saw a woman wearing what looked like an animal hide bikini. Blue markings covered almost every inch of her exposed skin, even her face. Her dark, wild hair reached her waist. She gazed as though she could see Berty, then said, "Seven sages. Seven seals. Seven secrets. Soon sinister steals."

Berty blinked. The image of the woman was gone. He stared into the depths of the claret crystal, wondering what had just happened. Seeing nothing more, he left the scepter to its mysteries.

While he walked across the bridge to Hope's chambers, a warm breeze caressed his cloak. Hope's bundle of branches was dark. He was sure that she had gone to bed hours before. Entering anyway, he magically lit a lantern. He carried it up to Hope's bedroom.

She slept peacefully in the center of her bed. As he smoothed her sheets around her, she opened her eyes halfway. "I'm just saying goodnight. Go back to sleep," he told her. Smiling, she closed her eyes. "See you at breakfast," he said before leaving her room.

Depositing the lantern where he found it, he returned to his chambers.

Morning arrived too quickly for Berty. Trying to shake the grogginess, he crossed the bridge to Hope's chambers. When he entered, he found breakfast waiting on the table. "Morning," he tried not to mumble.

Cheerfully, Hope hugged him, saying, "Morning, Uncle Berty. Are you having breakfast with us?"

"I am."

She squeezed him harder.

Once she let go, he added, "Need to make sure you have strength for archery this morning."

"Declan's back!" Waving her arms above her head, Hope danced around in place.

Seeing her happy made him happy. As soon as she had finished eating, she raced upstairs to collect her bow. She returned wearing her quiver. Bow in hand, she said, "I'm ready."

They met Declan in the Reception Room. He smiled at Hope as if he were remembering his own childhood lessons before leading them to the practice area.

Since Declan made no mention of his grandfather or the Watchers' Guild, Berty did not either. His mind wandered to the woman who appeared in the crystal. As Hope lobbed arrows at her target, Berty contemplated the meaning of nine words.

He understood *seven sages* to mean the Seven High Sages who crafted the scepter. The *seven seals* referred to the seven different circles incorporated into the Sages' Seal. There were plenty of things in the world that Berty did not know. The Sages and their secrets were another mystery to unravel. Three words out of the nine bothered Berty most—*soon sinister steals*. What was being stolen? Who was sinister? How soon was soon?

At the end of Hope's lesson, Declan joined Berty as they returned to the Empire Tree. "I'd like to start her on moving targets soon," said Declan.

"Whatever you think," Berty replied.

"Something on your mind, my Lord?" asked Declan.

He glanced at the concern on Declan's face. "Excessive

alliteration." Seeing Declan's eyebrows scrunch, he added, "I'll explain upstairs." As they entered the Reception Room, he called for Theodore.

Appearing near the stairs to the upper levels, Theodore said, "Yes, my Lord?"

"How does he do that?" Berty heard Hope ask.

"Magic," answered Freesia.

"I need to see the Advisory Council," Berty told him.

The four of them climbed the steps. Once they reached the landing to the Roundtable Room, Berty said, "I am so impressed with how quickly you have picked up archery, Hope." She beamed. "You have a great day. I will see you later."

Smiling, she ran up the stairs.

Berty and Declan entered the Roundtable Room. "The procession for the Guild Master starts at high noon," said Declan. "Will you walk?"

Looking at Declan, Berty saw more than just an Advisor—a friend. "Of course."

They took their seats around the Roundtable as the rest of the Advisory Council entered. Once everyone was seated, all eyes found Berty.

"Last night, a woman appeared to me from inside the scepter. She said, 'Seven sages. Seven seals. Seven secrets. Soon sinister steals.' When I blinked, she was gone," he said.

"Was she covered in blue markings?" asked Alfred.

"Yes."

"She was the Pixie Priestess," said Alfred.

"Not another prophecy to cloud another reign," Hatcher said.

"It's not a prophecy," said Estelle. "The stars would have indicated such an event."

"Are you sure?" Colvin asked.

Estelle's icy blue gaze cooled Colvin's fiery beard. "Prophecies are written in the stars. If the Pixies were to prophesize to the Emperor, then it would have been there," she explained.

"So you know what a prophecy says beforehand?" asked

Colvin.

"No. The stars only tell of a prophecy, not its contents," Estelle said.

"Pixies are not known for being straightforward," said Delyth. "I think the Priestess gave a warning. With all that has happened, it is just the beginning."

"I agree with Delyth, my Lord," Estelle said. "The stars, too, tell of something. Mars is at a strange angle with the Pleiades—also known as the Seven Sisters. It is the constellation that I was told to follow home from God Mountain. I have been watching it ever since. Other things are moving into positions unknown. Starjen can tell me nothing whilst in transition."

"Thank you, Estelle," said Berty. "Send messages to the Heads. We might not know what is coming, but we can prepare for something." His eyes swept the table. "That is all. Begin planning what needs to be done."

He heard the scraping of wood against wood as the Advisory Council left the Roundtable. Realizing that Silvia never told him exactly how she received her prophecy from the Pixie Priestess, he knew that he could not ask her. That knowledge did not matter anyway. All they could really do was wait.

Leaving with Declan, Berty followed him into the Sages' Grove. They stopped next to the line of gourd lanterns.

The Watchers' Guild door opened. Into the sunlight stepped a lone Watcher, her hood raised. The Watcher held her hands slightly cupped in front of her. Resting on top of her open hands was her wand. Behind her, two more Watchers emerged. They fell in line side by side with their hoods raised as well.

Two by two, eight hooded Watchers squeezed through the doorway carrying a large, wood and hay casket draped with a white cloth. The Watcher's Symbol of the open eye inside the six-pointed star was painted in black on the burial cloth.

Declan raised his hood as the dead Guild Master passed. Following his lead, so did Berty. More hooded Watchers poured out of the guild.

Stepping over the gourds, Declan and Berty joined the silent procession. As they headed towards the gates of the Sages' Grove, more hooded figures joined also. Since the new additions did not come out of the Watchers' Guild, Berty did not know their connection to the Guild or to the late Guild Master.

The front Watcher led the procession beyond the gates. They walked, emitting only the muffled crunching of boots rhythmically touching the forest floor. The procession stopped on the banks of a small lake. Feet from the water, the line spread to form a loose semi-circular group.

Everyone silently watched as the eight men stepped into the water with the casket still shoulder level. Each sloshing step brought them deeper into the lake. Once the water lapped their chests, the men dipped, resting the cloth-covered casket on the water's surface. They emerged from the lake with dry cloaks.

Watchers extracted their wands. They pointed them towards a spot in the sky. Red sparks emitted from each tip. They flew in an arched trajectory. The falling sparks ignited the pyre.

A small gasp escaped Berty's lips. Declan returned his wand to the inside folds of his cloak as the flames floated on top of the lake.

The water reflected the consuming fire, magnifying the luminosity. Reddish-orange flames spiked, reaching high into the sky moments before the lake swallowed the incinerating fire.

No one moved while they watched the lake surface ripple violently from the sunken epicenter. Unnaturally soon, the waves melted into a smooth mirror perfectly reflecting the surrounding forest.

Watchers began to lower their hoods. Turning away from the lake, they approached, either singly or in small groups, a man who stood unassumingly to the side. Each Watcher said, "Guild Master," to him as he or she passed.

After most of the Watchers had gone, Declan also approached the man. "Guild Master," he acknowledged before returning to Berty's side.

As the two of them walked away from the lake, Declan retrieved his wand from inside his cloak. "Kevin will make a good Guild Master," he said. "The glow surrounding him was bright."

"The glow?" asked Berty. He saw nothing.

"There is a magic that transfers from Guild Master to Guild Master," Declan explained. "The time between Guild Masters is when the magic begins its transition. During the transition, the Guild is masterless. Any Keeper can enter the Guild Master's private study."

"What did you find?" asked Berty in whisper.

"He knew what it was that I carry the moment he met me. The people known as the Lunatics revered the moon. Using the moon's magic, they built gargantuan stone structures. Their civilization is lost. Their structures are in ruins. Only my bow has retained the ancient magic they were able to harness from the moon. That is why it is one piece to opening the Cavern—its magic stems from elsewhere," said Declan, also in a whisper. "I also found references to things in the ancient tongue. Somethings called *Gullogbrand* and *Saðkuna Fróðir*. I'm probably not pronouncing those right."

He gazed at the trees for a few steps, then said, "Aaron murdered the former Guild Master just so he could pursue me during the transition when we were without Guild protection. Do you think he'll join forces with Leif?"

Berty remembered when he first met the wild looking Leif. "I believe they already were," he said. "He was so adamant against the last Empress having any contact with Watchers. The prophecy made a good cover for what he was really planning. If the scepter's crystal comes from the Cavern, then finding a way inside has always been the true goal."

Declan's wand moved slightly, causing him to alter their path. "The Empire Tree has a specific magical signature. My wand finds it easily," he told Berty.

Glancing at the direction of Declan's wand, Berty said, "It's nice to have something that always points you home."

About the Author

IE Castellano is an American author and poet living in the Eastern United States. Falling in love with the mechanics of the English language at an early age, she started writing poetry before venturing into fiction. With her propensity to ask, what if, she writes speculative fiction—authoring the dystopian sci-fi novel, *Tricentennial*, and the contemporary epic fantasy series, *the World In-between*.

Other books by IE Castellano:

The World In-between (Book 1)
Tricentennial

IE's blog: http://iecastellano.blogpost.com

JosDCreations: http://JosDCreations.com

www.ingramcontent.com/pod-product-compliance
Lightning Source LLC
Chambersburg PA
CBHW050402260626
47156CB00003B/840